THE MECHANICS' IN
ISSUE 5 AUTUMN 2(

The first Mechanics' Institute in London was founded in 1823 by George Birkbeck. "Mechanics" then meant skilled artisans, and the purpose of the Institute was to instruct them in the principles behind their craft. The Institute became Birkbeck College, part of London University, in 1920 but still maintains one foot in the academy and one in the outside world.

MIR

Birkbeck UNIVERSITY OF LONDON

The Mechanics' Institute Review
Issue 5 Autumn 2008

The Mechanics' Institute Review is published by MA Creative Writing, School of English and Humanities, Birkbeck, Malet Street, Bloomsbury, London WC1E 7HX

ISBN 978-0-9547933-5-7

Project Director: Julia Bell

The Editorial Team would like to thank Russell Celyn Jones, Sue Tyley and Anne-Marie Taylor for making this project possible.

For further copies or information, please contact Anne-Marie Taylor, MA Creative Writing, School of English and Humanities, Birkbeck, Malet Street, Bloomsbury, London, WC1E 7HX. Tel: 020 7079 0689. Email: a.taylor@bbk.ac.uk

Website: www.bbk.ac.uk/mir

Printed and bound by Antony Rowe, Bumpers Farm, Chippenham, Wiltshire

Cover design and typesetting by Raffaele Teo

Illustrations by Pete Williamson

The Mechanics' Institute Review is typeset in RotisSerif

TABLE OF CONTENTS

INTRODUCTION
Susan Elderkin

On the wall above my desk is a cartoon. It's by the Australian cartoonist Leunig. In the first box a little blob man sits on a chair in a doctor's consultation room. "Help me, doctor," he says. "I've got a book inside me." The kindly doctor perches on the edge of his desk, folds his hands, and points out to his patient that most people do, and perhaps he can refer him to a publisher. But the patient won't be fobbed off so easily. He wants the book surgically removed, or dissolved with herbs – anything rather than go through the painful process of writing it. "Life is so cruel," he wails in the final box. "I thought I could escape."

Almost everyone you meet these days wants to be a writer. It is practically a national epidemic. All round the country students are graduating from their first degrees and picking Creative Writing off the menu of MA courses as if it were a sensible career option. As law school leads to becoming a lawyer, and veterinary college to becoming a vet, an MA in Creative Writing surely leads to a publishing contract.

At its worst, this situation involves the fanning of unrealistic dreams by universities hungry for income. At its best, it plucks from the ranks an unsuspected genius who might otherwise have negotiated divorce settlements or castrated cats, and shoots them to literary stardom and a rather pleasant life.

Birkbeck is an unusual college in that all its classes are held in the evenings. This means that the students it attracts are like Leunig's blob man. They are people who already have proper lives, with jobs and families. They are people who are all too aware that there are more reliable ways of earning a living, more enjoyable ways of spending their time. People who should and do know better; but who nevertheless choose to close the door on everything else for long swathes of time and wrestle with their inner book – because the urge to write is strong, unfathomable and unrelenting.

During the last eighteen months, first as a writing fellow, then as a stand-in tutor, I've watched the Creative Writing students at Birkbeck – blob men and women all – wrestle with their inner books. An inner book becomes an outer book by a process that starts with the glimpse of something "other". An author must believe in this "other", explore it and get to know it, in order to realise the potential of the book inside.

At this point, whether a book gets written or not depends largely on faith. First, because an author has to listen to and obey the instructions of their inner book, and these instructions can be capricious. Often they seem to make no sense at all. A truly original book will command that its author go off on all sorts of apparently absurd tangents. And also because a book will only get written if the author sticks at it, returns day after day to the desk, however sunny it is outside, whatever mood they're in, and however lacking in charm the sentences emerging from their fingers appear to them that day. And believe me there will be days when the sentences lack charm. On days like these, faith is more important than talent.

When I was researching my first novel in Arizona, I experienced an extraordinary string of luck. When I needed a car, I met someone who lent me a car. When I needed a house, I met someone who lent me a house. It seemed as if fate wanted me to write my book as much as I wanted to. There's nothing like serendipity for bolstering one's faith.

When it was time to research my second book, I didn't dare hope for similar things to happen. But I carried the word serendipity around in my head, Joseph Campbell-style, all the same. I arrived in Derby, in north-west Australia, with no particular plan. I knew I wanted to spend time in some of the more remote Aboriginal communities in the Kimberley, but I didn't know how I would get to them. The Kimberley is notoriously difficult country. One unpaved road runs across it. It was still the dry season when I arrived, but when the rains came the rivers would flood and the Gibb River Road would turn to mud. I needed a four-wheel drive, and one of those engine snorkels for fording rivers. The idea of fording rivers by myself was pretty daunting, as the rivers were full of saltwater crocodiles, and you wouldn't have wanted to get stuck halfway. And besides, I didn't have a four-wheel drive.

Instead I had a mobile number with "Rossco" scribbled beneath it. Rossco had rescued my friend Natalie when the wet season came early one year and she was stranded the wrong side of a river. Natalie had pushed this piece of paper in my hand just before I left London. I called the number. Rossco said I'd find him at the bar in the Spinifex Hotel.

I knew who he was immediately. Big belly hanging over short shorts, flip-flops worn to a sliver, a grubby baseball cap facing backwards. His faded singlet gaped at the arms and a nipple ensconced in a nest of grey hair poked out. We got talking. I found out that he was a sparky, under contract to service air-conditioning units in Aboriginal schools in the Kimberley. This involved regular two-month trips around the entire region. At the end of each trip there was just time to pack a few beers in and catch up with mates at the Spini, before setting off and doing it all over again. He was leaving for his next trip in the morning. He had a four-wheel drive and the necessary apparatus to ford rivers.

I bought him more beer. By the end of the evening we'd struck a deal. I would go with him. Rossco would provide the food, the swags and the petrol; I'd provide the beer. Just before we parted company, Rossco gave me his business card. "Serendipity Electrical Services", it read. I almost fell off my chair.

Five months later I sat at my desk in London, opened my notebooks and began to write. For the first few months all went well. I had my main characters, some scenes, a rough idea of where it was going. And then, six months in, something changed. I re-read what I had written and found it prosaic. It was too grim, too gritty. It bored me. It hugged the ground like some creeping, crawling creature. It lacked wings. It lacked daring, invention, flight.

At about this time I was due to take up a two-month residency at an artists' colony in New Hampshire. I didn't like my novel. I was no longer sure if I even had a novel. But I had a plane ticket, and a tenant due to move into my flat. So I went, and for the next two months I dutifully got up every day, sat at my desk and stared at my screen. Sometimes I wrote a few paragraphs. Usually I erased them. I decided I would write another book, a different book. I started this other book. Then I realised this was just a distraction. I returned to my Australian book with a heavy heart. Day after day after day.

When I came back to London, I felt as if I'd made no progress at all. I'd hardly written a thing. But something must have happened during those long days of staring at the screen in New Hampshire, because the morning after I got back, I suddenly knew what to do. I sat down and created a whole new strand of the narrative. I liked it. It had wings. After that I wrote manically, seven days a week, charged to the gills. In a year, the novel was done.

The students whose work you're about to read have been on similar journeys: from joy to despair and back again. But reading their stories, you will see no signs of the birthing process. The blood, the tears, the sweat, the mucus – it has all been cleaned away. The stories appear to have written themselves, as all good stories do – to have been that way from their conception, creations of great ease and delight, penned in one afternoon before going out for an evening stroll or a pre-dinner vodka tonic. The really great thing is that the authors, too, on seeing their work between covers, perhaps for the first time, their name in the table of contents, a price on the back of the book – they will read them in much the same way, all pain eclipsed. And they'll marvel that these fully fledged stories, once just fragments embedded deep within them, now exist in the world on their own. This is why we write, and why we will write again.

STEALING JIMMY DEAN

Cynthia Medford Langley

"Ma'am, this is the operator. Will you accept a collect call from Mr KT Reynolds?"

I lean against the wall of the kitchen. Just my luck my goddamn mother is standing right next to me. If the first word out of my mouth is "yes", she'll know it's KT calling collect again, running up her bill.

"Right . . ." I say. Mom is taking her damn time packing up her cheese sandwich for lunch. Why the hell can't she just eat at the Burger King like everybody else at the Department of Health? I start flubbing off some conversation about fourth-period history, like it's Roxanne I'm talking to.

"Hey baby." That's KT's voice back behind the operator.

"Ma'am, if you do not accept the charges for this call I will have to disconnect you."

"Yes," I say, hoping enough seconds have passed that old eagle ears won't notice.

Operator hangs up and the line is suddenly clear between KT and me. I can hear him breathe. I can hear it just like he's up against my neck whispering to me. "How you doin' baby?"

"I'm a'right."

He yawns. "Your ma there?"

"You know it."

Finally, my mother shoves the sandwich in a Ziploc. With a hard look she catches my eyes and pulls them over to the clock with hers, pokes a kiss at the side of my head and abandons the kitchen. I hear her going down the stairs, packing her bag. She's got this whippy way of zipping up her coat that makes me think I'm going to have to take her to the hospital one day to get the skin of her neck extracted from it. Doesn't happen today though, thank God. The front door closes and a minute later her state car rattles down the driveway.

"Didn't you say you were going to call me last night? I waited." Through the phone I hear traffic, lots of cars, not just the occasional tractor trailer going by on Route 1 where KT used to room with Marco's family before he got kicked out.

"I got some good news," he tells me. It's his get-out-of-jail-free card, that phrase.

Still, I bite. "What?" My knees bend with the question.

"Got a car."

My teeth press gently into my lip. This crazy snake of energy runs all through me. I love the way he can just take a day and flip it upside down.

The phone is cradled tight up against my ear. I hear the rustle of his jacket, the little groan he makes when he stretches. It sounds just like when we wake up together in the morning, which we've done twice. The whole night together, I mean. Not just being together, which is more of a regular thing. Not so regular as if he had somewhere to live though. We're kind of stuck with motel rooms for the time being, and they're expensive. $28 for the night and you have to find a place that will let you rent underage. KT's an adult now but he doesn't have a driver's licence so renting the room still falls to me.

My real problem though is that if I get caught cutting school again I'll get expelled.

"Babe, you know if I come out to Trenton it has to be the whole day and I have to go to the doctor for a medical note. I've used up all my sick days."

"Who you talkin' to, Hope? You my lady. I know what have to happen when I call."

We say I love you about eight times each and I fly on out the door, hauling my book bag along so I look legit.

My hi-tops are open laced but my Wigwams hold them on, and I got the rhythm of how to walk in them so I can motivate pretty fast across town. I take all the back roads. I wore my jeans with the zips down the legs that KT likes but it adds a complication to the walk because some of the seams rub if you know what I mean. But I just keep going, not able to wait to see KT. He was so sweet on the phone. He's not always. When I said I was waiting last night, I left out that I was crying too. The worst thing in the world is when somebody says they love you and then doesn't show up. It's not really KT's fault because he doesn't have a phone, but still, whenever we're apart, I'm kind of always waiting for him not to come back. Underneath, I think I'm just not strong enough for the situation, but I try to be.

It's a long walk to Trenton on the back roads. See, in New Jersey, if I get expelled I get sent to the reject school. I've seen the kids who go there, freaks most of them. Some butt-ugly girls and guys that look like they've swallowed growth hormone. Quasimodo motherfuckers. Like to set fires 'n' all. Apart from that, today's complications include: risk two – if my mom catches me, I'm grounded. I won't be able to see KT at all and then we might break up. She hates KT since that time I came home tripping. She's right on the edge of hauling my ass into family therapy. Risk three is just your demographic-type problem. Flat out, there's some areas where it's not a great idea for a white girl to go. Altogether, you get the idea I'm running through a minefield.

Forty minutes later I round the corner between the tyre factory and the book distributor. I start checking out the cars in the parking lot of the Moorings Bar-n-Grill. KT and Marco usually go for nice cars, newish. 'Course, neither of them can hotwire so they're left with whatever they can find with the keys inside. People in some of the nicer suburbs, like with garages that are part of the house, leave their keys above the sun visor or in the ignition. This is troubling when you think about it. I mean, the ignition makes sense from a laziness standpoint, but you can't get me to understand the sun visor. I mean, you have to leave the keys somewhere you remember you put them. Why is it any harder to remember they are in the sun visor than in your handbag? Though, I suppose, if more than one person drives the car, it saves passing keys back and forth. But then, how hard is it to get an extra set of keys, and shouldn't you have a spare set anyway? You see, no matter which way you try to spread that shit, it comes out too thin. I think people just like feeling like they live in a neighbourhood that's too good for thievery. They want to believe it so much, they set out an invitation for you to try. You know, I realised that about all those gold chains you see the black guys down on Centre Street wearing. It ain't just about showing off they got some money. It's a dare. That gold means they're telling you they're hard enough to defend it. Snatching it means you're harder than the wearer. It's some medieval shit, I tell you.

We all wear silver. That gets snatched too. Never off me though. My baby always keeps me away from anything like that. That's why he leaves me behind sometimes. Him and his boys get up to some business females shouldn't be around. There's a high price for white girls in some places. A Jamaican tried to buy me off KT once when we were copping some herb. You know what was scary? I'm a free person in a free country so far as I understand but if KT had said yes there wouldn't have been a goddamn thing I could do about it. That Jamaican would have taken hold of me like a pink slip. Like I said before, there's places a white girl shouldn't go.

Most of the lot is full of empty vans and trucks. Then I see, right at the far side where the weeds grow out of the wall, a huge old Mercury about the size of a living room, parked nose in. The finish might have been black once but the paint is dead so it looks more like a dusty eggplant. I can see three heads in the front seat. The happiness I felt since KT told me about the car drops down and corrupts into something that feels like acid in my stomach. I know those heads. KT, Marco, and my ex-boyfriend Bobby Joe. I tell you, if there is proof I did something horrible in another life, it's Bobby Joe. He's going out with my best friend Roxanne now. Didn't exactly wait until we broke up to start, either.

I get this random attack of wanting to cry. KT hates crying though. That would be the day ruined for sure. I light a cigarette and start to reason on myself. Marco and Bobby Joe aren't always dicks and they might be leaving soon anyway. Either way I've got KT. He called me when he could have just spent the day with his boys. Fact, that's probably why he didn't call last night. He was busy getting the car so we could be together. Yeah.

The nearer I am to the car the more I can hear the music. Marco stole that new Run DMC tape and he turns the bass way up whenever he's got anything to play it in. KT is watching me in the side-view mirror and when I get near the door opens and he steps out. He's wearing Marco's old sheepskin and it falls open and I can see he's losing weight. Not a lot but he didn't have any to lose in the first place. Bobby Joe and Marco are bigger than him and the three of them could eat like horses except none of them have jobs.

KT smiles and waits for me to come up and get inside that coat with him. For my life I can't tell you why he has such an effect on me. I mean, if I have a type it's a man with dark hair, probably dark eyes too, with strong arms and a broad back. What I have my arms around inside this sheepskin is a blond, blue-eyed man only a couple of inches taller than me and probably only ten pounds heavier than me now that he's not eating enough. His teeth are crooked and he has a claw-shaped scar on his head from when he got hit with a bat in some dealer's house. That scar still hurts him sometimes. Nobody says it out loud but we all think it's going to kill him someday, like some lodge of badness that will break open and pollute his life force. I have to tell you it's a trap to start loving anyone you feel sorry for. You stick one hand down in that quicksand and then another and soon enough you're in there too.

I'm not quite done being held but he's done holding me. He pushes me off him, puts his hand on the back of my neck and leads me over to the car. Bobby Joe and Marco can see I'm not too happy and their eyes get these little sparklers of mean in them – tickled that I can't do anything about the situation. But that amusement passes in a second and I can see they're all electric jumpy, like when they've found something good and easy to steal and they're making plans.

Bobby Joe, the only one with a licence, is behind the wheel. "How you doin', Hope? You with us today?" he asks.

I relax a little. I don't mind hanging with all of them as long as it's friendly. Also, while they can be dicks, there's no way they'd let anyone else hurt me. I kind of like that feeling since I spend a lot of time worrying about rape and mugging. I don't know why, maybe not having my dad around plus all the shit you hear on the news, but it does seem sometimes like the whole world is waiting to snatch away whatever little bit of beauty you've got, even if it's just your sweetness or the way you used to trust people.

I lean down and look around the inside of the car. It's got white leather upholstery and a huge wood steering wheel. Furry dice hang from the rear-view mirror. "Wow! This is cool," I say, and they all smile. "Bet it's fast too. You could fit about ten people in this bitch." I look into the back seat, admiring the space and suddenly stop. "Who the fuck is that?" I stand straight up, one hand on my hip. The boys are all grinning. I try again: "Who the FUCK is THAT?"

"That's Jimmy Dean, baby," KT, who still has a hand on my neck, says.

"What the . . . ? What in the fuck are you doing with that old black man in the back of your car?" I lean down again, staying far back from the door. The man is sprawled across the back seat and I watch him in cold horror, waiting for him to draw a breath. He does. He has dark plum skin and thick hands. A trilby sits cocked on his head, pushed up by the back of the seat where his head rests. "Is he a bum? What's a bum doing in the car?"

The boys are all laughing now. "It's Jimmy Dean, woman. I told you so."

While we're in the middle of all this I'm gonna have to go back to demographics and tell you that Bobby Joe is a strawberry blond with a moustache to match and Marco is Italian with brown hair and green eyes. Them and KT been to juvie, Marco for five years, so every one of them talks like the black people they grew up around but not one of them would touch a black girl and they don't go into black neighbourhoods except to buy drugs. This place is like, divided.

"Is he hurt?" I ask.

KT's hand is tight on my neck. "He's just company for the day."

Funny enough, it's Bobby Joe who takes pity on me first. He pulls a wallet off the dashboard and hands it to me. It's leather, rubbed smooth and rounded at the corners. Inside, behind a plastic window, is a licence with a picture of a dark face, and the name Dean, James, as clear as day. He's fifty according to his birthdate, and lives over in Cadwalader Park. Oh, please tell me they weren't over there in the middle of the night, I think. But I know I'll find out soon enough. These boys like to hold on to a story like a cat with a bug but sooner or later they get tired and let it go.

KT looks in at the other two. "A dude's gotta sit in the back."

They agree and Marco gets out of the car. He looks down at me. "Ain't no lady gonna sit in the back with old Jimmy Dean." He winks at me. "You sit in the front with KT."

It's a Monday which means I got my lunch money off my mom in the morning. That gives us $5 if we can find a nickel bag, but most people just want to sell dimes. There ain't nothing in Jimmy's wallet. We decide to drive to the 7-Eleven so the boys can steal some breakfast.

"Wallet got cleaned out last night," Bobby Joe sniggered. "How else you think we end up with this dude?"

I want the story and so I play up to Bobby Joe, looking way up at him from the crook of KT's arm. He could never resist that look and it works again. Turns out that the boys had decided to stay out the night together since KT had nowhere to sleep. It's still cold at night, only being April, and when the Moorings closed they started to wander over West Trenton where one of the illegal bars that's open late might serve them without ID. By the time they found one they were way down by Stuyvesant Avenue. I cut in here: "Jesus fuckin' Christ! Stuyvesant at one o'clock in the morning?" KT's arm clamps around my neck and I shut up and let Bobby Joe finish the story.

"Yeah, woman." He cuts his eyes down at me. "We men. Ain't gotta worry. We go in any place we want. Don't matter if it black, Puerto Rican. Anyway, stop distractin' me."

"She ain't distractin' you, you still drunk from last night." Marco speaks up from the back. "We found this place called Oscar's."

"Oswald's."

"Oscar's, you pussy."

"Oswald's fucking bar. Down in some basement. Dark as could be. Walls black, furniture black."

"People black as fuckin' night," KT adds.

Old Jimmy Dean groans, shifts himself and slumps again with his head cocked towards the window. Marco lifts his hat delicately and moves it so his eyes are covered. "Don't want him wakin' up now, do we?" he says, his face one big grin.

Bobby Joe checks him out in the rear-view and then keeps talking. "Anyway, we meet up with this old dude, asks us do we want a drink. So, we says yes. Sits down, and he's buyin' rounds. Then he tells us we just met Jimmy Dean. 'Where?' we say. That's when he get out his wallet and show us that licence. 'Course we also notice that dude must have just got paid or somethin' 'cause he got plenty money. So we stay there and drink till the bartender throw us out."

"So this is his car?" I ask.

"Way it turn out," KT says in my ear, "he was too drunk to walk, let alone drive, so we tell him we drive him home."

"And that was about six-seven hours ago," Marco calls out. One thing about Marco, no matter how much he might piss you off, when he's laughing you have to laugh with him.

We're still laughing when we pull into the 7-Eleven. "What we gonna do with her?" Bobby Joe asks. "Can't bring her in the shop in case we get caught."

"Can't leave her out here, man," KT says. "Not leavin' my woman with dude in the back seat."

"Can't she stand over by the door?" Bobby Joe asks.

"It's cold, man," Marco offers up. "And what if you got to run? Females can't run."

I know there's no point entering this argument so I just wait. It's finally decided that Bobby Joe and KT will go into the store while Marco hangs in the back with Jimmy Dean. I'm supposed to stay where I am.

It's always easier to talk to them one at a time, so when the two leave I turn around and meet Marco's eyes. His face squinches up and we laugh for a minute just because of the charge in the air.

"So how come you all didn't just leave him somewhere?"

"Nights is cold when you outside. I mean, bad enough we drink up all dude's money and take his car – but leave him out in the weather to sleep as well? Even I ain't that hard."

I nod and he nods along, and then he's laughing again. "Anyway, if the cops found him, they'd start lookin' for the car and we'd be in jail again. Got five warrants on me already. Now, long as we got Jimmy, we got wheels and a place to hang out."

He looks over at the dozing figure, drawing my eyes to that corner of the car. Jimmy looks like he made a bit of an effort last night. Wearing brown trousers with a sharp crease down the front and he's got some wicked pattern shirt on – some kind of burgundy-and-gold fleur-de-lys pineapple mix. His tie is loose, dark red with an eight-ball tie tack. Marco says, "Check out dude's shoes." I kneel up on the seat and look over.

"Fuckin' A!" I gasp. Brogues with extra-long toe boxes, look like a leather collage. Maroon fleurs-de-lys decorate the toes, strip of yellow reaches from the arch to the laces, and round the back, a maroon heel. New soles and shined to gleam. "Maybe he is Jimmy Dean," I say.

"You think Jimmy Dean come back to life as an old black man?"

"Not when he first come back. Maybe came back as a boy and grew old like he should have the first time, just in a different body."

Marco, who loves nothing more than chance to chew over a philosophy, rubs his chin, his face gone serious. "So you think Jimmy Dean die a rich famous white kid and come back a poor black kid. That make sense in a way." We go quiet a minute. "Maybe if I die today I come back a rich black man!" he shouts. "I come back as Michael Jordon, or, fuck that, I want to play for the NFL. If we die today I'm gonna come back as Herschel Walker."

The doors of the car open and KT and Bobby Joe get in in a hurry. "Be cool, man," KT says, "and let's just get the fuck out of here."

I wait until we are heading down Spruce Street before giggling, "If we die today Marco's gonna come back to life as Herschel Walker." Then I look down at the bag KT's got at his feet. "How did you . . . ?"

Bobby Joe laughs. "That girl in there is sweatin' me. I ask her if I can have a plastic bag because I got a bottle of oil leakin' in my trunk. Then I hand it off to KT who say he gettin' a soda. Then I just start layin' it on and while she payin' attention to me, KT go shoppin'."

KT starts pulling food out. Doritos go in the back seat with Marco who opens them and puts the governor on – gripping the pack so the boys can't get more than a handful at a time. We work on them while KT shows us what else he got. Sodas, Slim Jims, and three burritos. "They was only three in the case. You could have some a mine," he says to me. Then he pulls out a blue plastic container.

"Nigger, what is that?" shouts Bobby Joe.

KT turns it around. "Muscular Dystrophy Association" it says. KT shakes it and coins rattle.

Bobby Joe whoops. "How the fuck did you get that? I been eyeballin' that thing for months now."

KT reaches out and high-fives Bobby Joe, a loud noise above my head, then with Marco over the back of the seat. I spread the empty bag over his lap while he pries the jar open and dumps out the change. There are a lot of pennies but plenty of quarters too. He starts counting. Nine dollars, enough to get a dime bag without even touching my lunch money. We lock the doors and head down Donnelly Homes. The two guys who work the lot near the fish place are usually out from seven a.m.

While we drive, in that buzz of expectation, conversation starts back up. "Now what's this about Marco coming back to life in the NFL?"

"Well, we figure maybe that Jimmy Dean back there really is Jimmy Dean, come back from the dead, you know? And if so, since we met him, maybe his magic will rub off or something. He was a rich young white dude and now he's a poor old black dude. Maybe we're in the middle of some story and we'll all die today and come back as some kind of opposite. Marco figures he's coming back as a black NFL player."

"Why you gotta be black, man?" Bobby Joe wants to know.

"'Cause that's how it work, man, ain't you listenin'? Can't come back exactly the same."

"But you already play football."

"You *is* still drunk, you dumb-ass motherfucker. And Jimmy Dean had some crazy shoes when he was alive too, you could see it in old pictures. See, some of the shit got to be the same. With me, the football is the same part."

Bobby Joe is nodding. KT has his lips pursed together, his hands gripped around fists of change while he thinks the situation over. "I'm gonna be Martin Luther King," he says. We all look at him. He smiles. "I'm a bad white dude now, so I'm gonna come back as a good black dude."

"I heard that bastard had women comin' out his ears," Marco says. "Good choice. You gonna be hooked up."

"Hey!" I protest, but then laugh. I'm thinking about who I want to be.

Bobby Joe stops at a red light and a cop car glides through the intersection. "Five-oh." We hold completely still, knowing nothing draws a cop's attention like looking at them. When the light goes green he steps on the gas really soft, not squealing wheels like he likes to do. When we're rolling he says, "I'm gonna be Eddie Murphy. That bitch is loaded. I seen a picture of his girlfriend too. She ain't black neither. Got some green eyes."

"I seen that girl," Marco shouts. "Big titties like Lisa Lisa. She Chinese or something though."

"I could deal with that. Anyway, Eddie Murphy's funny as hell. I'm gonna be him. Also, you see him in *Beverly Hills Cop*? He can run, and kick ass."

"So what about you?" Marco asks me.

I've been thinking. I never had to look for a black role model before but now I've asked the question there might be a few people I want to be. "Janet Jackson! She's beautiful and rich and she can sing and she has this big family that loves her. That's who I'm gonna be."

"Statey!" Bobby Joe suddenly calls out. This normally means a state trooper, a warning on the highway to slow down. Here it means a state car has gone by. KT pulls me down across his lap. All state cars are treated like they could be my mother. After a few minutes he lets me go and I bob back up again. "Yeah, Janet," I say.

We get the herb without a hitch but there's nowhere really safe to park so we drive and light up. I've got that sweet spiky smoke in my lungs when I say, "There's only one hitch to the plan: we have to die today." The stuff we are smoking is cheap, but it's got us high and the day is turning warm. We have a car, cigarettes, food. We're mellow.

"There's lots worse than dying," Marco says quite peacefully. Then suddenly he sits bolt upright. "Holy shit, man, what day is it?"

"Don't know. Car ain't got no calendar."

Marco slaps the back of the seat behind KT. "Ain't we got court today?"

"You gettin' paranoid, man. You ain't got to go to court every day." Bobby Joe laughs. The whites of his eyes are gone near as red as Jimmy Dean's shoes. I get the Visine out of my purse and offer it around.

KT is bobbing his head to music no one else can hear. Whenever I ask him about it, all he says is "Black Sabbath". He barely moves when Marco hits the seat, only asks, "You mean the Hamilton one for the Grand Am? If we had court, we shoulda gone this mornin'."

We are on the third joint now and everything in the world is funny to me. "Hamilton's not far, is it Bobby Joe?" I laugh.

Marco's leaning over the seat. "Yeah, that's it! They can't put us in contempt if we show up on the same day."

"Nigger, they can."

"Nah, man. I seen it a hundred times. Somebody always get there late. If they got to reschedule you, it cost more money for them. We got to go."

KT starts scrounging in his pockets. "If we got to go to court, they must be a letter somewhere. I always keep the letter till I'm done."

Marco slaps the seat again. "We got to go to court, man, or that be six warrants. Go police station, Bobby Joe."

"Man! I ain't drivin' up to no police station with everybody high in a stolen car with a drunk old man come back from the dead in the back seat!"

But there we end up, in the parking lot of the municipal building.

"So what's the plan, then?" Bobby Joe wants to know.

Marco leans forward. "Me and KT go in and find out if we supposed to be in court. You take the car an' Jimmy Dean an' Janet Jackson here an' come back in twenty minutes. If we outside, all's cool. If we not, it mean we might be in court. So you come back once an hour to see if we out."

When they get out, I slide into the space KT vacated so I'm not right up next to Bobby Joe.

"Now what?" he asks.

"We near Vo-Tech. Let's go see Roxanne."

"Oh, shit, yeah," Bobby Joe says, reminded of his girlfriend. He looks at me quick. "Don't tell her I didn't think of it."

Of course I won't. But she's not gonna like me and him driving around alone together either. Just like I didn't like her kissing him when he was my boyfriend. I smile to myself.

We get to Vo-Tech between classes. Clumps of students stand smoking at the edges of the parking lot within the wings of a great red brick building. Roxanne is in the health occupations course so she's over with the clump of girls in white lab coats. To their right are the hairdressers and nail technicians, in pink smocks. To their left are the boys from machine shop in brown and auto mechanics in blue. Bobby Joe finds an empty space next to an Explorer and backs in, trying to keep Jimmy Dean as far from view as possible.

"I'm just gonna go find Roxanne. You wait here."

I look at Jimmy in the back seat. Though he has not moved, he is a big man. And what with all he's drunk I'm sort of waiting for him to throw up, if nothing else. Bobby Joe follows my eyes. "If he does anything, just shout. I ain't goin' far."

When he gets out of the car I remember that coming to see Roxanne was my idea. I'm still going to tell KT that he left me alone in the car though. I light a cigarette. I'm coming down a little, but still very chilled. Then I hear Jimmy shifting around in the back seat. I wait, stock still, for him to settle down like usual, but this time he doesn't. A deep voice garbles out, "Gotta piss."

What do I do? I don't want to turn around and look at him. In amongst all those smocks I can see some teachers, so I can't honk the horn. "Just wait," I say.

I hear the unmistakable sound of his fly being drawn down. "Not in here!" I shout, whipping around in my seat. "Outside!"

Jimmy opens the car door and rolls out onto the tarmac. I see a few of the brown-coat boys look over. Fuck. I get out of the car and walk to the front of the Explorer. Back behind me Jimmy is staggering to his feet, holding on to his purple car. His hat has fallen off and his head is shiny as an eight ball and I wonder, crazily, if that is the inspiration for his tie tack. I scan the crowd for Bobby Joe. More of the brown coats are looking at Jimmy Dean and now some of the blue coats too. I spot Bobby Joe, head and shoulders taller than the pink coats surrounding him. I call his name, but he doesn't hear me. Jimmy is now having a piss back between his car and a Honda, without bothering to turn away from the crowd of onlookers.

"Bobby Joe! BOBBY JOE!" I shout. Roxanne sees me and her eyes narrow. She might be my best friend but all I can think is, I hope she sees how it feels to have your friend spending time with your boyfriend. Bobby Joe takes off without a word and runs over to me.

By now, the brown and blue coats have started calling to white and pink coats and a flock of girls with permed hair sprayed up high in banana clips have gathered around to squeal at the spectacle of Jimmy Dean pissing. A few shriek and cover their eyes. Blue and brown coats are posturing, the larger ones coming to the front to form a defence for the startled girls.

Bobby Joe tries to run up on Jimmy Dean but there's nothing he can do until the man is empty. Finally Jimmy stops and Bobby Joe grabs him, telling him to zip his fly, and bundles him back into the car. "Get in," he shouts to me. The engine fires up and Bobby Joe squeals out. I see Roxanne in the wing mirror, her arm crossed over her belly and her hip shot out.

"Sorry," I start to say to Bobby Joe.

"What you sorry for? Wasn't nothin' else you could do. I'm sorry I left you alone with him." He gives me a smile. "Wasn't no way to treat a superstar, Janet."

I return the smile. "Well, Eddie Murphy couldn't have cleaned up that mess faster. You got him right into the car and got us out of there. That wasn't easy. High-speed driving an' all."

Back at the municipal building, Marco and KT are standing at the side of the road. We slow down and let them in, barely stopping.

James Dean has leaned back in his seat again. Marco gives him a soda from the bag and he drinks half of it before his hand begins to tilt, spilling Dr Pepper down his pretty shirt. Marco takes the can and flings it out the window and then dabs at the stain with a napkin.

The nurse tries to give me a hard time about the school note, saying I didn't really have an appointment. I would normally start to sweat and scheme at that sort of confrontation but I feel strong somehow, new, not like me at all.

"I'm in a show tonight. I'm singing," I hear myself say. "There's a talent agent coming. My mother didn't want me to miss my big break so she made me come here to see if someone can have a look at my throat. There's strep going around."

"I used to sing," the nurse says. Now, I've never sung anywhere outside my bedroom but we're looking at each other, her at a memory and me at a dream. "Have a seat. I'll get you in to see the doctor."

I'm in and out, relieved at a clean bill of health, which I have to remind myself was never actually in jeopardy.

"Break a leg," she says, as she hands me the school note she's typed up.

In the parking lot I see a couple of white boys standing around an old black man. Thing is, the white boys ain't mine but the old black man is Jimmy Dean. They're up in his face about something. The car is gone from the kerb. I may not know Jimmy too well but when one of them starts pushing him I remember about possession being nine-tenths of the law. I don't know what that really means, but to me it means Jimmy Dean is my responsibility now. There is no way I can beat up even one of these white guys let alone three so I do the only thing I know how. I tilt my head back and holler, "KT!!!!!!"

Don't you know, like a shot, that old purple car spins around the corner and screeches to a halt right where I am standing. I point wildly and KT runs up on the white boys, Marco and Bobby Joe at his back. My baby might be small but he's lean and that makes him the fastest of the three. In a second he's between the boys and old Jimmy. I'm thinking there is going to be a fight, what with three on three.

"What's the trouble now?" he asks.

I nearly choke, having expected him to start kicking people in the head.

The white boys look at each other.

"Nothin', man. Thought dude was trouble," one of them, looking too small for his Air Jordans, says.

"He not causin' no trouble though, is he?"

Another, a boy with a fat gold Italian horn on his neck, jumps in to defend his friend. "Ain't somewhere you usually see a nigger, man. Just wanted to know what he's doing here."

"He ain't no nigger. Just a old man. You can't go accusin' nobody just 'cause they black," KT says. "How you know he ain't have to go to the doctor?"

Marco and Bobby Joe are standing with their arms folded, sort of spellbound like me. The boys all look at each other while Jimmy and me wait for a result. The guy in the Air Jordans extends a palm. Suddenly everybody is shaking hands and we have Jimmy bundled back into the car. He's not done much but look at everyone while it was all going on but back in the car he says, "Brother," before closing his eyes again.

We're stewing around in some good vibe and when we drive off we seem to float, and not just for that luxury suspension.

"God, you know what?" I ask. I turn to Marco who is most likely to support me on this one. "Jimmy's like a charm. We're all turning into what we thought we'd come back as, and didn't have to die to do it." I fill them in on Bobby Joe's heroics and my result with the note for school. KT nods like he's really thinking on it.

Marco is looking pale though. "What if we actually dead?"

"Pussy, we ain't dead," Bobby Joe growls.

"Now how you know that for certain?" KT challenges.

"Yeah, all the time in movies people don't know they die. You don't know they dead neither till halfway through the story when they have a conversation just like this," Marco adds.

"I'm fuckin' sure we ain't dead." Bobby Joe lights a cigarette, as if to prove the dead can't smoke.

"When do you think we died?" I ask.

Marco is rubbing his arms. "Maybe somebody done shot us in that bar last night."

"Then how'd I get here?" I want to know.

"Yeah, we have to die after she get here," KT adds supportively.

"Maybe that woman in the 7-Eleven shot us for robbery."

"Or, could have had a car accident just when you was duckin' from that statey."

"What if we was caught in a drug shoot-out when we was coppin'?"

"Or we been poisoned by 7-Eleven burritos."

All of a sudden Jimmy moans out, "Ain't nobody dead." But his voice sounds like some ghost up out of the Deep South and everybody's eyes go wide. We're about to have a large-scale freak-out when old Jimmy pipes up again. "Wanna go home. Gotta get . . ."

"Gotta get what?" Marco asks, like he's in a seance.

I look up at the Sovereign Bank as we drive by. It's only two p.m. "I can't be on the street until three thirty," I say, "dead or not."

As if to demonstrate my point, Bobby Joe yells out, "Statey!" and KT pushes my head down to his knee.

When I can sit up again Jimmy Dean moans out that he wants to go home.

"I got a idea," Bobby Joe says. "Why don't we take him home to get what he needs, then drive back to the Moorings and let Jimmy have his car back?"

I get out Jimmy's wallet to confirm the street address. "Cadwalader

Park." I shake my head. "Jesus."

I've been to some bad areas with the boys, but not Cadwalader Park. I want to suggest bringing him back after three thirty when I can go home, but for one I don't want to look chicken, for two, Jimmy's kept on moaning since he started and there's not much else to do to appease him, and three, I love hanging out with the boys when everybody's happy like this.

Cadwalader Park used to be rich, but now it's a hole. Old mansions falling down around the edges of a big park. Lots of them boarded up, with homeless squatting inside, and rats. The ones that aren't are full of extended families tight as tribes. I feel sad when I look around. It isn't hard to imagine the big old houses in their heyday. Gingerbread detail broken and paint peeling off in thick ripples. Porches sagging under disused furniture and old tyres. A few wear the angry upward smudges of fire above the boarded windows.

Jimmy's house is the last on a street that overlooks the park.

"Now what do you got to get?" Bobby Joe asks, but Jimmy has opened his door and is already standing in the driveway.

I look around nervously, trying to see if any neighbours are looking out their windows. Jimmy is halfway up his steps when Marco suddenly asks, "Which keys you give him?"

"There's only one set, man. Gave him the ones I was drivin' with."

"So if he goes in that house and don't come out, we fucked."

Bobby Joe opens his mouth but thinks better of it and jumps out of the car, followed by KT and Marco. I watch through the windshield as they run up on him, trying to make it look like they are helping him up the steps. This is so bad. Jimmy lets out a string of complaints and sits down heavily on the steps. No matter how the boys try to budge him, he won't get up and instead raises up his arms like he's being arrested.

I get out of the car. KT shoots me a look that says get back in but I can't see the point of being trapped in there without any keys if we suddenly have to run. We're kind of in the middle of a couple of felonies and I don't want to wind up as evidence in the stolen car.

Bobby Joe and Marco are leaning down, each with an arm under Jimmy's shoulders, ready to hoist him to his feet. "Nah, nah, nah," Jimmy's saying. "Gotta go home."

At the bottom of the steps I look up. Marco, KT and Bobby Joe are like the warriors of some primitive village that me and my friends live in. They are the toughest and the meanest among us and so everybody has to make sure to be on their good side. As a girl, the easiest way to do that is to go out with one of them. Roxanne's been out with all three. I've nearly caught up.

All of a sudden, something about the arrangement of this scene clicks. There's Jimmy in his fine clothes, sitting on the porch of a house he owns, even if it's coming apart in places. He's got a car, money in his wallet and going by the size of the house, maybe family too. So what made us all call him a poor black man? So far as I can see he's got more than we do.

"Hey, Jimmy," I say.

He stops struggling and looks at me.

"Jimmy, I'm not from around here and I don't belong here and unless you help us I can't quite see how I'm going to get home either. If you just come on back to North Trenton with us, I give you my word we'll give you the keys and you can drive right on back home."

I can't fathom how much alcohol must be in Jimmy Dean's system because after making his slow way down the steps he dozes off in the back of the car again. In the Moorings parking lot Bobby Joe turns off the ignition and him and KT open the doors. Before getting out we all stop and turn around to have one last look at James Dean. He's got a brown stain down his shirt and we've used up nearly a full tank of gas. He's got no money and probably wants his bed more than a starving man wants food. But all in all, I think it was a pretty caring kidnapping.

We're across the street. The boys have decided to walk me home. Suddenly Bobby Joe looks down and says, "What the fuck? I took Jimmy's keys."

"Shit, give 'em back or he gonna be stuck there."

"I told him he could go home. I promised," I add.

Jimmy Dean is standing by the open driver's-side door, feeling his pockets. He looks over at us. But just as Bobby Joe turns to head back with the keys, a cop car rounds the corner and clocks us. The siren whines out as the lights come on.

Seeing us jump, Jimmy meets our startled eyes and holds out his hands. The cop car is nearly on us. In a flash Marco grabs the key ring out from Bobby Joe, takes a running step forward and throws those keys a good thirty yards. They sail, glistening, in a perfect arc and old Jimmy Dean catches them like a Super Bowl pass in his big cupped hands. Without another blink we haul ass out of there.

And despite everything that got said here, you can trust me about one thing. I didn't go to jail that day or any other. Females damn well can run.

COMMISSION
Jon Elsom

Nathan's shadow loomed before him on the pavement like a comic-book villain as he turned with a sigh into a road called Sunset Cedars. He stopped and looked ahead at the stand of cedars which did indeed rise above the farthest houses and which were, too, bathed in a ludicrously pretty evening light.

Perfect, he thought. Just fucking perfect.

He shifted his rucksack on his aching back and set off into the cul-de-sac. This was the eighth such enclave he had explored that day; he had soon discovered that the neighbourhood of Osmington, Western Australia, was comfortable, clean, middle class and unflinchingly cheerful – in other words, identical to all the other neighbourhoods strung out like polite parasites along the Margaret River. Since starting the job five days ago the sweltering hours between noon and nine p.m. had yielded nothing in the way of commission – his only remuneration – but no end of faces chiselled into permanent smiles on impossibly pleasant people who, if they were at all irritated at the interruption to their domestic routine by a stranger knocking on their door, showed no sign of it.

Now, after less than a week of trudging around these cheery environs, Nathan longed for a frosty reception. He yearned for a frown, hankered after an impatient glance at a watch, could only dream of a door being slammed in his face. Surely a sigh wasn't too much to ask? Where were the caustic widowers, the damaged divorcées, the decrepit pensioners embittered by exhausted prostates and cartoon-sized corns?

Nathan opened the wrought-iron gate of the first house he came to, noting the tricycle in the pristine front garden. Or was it a yard? He still wasn't sure where this country stood; sometimes they thought they were American, other times English. He looked up at the house. Classic example of the architectural style of neo-shit. Dark wood cladding rubbed shoulders with beige stone. Latticework of lead decorated the windows. A huge gable sat atop the open carport, adorned with a hand-painted name sign which read "Bonhomie". Nathan tried to imagine living at an address which began "Bonhomie, Sunset Cedars", and for an instant saw himself lying in a reddened bathtub with both wrists opened.

Avoiding the susurrating sprinklers which doused gasping flowerbeds alongside the path, Nathan stepped up to the front door and rattled the cast-iron knocker. The door opened to reveal yet another smiling ponytailed clone, this one in white cotton dungarees. Nathan took a deep breath and, allowing the clone a brief "Hello," launched himself.

"Hi! How you doing? I was just in the neighbourhood for today only and thought I'd give you a call because we're part of the team who brought *Sesame Street* to the TV for kids! Have you got kids?"

I mean children, not goats.

"Yes," said the clone.

I know you have.

"Great! Well we've put together a brand-new programme for kids, designed not only to entertain, but educate as well!"

"Oh, right."

Let me in.

"And I wondered, if you've got a tiny amount of time to spare for your kids' education – just five minutes is all it'll take – whether you'd like to be among the very first to hear about our brand-new programme and take advantage of it – to help your kids!" Still not goats. Let me in.

"Oh." She's smiling. I'm in. "Well, I'm doing some baking . . ." Of course you are. "But maybe I could spare five minutes." How could you not, for your kids?

The she-clone in the doorway wiped her hands on a tea towel that she seemed to have produced from nowhere – maybe a small compartment in her back – and looked behind her as a little blonde mini-clone out of a washing-up-liquid ad ran up and hugged her thigh.

Let me in, you horrible, perfect people.

"Come in."

Nathan stepped across the threshold, savouring the morsel of triumph. For all the endless goodwill of the people who inhabited this shining, disinfected corner of the world, clearing the first significant hurdle of the doorstep was something he got to do only two or three times a day.

The clone, who introduced herself as Naomi, showed Nathan into a spectacular open-plan living/kitchen/dining room which appeared to cover a large proportion of Western Australia, and offered him a seat on a colossal sofa. No sooner had he lost himself in it than four more glittering children appeared, homing in on the she-beacon that was their mother.

It's *The Sound of* fucking *Music.*

Nathan watched as Naomi issued all five children with various impromptu orders, assigning each a mission she managed to make sound both fascinating and imperative. As the children dispersed and Naomi sat opposite him Nathan found himself almost liking this woman. She was clearly a clone in control. He felt a little bad for the deception he was about to reveal.

"Your husband home?" he ventured.

"No, no. It's his poker night. With the boys." She rolled her eyes a little, at once showing tolerant affection for her husband and establishing the informal tone for a conversation with a complete stranger to which Nathan had quickly grown accustomed since arriving in Australia.

"So what's this programme all about?" Naomi said through a broad smile.

"Well, it's a brand-new programme we've developed especially for kids." Weasel. "It's designed to teach them, in a fun way, all they need to know for the best start in life."

"Sounds good. When's it coming on?"

No avoiding it now. "Well, it's not a TV programme as such, although as I say we are part of the team responsible for the brilliant *Sesame Street*! It's a programme of entertainment and education which features fantastic things like this –"

Nathan pulled five folded charts from his rucksack. Opening each in turn, laying them on the glass coffee table before Naomi, he guided her through the multicoloured, annotated illustrations which depicted the greatest moments in history, the top-fifty species of tree, the night sky of the southern hemisphere, a cross-section of a man's body with garish internal organs, and how to design, engineer, construct and maintain a suspension bridge. Word perfect, he spoke rapidly, allowing no opportunity for intervention, and grew more enthusiastic with every new point.

Exactly fifteen minutes later Nathan had completed his tour through the coloured charts, explained that their contents actually came printed within a series of beautiful books, produced and deified the example tome bound in cocoa-brown cloth, and deftly constructed and demonstrated the handy, flat-packed plastic Dollar Dropper box (which comes free and is a fantastic saving aid – and who couldn't give up five cigarettes a day or buy a cheaper brand of perfume to help their kids?), all without once uttering the word "encyclopaedia".

Nathan sat back, spent. In doing so he was aware he was breaking a golden rule – probably *the* golden rule – of salesmanship: never stop talking. Hadn't they gone over this a hundred times back at the training centre in Perth? Never stop talking; even when you're not talking. Nuances of body language, meanings of facial expression – Christ, how open his *eyes* should be at given times. They had taught him how to sell even when silent.

The trouble was, whenever Nathan completed a "pitch" he simply needed time to recover. The physical and mental demands of a technically precise and emotionally charged performance exhausted him. He also felt an insuppressible shame at the deception he had perpetrated to get in the door, and embarrassment at the revealing of it. With these sensations came, too, an attendant feeling of grubbiness, which crawled across his body like maggots on a dead badger.

Nathan suspected he was not a born salesman.

Naomi regarded him with an expression that Nathan knew at once was not a till-ringer.

"Well, the books certainly are beautiful, Nathan, and I'm sure they *would* be great for the kids, but we've already got a set of *Encyclopaedia Britannica*."

With a leaden heart, Nathan pasted a smile on his mouth and responded the way he knew he must.

"Ah, well, that's absolutely *fine*! Because actually we're not the same as *Britannica*. Of course, if you want to know the basics, you can't fault them. But if you *really* want your kids to have a head start . . ." Oh, the shame. " . . . then the detail in our *Globe Book* is second to none, *and* you get not one but *two* beautifully bound yearbooks every year as well as the initial set of thirteen. It really is the only way to make sure your kids succeed in life."

Shoot me now.

Naomi smiled. A pleasant smile, without a doubt, but something else now, too. Nathan recognised it, and shuddered.

Please, not the sympathy. Anything but that.

"Ah, that's a lovely thought, Nathan, but you see the other thing is we're really into computers in this house." The C-word. "My husband Jim's got his own computer company in Perth – he's doing really well – and so we're all geared up here which is great."

Nathan drew himself up from the ashes, ready to deliver his stock response concerning the unrivalled and irreplaceable beauty of the printed page, but found that he just did not have the heart for it. Breaking the golden rule again he allowed Naomi to continue.

"And also lately all Jim talks about is the next big thing – the Information Superhighway. He swears by it. Says it's going to change how we learn about all sorts of things. He's shown me a few things and they look pretty exciting."

Nathan shifted on the sofa. There it was again. This was the third time someone had mentioned this "Information Superhighway". No one had told him about *that* at the training centre. He was fairly confident it wasn't an actual road, but if not that then what? He resolved to ask Aidan, his sales director, about it back at the camp.

Five minutes later Nathan was standing with Naomi at the front door. He found himself infused, as always when he failed to make a sale, with both relief at not having separated a probably very nice person from eight hundred dollars and despair at once again having earned no commission. They had quickly processed the usual niceties to conclude the meeting, featuring the usual questions: where was he from; how long had he been in Australia; what did he do before; how long was he staying; did he have any relatives here; where was he headed next? (England, a place called Crowley Green; six months; graduated from uni; as long as he could afford to; his mother had a cousin in Broome; don't know.)

As Nathan was about to take his leave one of the mini-clones reappeared at the top of the stairs.

"Mummeee! Georgie's on my Scalextric and she won't get off!"

Naomi looked briefly beleaguered then made a quick recovery.

"All right, darling. Mummy'll be right there. Nathan, would you excuse me? I'm sure this'll be another thirty-second crisis."

As Naomi floated upstairs, Nathan pondered how a moment before when the child had screamed out it was as though Naomi's mask had slipped for a second. He had seen in her, however fleetingly, something else. Tiredness, he thought. She had looked more tired than he'd ever seen anyone look.

Nathan stood in the corner of the open-plan whatever room. He stared out across the vast, plush space. It seemed to go on for ever. Way off in the kitchen area where the floor became designer slate he was sure he could see the curvature of the Earth. A pang of loneliness stabbed suddenly through him. Not for the first time since arriving in Australia he felt the physical fullness of the distance that separated him from everything and everyone he knew. Nathan looked around at the impressive tableau of affluent domesticity. How could they afford all this stuff? Right now, he had nothing in his Westpac account and fifty pounds credit on his Mastercard for emergencies. Why, oh why, he asked himself, could he not have spent his travel money just a little more wisely?

Thailand had been so cheap. Four glorious months of living in wooden shacks on perfect beaches. Arriving in Perth on a high, Nathan had been swept away by the charm of the city by the sea. Night after night of drinking and clubbing. The money had run out after six weeks. All his ambitious travel plans were suddenly in jeopardy, the destinations he had long researched now as good as a million miles away. Then he had seen the ad in the *WA Gazette*. Scanning the job pages with a Captain Morgan headache and pins sticking into his eyes the words had danced before him:

> **Want to earn serious $$$ and see Oz?**
> Amazing financial returns and extensive, all-expenses-paid travel across Australia. Your lust for life is required, experience is not. Call 1 800 456 1800 right away!!!

Now, two weeks later, here he was, a fully trained, fully crap door-to-door encyclopaedia salesman who had travelled an extensive ninety miles south of Perth and received the inarguably amazing financial return of nothing.

Next to where Nathan stood a forest of silver, gold and pewter photo frames grew out of a gleaming mahogany sidething. Looking at the photographs within them sent him spiralling further. Here were three, maybe four, generations of familial perfection. Hair shone, torsos tensed and teeth dazzled from a series of spectacular coastal locations.

Someone's framed the entire fucking Kays catalogue.

He picked up the nearest frame, surprised by its weight. In the photograph which sat inside wide gilt borders were two men. One of them Nathan recognised as Bob Hawke, the prime minister. The other man, with his pleasantly lined, tanned face, sandy hair, blue eyes and home-spun smile, could only be, judging by his appearance in most of the other photos on display, Naomi's husband, Jim. He was receiving some kind of award. So, the perfect family and a business genius too.

You lucky, shiny, arse-thumpingly irritating bugger.

Nathan turned the frame. The rear was gilt, too; hallmarked. At the top was an inscription engraved in, to Nathan's mind, an unnecessarily florid typeface:

> *Dear N,*
> *Next stop the moon!*
> *Love, J x*

Oh, holy crap. You didn't actually ask the engraver to write that.

He looked at the photo again. What kind of smug bastard bought a solid-gold photo frame to hold a picture of himself and gave it to his wife?

Nathan's thoughts were interrupted by a cacophony from upstairs. Naomi had opened one of the bedroom doors to return downstairs. He heard her voice cajoling the children to play quietly. She then reappeared on the upper landing, smiling down at him. As she descended the impressive staircase Nathan barely registered that he had lowered his hand to his rucksack and slipped the photo frame into it.

"Sorry about that, Nathan. Another disaster averted."

"No problem. Look, thanks for your time. Sorry to disturb you."

"Oh, not at all. It was really nice to meet you and I'm sorry I couldn't help you out. I guess you guys work on commission."

"Yes. Bit thin on the ground, unfortunately."

"Yeah, it must be tough. But there are heaps of families to try round here. I'm sure you'll get something out of someone."

Outside, the sun had sunk behind the eponymous cedars. Nathan glided out of the cul-de-sac.

Thief.

He made his way along a wider residential road called Cook Avenue, passing some young children gathered reverentially around an older boy on a motorbike. He passed three more turn-offs then veered into the next, another cul-de-sac, called Willowmere. He sat on a wall near the entrance and tried to remain calm.

Thief.

He took his rucksack off and put it next to him on the wall, relieved not to be touching it.

Nathan assessed how he felt. There was no doubt that, amongst other things, he was exhilarated. His heart hammered, his temples throbbed. He felt moisture above his upper lip. He thought again of the weight of the photo frame in his hand, saw the etched hallmark. I could get a hundred bucks for it. Maybe two. Pawn it in Perth, get a room and a proper job. Or a better shit job. Earn some money, travel on.

Nathan knew it was only a photo frame – not exactly a serious haul. Now I'm thinking like a fucking wise-guy. But it was a way out. He could leave the campsite tonight, after the Evening Motivation session, once the sales staff had sunk into over-submissive campbeds in the dormitory tent. Pack his stuff and sneak out. Hitch a ride to Perth.

But as he sat there on the wall, try as he might, Nathan found he could summon no enthusiasm for his plan. He felt a new heaviness in his belly. A queasy feeling, too. His pulse still raced a little but not now with exhilaration. He thought about the photo frame again. This was his first foray into larceny. He was already beginning to wonder if, as with the role of salesman, he was quite cut out for it.

To take his mind off things, Nathan decided to press on with his rounds. He glanced at his watch. 7:05 p.m. Two more hours. Maybe, just maybe, there was some commission out there. He put his rucksack back on, trying not to notice the added weight, and ventured further into Willowmere.

Just over an hour later, in Kookaburra Close, Nathan trudged away from another front door as it closed with a polite finality.

He found an ornamental bench and checked his logsheet. Forty-three houses since seven o'clock. Twenty-eight no replies, twelve unsuccessful doorstep pitches. Just one doomed full presentation to an emotionally and financially bereft widower. The remaining two calls had been aborts, which he still refused to write on his logsheet the way Aidan had demonstrated: ABOrt.

"You'll never sell to an Abo," Aidan had announced. "The Abos don't have money, so you don't give them time. ABOrt!"

At first, in protest at this policy, Nathan had given the occasional native Aboriginal family he encountered the same energies he afforded their white neighbours. He soon found, though, that the houses of these indigenous people were more down at heel and he never sensed the remotest possibility of a sale. In fact, he felt all the more guilty at attempting to wheedle a substantial sum of money from people who clearly had none to spare. Thus he avoided it, his own version of the doorstep abort a creatively truncated pitch: "Hi! How you doing?" You're Aboriginal. "I was in the neighbourhood and thought I'd give you a call because I'm selling encyclopaedias. They cost eight hundred dollars!"

Nathan slumped lower on the bench, exhausted. On any other day he would be spent by this time, he knew. But today it was not just bone-tiredness.

The guilt at first had been a small, foreign object lodged deep in the pit of his stomach, discernible, but washed over by surging adrenalin. As he had slogged on for the last hour, though, he had felt his feet become more and more weighted, his body temperature rising and falling suddenly and the hard, strange new object in his belly had become as real and defined as the one in his rucksack.

Fuck. Shouldn't have done it. Why did I do it?

Thief.

Take it back. Yeah, right. Twat. How?

Just take it back. Confess. Say sorry.

Not going to happen.

But I don't want it.

Take it back, you know you have to.

I know. I know. I'll take the fucker back.

Don't know what I'll say. I'll think of something. I will.

That's it. I'm taking it back.

I'm taking it back.

Fuck.

Nathan made his way along Kookaburra Close. The light was fading fast and lamps were clicking on in the houses around him. As if in judgement, a pair of curtains was pulled shut as he passed by. He ran through various strategies for regaining entry to the house in Sunset Cedars and returning the photo frame. He found it surprisingly easy to think of them; five days of bending the truth had served him well.

Just as he was about to leave the close he noticed a house set back further from the road than the others. He must have missed it earlier and now saw the front garden was ablaze with children's toys. In the living room someone was moving around in enticing lamp light. Nathan sighed and checked his watch. Time for one more? He would prefer to eat his own feet than go through his sales pitch once more that day, but this was a prime contender if ever he saw one. After all, he was taking the photo frame back. His financial situation would be unchanged. And after another disastrous day he would be yet again, back at camp that night, Sales Fuckwit of the Day.

The door opened to reveal a diminutive thirty-something redhead with a generous application of make-up and her hair gathered high, bronze spirals cascading in front of each ear.

"Hi! How you doing?" All tarted up. "I was just in the neighbourhood for today only and thought I'd give you a call" clearly not at a good time as it looks like you're planning on getting laid "because we're part of the team who brought *Sesame Street* to the TV for kids! Have you got kids?"

"Er, yes I have. But they're having a sleepover at a friend's and I'm afraid this really isn't a good time."

Obviously will be for someone. "Great! Well we've put together a brand-new programme for kids, designed not only to entertain, but educate as well!"

Wasting my time here.

"Oh, that's great, but as I say I'm –" The woman broke off as she heard a voice behind her.

"Right! I've got the champers open. Let's – Oh, I didn't hear the doorbell."

Beyond the redhead a man stood in the living room with an open bottle of champagne and two glasses, looking surprised. He was a tanned forty-something in pale jeans and a faded-yellow Lacoste shirt. Blue eyes peered out at Nathan from beneath freshly combed sandy hair.

Jimbo, you dirty bastard.

After a brief silence Nathan was the first to speak.

"I'm really sorry to bother you both. It looks like you're settling down to a nice cosy evening."

"That's right, we are. Sorry!" the woman in the doorway replied.

"I won't take up any more of your time."

"Oh, no worries."

Although . . .

"Although . . . maybe if I could just have a word with your . . . husband . . . here?"

"I'm sorry, I really don't think we –"

The redhead broke off again as Nathan called out past her: "Jim, isn't it?"

The man, who was bending to put the champagne and glasses on a coffee table, stood up quickly.

"Who wants to know?" he said, taking a few steps towards the door.

"Ah. My name's Nathan. I'm . . . I guess you could say I'm an acquaintance of . . . Naomi."

The man hurried to the door. Before he got there, Nathan hopped across the threshold past the dismayed redhead.

"Listen mate," said the man, "I don't know who the bloody hell you are but you'd better get out of this house right now."

"Er, well, as I said, my name's Nathan. So you do know who I am." I'm going to get my head kicked in. "Which is nice, because, as you can see, I know who you are too."

Nathan turned to the woman who now looked as though she felt sick.

"I'm sorry, er . . . ma'am . . ." Ma'am? ". . . but, you see, I need to have a quick talk with Jim here. It really won't take long, but I wonder if you'd mind very much giving us a couple of minutes?"

The woman looked stupefied. She then turned to the man.

"Jim, what's going on? Get rid of him will you? Right now." She marched out of the living room.

"Look mate. You explain yourself right now. You've got thirty seconds and then I'll break your nose if you're still standing here," said Jim.

"Gosh," Nathan said. "Thirty seconds. Well, it usually takes a full fifteen minutes but I'll try my best."

Nathan strode along Cook Avenue. It was dark now and ornate street lamps illuminated the path ahead. The air was warm and filled with the trilling of recently awoken cicadas, interrupted only by the occasional car purring home.

Job satisfaction, Nathan considered, can be found in the least expected places.

It hadn't taken too long for Jim to calm down once Nathan had outlined his proposal – which was not just a one-day-only offer but entirely exclusive to Jim. He had explained that whilst it was possible that back in Sunset Cedars Naomi might happen to hear her husband was not in fact out playing poker, it was also a mere matter of putting pen to paper to prevent it. A simple business transaction. And it wasn't as if Jim wasn't getting anything out of the deal. Quite apart from the guarantee that his nominal poker nights would to all intents and purposes remain poker nights, Jim was getting not one but two sets of beautifully bound *Globe Book* encyclopaedias, one for each of the homes that he was, in various ways, residing in. Not to mention the two biannual yearbooks for each address for the next five years. After all, you never knew when the urge for reference could strike. And the Information Superhighway couldn't help him out every time, could it?

Finally, Nathan had explained just how simple payment could be, and with not one whiff of a plastic, flat-packed Dollar Dropper. A simple cheque for the full amount now, less his commission which after some brief mental gymnastics Nathan calculated to be two hundred and twenty dollars. This, Nathan would accept in cash, to avoid having to wait for his sales director to pay it to him. The only hitch had come when Jim discovered he had only a hundred and fifty dollars on him, but after a spirited consultation in the kitchen with the redhead Jim had returned and furnished Nathan with the remainder.

Nathan continued walking up Cook Avenue. He had twenty minutes before the minibus arrived to return him and a dozen sweaty sales colleagues to the characterless campsite off the highway.

Nathan would not be crowned Salesman of the Day, he had decided, even if no one else had secured two sales. No, once again he would be denounced as a commission-free zone and treated as a pariah at the evening's festivities. Then in the middle of the night he would quietly rise, pack, leave Jim's cheque and a note for Aidan to find in the morning, and take his leave.

This time tomorrow, he predicted, he would be in a cosy bar in Perth, cold VB in hand, regaling Swedish twin sisters with tales of incorrigible derring-do.

But first, one more thing.

"Hello again." Naomi's smile was as welcoming as before, but Nathan noticed bags under her eyes now she was lit by the automatic porch light. Nathan thought again how likeable she was.

"I'm so sorry to bother you again," he said. But your husband is a two-timing bastard who should have his dick cut off.

"It's OK – I just got the kids off to bed. For the time being, of course." Again, the comfortable familiarity.

"I won't keep you long. It's just that I think I left my pen here. I must have dropped it when I was on the sofa doing my presentation. I wouldn't have bothered you, but it's got personal value – my grandmother gave it to me just before she died." Not a complete lie. She did die.

"Oh gosh, well, let's see if we can find it. Come in."

Yes.

Nathan closed the door behind him.

"I won't come right in. My shoes are a bit muddy – all those sprinklers out there."

"Oh, that's OK. You wait there and I'll see if I can find it."

Nathan reached behind him and pulled the photo frame out of the waistband of his jeans. As Naomi crouched on all fours between the sofa and coffee table he slipped the frame onto the mahogany sideboard.

"Nope. No sign of it I'm afraid, Nathan. It's not under the sofa and . . . no . . . it's not under the cushions . . . or down the back either. That's such a shame. Maybe you left it somewhere else." Naomi rose stiffly and walked back towards Nathan.

"Yes, I must have. Look, I'll go to the next house I went into and ask them. I'm sure it'll turn up."

"Yeah. Things usually do turn up, if you look hard enough."

No shit.

"Thanks for looking. I really appreciate it."

Nathan turned to go and opened the door. He was about to bid her goodnight and leave, but instead turned around again.

"Naomi."

"Yeah?"

"Um, well. There's something I think I should tell you."

"Oh really?"

"Mm. It's just . . . well, this is a bit difficult . . . I've just met your husband."

"Jim? But he's over in Waverley, playing poker."

"Well, that's just it. You see, he's not. He's actually here in Osmington and . . . he's not with . . . the boys. He's with –"

"That's quite impossible." Naomi's voice cut through Nathan's.

"Er, sorry?"

"It's impossible. As I said, Nathan, he's in Waverley."

"But I –"

"Playing poker. With the boys. Like he does most Friday nights."

Nathan looked at Naomi, taken aback by a new, flat clearness in her eyes. He opened his mouth to speak then closed it, leaving a silence as infinite as the immaculate house around him.

"Right," he said. "Of course, he's playing poker. I must have been mistaken. Sorry."

*

The front door clicked shut behind him as Nathan turned out of Naomi's garden. He closed the wrought-iron gate and headed for the entrance to the cul-de-sac.

The warm air was fragrant and sweet and the cicadas were building up an impressive crescendo. Nearby a toad hopped across a pristine lawn through a pool of solar-powered light and slipped into an ornamental pond. An exhausted cat slunk its way home, close to the wall.

Nathan was eager to reach the edge of the estate and his pick-up point, but he paused at the entrance to Sunset Cedars and looked back.

The houses had receded into shadow now, frowning out through lamp-lit windows. From somewhere a nightbird cried. All around in the gardens, the water sprinklers whispered their secrets to each other.

Nathan hoisted his rucksack higher on his back and turned to go.

A YEAR OF NOT CALLING
Thomas Jerome Seabrook

After a while I forget what I'm reading about. I haul myself up out of my chair and set my book down on the arm. I'm not sure if it's my knees or the floorboards that creak as I make my way out across the hall – both seem to need easing back into life. I go into the kitchen and clean away last night's bottles as I wait for the kettle to boil.

This house is much the same now as it was when we bought it. We'd had an overspill of furniture when we first moved in together. Some of it went to friends but after we bought this place anything that hadn't been ruined by five years of cold and damp in my parents' garage came here. Tables, dressers, armchairs. Some of it not even ours to begin with – hand-me-downs from aunts and godparents. We bought a few new bits – a bed, one of those fridges with an ice dispenser in the front – but mostly made do with what we had already. Anne called it shabby chic.

I pour myself a coffee and swing open the back door. I hear gulls chattering out across the estuary. There's a light on in the shed in the garden next to mine. My neighbour, Richard. We introduced ourselves once, but haven't said a lot more since. He seems to spend most of his days out there – doing what, I'm not sure. The young couple on the other side told me once that he makes model boats, but I've never seen any evidence of it. I remember talking to them about him before we bought the house. Keeps himself to himself, they said, since his wife died. Lived there with her and her lover. Didn't seem to mind – said women got on his nerves after a while, so he was only too happy to have someone else there to keep her busy while he worked on his boats.

The letter arrived on Wednesday. There was a time when I might have struggled to remember such a thing. In London, the post came with such comforting regularity that I could organise my morning around it. I would try to be at my desk before the first lot hit the mat, and wouldn't get up for coffee until after the second lot tumbled through. Here, though, it's more sporadic. Only a handful of people know I'm here; fewer still write or visit.

Most of the letters I do get are written by hand, which means I usually have a fair idea of what to expect before I open them. I recognised the handwriting on this one at once. I don't know if I was expecting Anne to write, but I wasn't surprised that she had. I held the envelope up to the light, hoping to get some sense of what it might say from the thickness of the paper or the force with which the address had been scored into it. I got little sense of either, so set it down on the dresser by the door, unopened, and carried on about my business in the hope that I might soon be able to forget about it.

We bought this house two summers ago. We would once have scoffed at the idea of weekend cottages and the need to get out of the city. I remember Anne telling me, only half joking, that she was too beautiful to live in a place where nobody would see her. I tended to agree. But these things change. I'd never been too keen on the idea of having children, but it was hard not to be awed by the changes in Anne and the mysterious creature growing inside her. I laid my head on her belly and started to give serious thought to buying somewhere outside London. Maybe not a new home exactly but somewhere we could escape to once in a while. Close enough that we could drive back into town in the morning if we needed to.

The institute was OK with my coming in less often. I'd never been much of a team builder so it didn't make a lot of difference where my desk was. Why not make it somewhere we could wake to the gentle brushing of the tide against stony sand, or take afternoon walks out across the mud as it dried between our toes?

Yesterday, Friday, I woke slowly, my head heavy from drink and another night's broken sleep. I went out into the hallway after breakfast to see if any new post had arrived, but it hadn't. Anne's letter was still there on the dresser. I held it up in front of me again. There had always been something odd about her handwriting. It had the flamboyance one might expect of an actress, but there was something of the schoolgirl to it, too. The *M*s swirled extravagantly, but the *A*s were perfectly round. That was Anne all over, I suppose.

I caught a glimpse of myself in the mirror above the dresser. I looked tired. The thought of Anne writing after all this time unnerved me. What good could come of it? I hadn't seen her for a year, and we hadn't talked in any meaningful sense for even longer. There was little that could be said now that would do anything but bring back the pain of the past few years.

I thought about burning the letter. I threw it away but dug it back out of the bin a few minutes later. I didn't want to read it, but I couldn't destroy it, either. I took it into the front room, rolled open my desk, and pushed it into a slim shelf between bank statements and parish circulars. At least there I wouldn't have to see it.

The tide is out this evening, and the sun is still just about within reach. Whatever Richard is doing over there in his shed, he does it in silence. I look out across the mudflats at patches of low, scrubby marsh and narrow creeks that look like they've been carved out of the ground with a butter knife. A few boats are stood here and there on tiptoed keels, precarious-looking but perfectly still. Scratched plastic buoys roll around in the light breeze, lost without a current to bob up and down in. Factory chimneys cough and splutter gently across the water.

I turn back towards the house and make a mental note to do something about the clumps of greying paint that hang from the door and window frames. Not much has changed since I came back here. The young couple next door has been replaced by another, slightly older, from Upminster. They don't say very much. He raises a hand once in a while; she shows a few teeth. They work long hours during the week, but are always up by nine on Sundays to dig and drill and bang. They'll sell it as soon as they're done, I'm sure, and then somebody else can rip out the kitchen.

I hear a sound from Richard's shed, something metallic bouncing two or three times on concrete. I look over to where the sound came from and see Richard peering back at me through a thick Perspex window. He disappears for a moment, and then re-emerges from the door at the side of the shed. I take a sip of cold coffee, and realise I've been standing out here for quite a while.

Richard meets me at the fence, leaning forward on his forearms as if he's standing on tiptoes. The hair on the top of his head seems to have emigrated to his eyebrows, which stick out at the sides and are starting to merge in the centre.

"You look tired, Matthew."

I shrug.

"Not sleeping?"

"Not a lot," I say. "It's the foxes. They seem to spend all night fighting in my garden. Howling like bloody hyenas."

He smiles, and seems friendlier than I remember.

"You know what'll get rid of 'em, don't you?" he asks. I don't. "Mark your territory."

"You want me to piss all over my back garden?"

"Why not? Can't hurt."

I wonder about that.

"What are you doing over there anyway?" I ask.

"Makin' a boat. Have a look if you like. Come round the back."

I don't know much about boats, but I go anyway.

In the end I just had to leave. I put a few things in a bag – books, clothes, toothbrush – and went. I didn't tell Anne, but it didn't feel like I needed to. She was sleeping in the front room by then, and we only seemed to speak to each other when it became absolutely necessary to share information.

I didn't have much of a plan when I got in the car, but once I started driving it seemed obvious. The house had sat empty for months. We'd talked about spending our summers here, and maybe moving down permanently once Michael got a bit older; the schools were meant to be good. None of that happened, of course. We'd barely spent a night here since the year we bought it. Perhaps that's what drew me back.

I let myself in and looked around. I felt relief at first. The weight was gone. I spent a few days reading, walking, watching the tide come in and go out, following the last rays of the sun across the purple-grey mud. The house that was meant to provide our escape from the city became my refuge from the world.

I didn't think about Anne for a while, but then she started to creep back in snatches, like the drip of a tap that kept leaking however hard I tightened the nut. Little things came and went in my mind. The way she picked the toppings off her pizza and ate the dough first. The faces she pulled when she curled her eyelashes. And then after: the jogging-bottoms, the endless hours of daytime television. Boxes of tissues but no tears.

Richard's shed is bigger and cleaner than I expected it to be. There's a workbench running down one side of it, stacked up at each end with pots of paint and varnish, clamps and brushes, hammers and chisels and electrical components. In the middle is the scaled-down hull of a boat held in a vice between two bright spotlights.

"That one's not quite ready," he says. "Still got the riggin' to do." He gestures towards a sheet of sailcloth marked out but not yet cut.

I take a step closer. The hull is made up of hundreds of thin hardwood slats formed into an elegant curve, with miniature cannon pointing out from the lower deck. The front narrows to a point in the shape of an elephant's tusk. The nest at the top of the mainmast looks like it has been slotted together from pieces smaller than matchsticks.

Richard carries on talking, but I stop listening for a moment. I find myself looking through the open doorway across the garden instead, out over the sea. When the sun goes down it's hard to tell whether the tide is on its way in or out. I remember there being some way of figuring it out from the direction the boats are facing. Anne would know.

"Got more in the house, if you're interested," Richard says. I am.

Going into his house is like looking at mine through a dirty mirror. The layout of the rooms is the same but everything in them seems like it's been there for years and is now slowly fading to dust. A pair of small, bare shelves stick out from one wall of the kitchen; a boiler hangs exposed in the far corner. An assortment of ill-matched, tea-stained cups are piled up on a scratched wooden tabletop. There's a radio in the corner; Eddie Mair is laughing to himself about something. Richard pulls a cord to switch on the light by the stairs.

"They're up here," he says.

Michael died in his sleep. If his arrival brought unprecedented joy and happiness to us both, his death brought only silence. Friends kept away at first, then came flooding to see us, but they didn't know what to say or do, and soon dropped into the background. We weren't sure what to say to them, either. Anne's mother stayed with us in the beginning, but she too left after a couple of weeks. There was only so much she could do to keep out of our way.

Anne and I began to avoid each other, as well. We weren't conscious of it – it just happened. Several days could pass without us saying much more than goodnight or good morning. We ate separately out of cartons pulled from the fridge and warmed up in the microwave.

I wanted Anne to scream but she didn't. I wanted her to cry out as she stood in the doorway and watched me dismantle the cot and pack it carefully into piles of long thin bits and corner brackets and screws. I wanted her to tell me how much of a heartless bastard I was as I tied everything up in a pink sack and put it out behind the bins late at night so the neighbours couldn't see. I only saw her cry once, while we were watching P. J. Harvey on *Newsnight Review*. Neither of us said anything.

I spent my evenings in the spare room, sat in front of a desk covered in Post-it notes and articles printed out from the Internet, my head filled with facts and statistics about toxic chemicals in mattress fabrics, low birth weights, deficiencies in Medium-Chain Acyl-Coenzyme A Dehydrogenase.

Upstairs is a room crammed with unmade single beds, on each of which are two or three of Richard's boats. A few more are balanced carefully on shelves above a sealed-up fireplace. I know little about boats, but recognise some of them from books.

"HMS Bellona," Richard says. "Laid down 1758. Fought in the War of Independence."

He leads me around the room, pointing out features of each boat as we pass it – the complexities of the rigging, the particular way the boards of the deck have been arranged, how realistic the paintwork is. He seems glad to have somebody to show all of this to.

"These are amazing, Richard," I tell him.

"I started making 'em for my son, John," he says, "'cept he wasn't my son, not that I knew that at the time. Peggie had a friend. Used to go swimming together. That's how they met, you know. Out there in the sea. Didn't think a lot about it at the time, just that it was nice, her having someone to go out there with. Never was much of a swimmer m'self. He came and lived with us eventually. Wanted to be with his boy. Couldn't really blame him. I wanted to be with him too."

"What's John doing these days?" I ask.

"He lives in America. Far as I know he's married now. I hear things from time to time. Not a lot, though."

We go back downstairs. Richard puts the kettle on. We talk some more about his boats, and his wife. Most of it tallies with what I'd heard before, but it seems sadder this time. I think about telling him about Michael but I don't. Another time, maybe. I remember I have other things I should be doing and make my excuses. Richard tells me it's been nice having someone to talk to, that I should pop in again sometime. He's got some books I might like.

I make my way out around the back of the house and stop at the end of the garden to listen to the breeze and the light lapping of the tide against pebbles and sand. The factories across the water blink and flash orange and red like a distant amusement arcade. Everything else is still. I stand for a moment and think about the letter, how it's about time I opened it.

I go inside, pull the envelope out from where I left it and tear across the top with my forefinger. There are three pages inside, tightly written, front and back. I can't help but scan the whole thing before reading it properly. Some parts look kinder than others, but one line sticks out among the rest. *At least let me speak to you. You owe me that much.*

That much I know.

BOOZEHOUNDS
Philip Makatrewicz

It was just gone noon when Paddy Gombrowicz emerged from his bedroom, adjusting his dressing gown and scratching his armpit. And, as he plunged his hand down his boxer shorts to make the required adjustments, he surveyed the scene. There was crap everywhere. A patch of sticky brown stuff on the floor. Probably the last of the *powidła* he had bought as a treat from the Polish deli on Streatham High Street. Empty bottles and their casually discarded caps littered the floor. Two days' worth of dirty plates and cups. He allowed himself a groan. One extra hourlet of sleep and he wouldn't have had this pain in the arse of a headache. He needed fortification. His eyes landed on the dog-end of a joint among the overspill of the ashtray. He shrugged, wiped it clean of ash on the sleeve of his dressing gown, and lit it. It offered up a couple of sour tokes and then it was gone.

There was nothing for it. Paddy began to harvest the rubbish from the floor like a child collecting shells on the beach. Poker chips. The ace of spades. Three jokers laughed at him from the hardwood floor.

On the battered old couch a creature stirred. Paddy threw a fistful of bottle caps in its direction.

"What the fuck was that for?" it yelped.

"I felt like it."

"Bastard."

"Now, now," Paddy grinned, "no need to get wound up."

The creature rolled off the couch in a loose heap of sweaty limbs and landed in an ashtray.

"*Kurwa jasna!*" it swore.

Paddy laughed. "*Chwała bogu.* A miracle. Someone who feels worse than I do."

The creature began to lick the ash off its testicles in a slovenly fashion, lapping its lazy tongue over the rough pink skin before deciding it could no longer be bothered.

"Do you have to do that when I'm here?"

"It's not my fault I'm completely shameless."

"How can you be shameless if you know what you're doing is revolting?"

"Let's not go through that again. You know the answer."

Paddy sighed. "I just can't seem to get used to seeing my little brother lick his balls in front of me, that's all."

"*Przepraszam.* I'm sorry. I'll try not to do it in future."

Paddy shook several cigarette packets and muttered "Thank Christ for that," when one proved not to be empty. Two Marlboros. Reds as well. A bonus. He put one of them to his lips and set it alight, inhaling deeply, pensively, as if the smoke contained an answer that would percolate into his bloodstream and then disperse through his entire body until it finally hit his brain.

"Patrik . . ." It felt strange to hear his proper name. His Polish name. It was as if his brother was talking to a different person.

"Yes, Jacek?"

"Where are Stanisław and Bogdan?"

"*U Mamy.* They've gone to Mama's."

"Oh."

Jack looked around him for a second, focused on a patch of the floor and sniffed. Paddy wondered what he could possibly be smelling.

"She doesn't know about me yet, does she?"

"No."

"Where does she think I am?"

"France."

"France?"

"She thinks you've run off with a French girl. She says she doesn't mind, she just wishes that you'd call to let her know you're OK. I know, I know," he said as Jack emitted a series of high-pitched little whines and buried his face between his paws. "It was Stan who came up with that little gem, so now we have to go with it until we find a way of getting you out of this mess. Mama believes it though. 'Such a good-looking boy,' she says. 'I always said there's not a girl in the world who could resist that twinkle in his eye. I mean all of you have it, but my little brown-eyed boy . . .'"

Jack began to pad around the room, placing his paws gingerly in the spaces between all the detritus scattered about the floor. "I miss wearing shoes," he said.

"I know you do, kid. I know you do."

Paddy looked down at Jack, who was now standing next to him, his tongue hanging from his mouth, his head by his brother's knees. Paddy bent down and held the cigarette in Jack's mouth, allowing him to take a couple of drags. He looked at his brother's wagging tail and for half a second his eyes threatened to well up.

"Last night's brainstorming session didn't help much, did it?" asked Jack.

"Did you really think it would?"

"I guess n–"

Without finishing the word Jack suddenly began barking uncontrollably, first at the wall, and then at the ceiling. Paddy, his head still pounding, held his fingers to his temples and screwed up his face in pain. "Will you shut up?" he pleaded, all the time looking around for the cause of the consternation. It was a moment before he realised that the sun must have come out again from behind the clouds, and was to blame for Jack's distress. For a swathe of golden light had sluiced through the funky gloom from a gap in the curtains. It was reflecting off his watch, creating a quivering disc of light that now danced over the cracks in the ceiling. Jack had seen the disc and made a sworn enemy of it. "Please, Jack, think of my poor head . . ."

Jack seemed oblivious to his brother's request and continued persecuting his new-found foe until Paddy removed his watch and put it face down on the table. A guilty silence enveloped the room. Jack bowed his head and put his tail between his legs. "Sorry. I just seem to lose control when that happens."

"It's all right. I should know by now." Paddy placed a hand on his brother's back and began gently stroking the fur on his neck, working his way up behind his pointy ears, and down beneath his muzzle to purrs of canine pleasure. "Why don't you grab a quick drink of water and then I'll take you for a walk."

He couldn't help a little smile when he saw Jack's tail slowly begin to wag again, although it quickly disappeared when his brother ignored the saucepan half filled with water on the floor. Instead, Jack made his way to the toilet and began to drink greedily from the bowl. He had never done that before. If someone had suggested he do it he would have said, "What do you think I am? A dog or something?" And Paddy would have said, "No, of course not. You're my brother."

"Any luck finding that bastard Rodrigo?" Stan slurred.

Paddy checked the clock and saw that it was five in the afternoon. The twins had just got back and the day was as good as gone already.

"No. I was stuck here looking after our little brother. I took him for a walk. And where the fuck have you two been?"

"We told you. We went to Mama's," said Dan.

"I see. And when did she move into a pub?"

"What pub?" cried Dan, his already rufous cheeks reddening further, his eyes refusing to leave the floor.

"Honestly Paddy, we don't know what you're talking about. Mama says hi, by the way," added Stan, shifting his weight guiltily from foot to foot.

Paddy narrowed his eyes. The twins stood there, shamefaced and unshaven. They were both still wearing the same clothes they'd had on the previous night. Of the two it was Dan who was growing fatter faster. It seemed to Paddy as if the blood had recently been flowing away from his brain and into his stomach.

"Don't give me that. The pair of you stink of booze and fags. I've only just managed to clear this place up after last night. Have you forgotten about him?"

Paddy pointed to Jack, who was in the corner wrestling energetically with an old tweed slipper. It was one of a pair that Paddy had bought him to chew on from a charity shop on their walk to the Common that afternoon. As they all watched him he paused, surrendered the slipper and looked up at his brothers. His long tongue hung from his mouth, his tail offering a couple of tentative wags.

"What?" he barked.

"Here boy," said Stan, genuflecting and slapping his thigh in encouragement.

"*Spierdalaj.* Arsehole. Don't treat me like a dog."

"All right, then. Will you come for this?" He produced a pack of cigarettes from his pocket, pulled one out, struck a match and lit it. "Ah, that's good," he sighed.

Jack began to wag his tail harder. He cocked his head to one side and emitted a series of whines and whimpers, all the time gazing imploringly at the glowing cherry.

"It's not just good, it's fantastic." Stan exhaled a plume of grey smoke whose tendrils stretched luxuriously towards Jack's twitching nose. Paddy fumed as he watched Dan sway on his feet, struggling to contain his laughter as Jack began inching towards the cigarette, whimpering.

"He's still your fucking brother! What're you trying to do to the kid?" cried Paddy, swatting the cigarette from Stan's hand. He lit another cigarette, walked over to Jack and held it in front of his mouth. "Here you go, Jack."

Jack pulled hard on the cigarette. After a couple of drags he coughed twice from the very back of his throat, his head jerking back each time with a violent spasm.

"Shit! Are you OK?"

"I think so," replied Jack. "That cigarette tastes funny."

Paddy took a drag on it. "Tastes fine to me. Here, have another go on it."

"I think I'll pass. I'm thirsty. I need a drink."

"Vodka?" said Paddy. "I've got a bottle stashed."

"No thanks."

"I'll fill your pan up."

"Don't worry about it," said Jack, setting off at a languid trot.

Paddy couldn't think of anything else to offer his brother. He looked at the twins as they heard a lapping sound from the toilet. They saw what was happening. He was glad that now they seemed worried too.

"What were you saying about vodka?" asked Stan as he collapsed into an armchair and slid with the same movement into a slump.

"All right, all right," said Paddy, climbing onto a chair and reaching up to the top of the empty bookcase where his bottle was stashed. "I think we could all do with one."

"Where are the cards?" cried Stan.

"No cards," said Paddy flatly, feeling himself sober up all of a sudden. Eight in the p.m. was no time to be plastered. He hadn't left his armchair for over two hours, even though he'd been bursting for a piss for the last twenty minutes. They hadn't begun to think about dinner yet, and when they did they'd remember that there was nothing to eat in the flat but half an onion and a hunk of mouldy cheese. Nor had they made back enough of the money that they had lost to waste on groceries. It seemed unlikely that the twins would remember about that thing called food any time soon, and there was canned dog food for Jack, which was fine ever since he had developed a taste for the stuff.

"Oh, come on," said Dan. "I'm in the mood for a little game."

"No. That's what got us into this mess in the first place."

"And maybe it's what will get us out of it," argued Stan as he tried to find a space in the ashtray to stub out his cigarette.

"Not if we sit around here and play amongst ourselves it won't."

Stan and Dan fell silent. Paddy grimaced. There was nothing they could come up with against that. "And he's getting worse," he said.

"Who is?" asked Dan.

"Jack, you moron."

"Oh."

"Haven't you bloody noticed? I know the pair of you spend half your lives with your heads up each other's arses, but your brother's turned into a dog, he's been a dog for nearly two weeks, and he's starting to act more and more like a dog every day. He's only nineteen, for God's sake. You think he's finding this easy to deal with?"

Stan and Dan exchanged one of the looks they frequently did with one another. Mama had once told Paddy that as the oldest brother he should look after Jack more than Stan and Dan, as the twins would always look after themselves. Twin before kin, he had thought.

"Oh, will one of you just say it . . ."

Stan shrugged. "All right. It's your fault."

Paddy sucked in so much air that he momentarily threatened to explode. Then he did explode. "You selfish bastards! You selfish, fucking forgetful bastards! If Mama only knew about the pair of you, what a pair of little selfish fucking bastards you are! Have you forgotten how it happened? Have you completely forgotten about how I was only trying to bail you two idiots out?"

"*Być może.* Could be. But we didn't ask you to step into our hole and keep digging. You messed up, Paddy. You did. Just admit it for once," countered Stan.

"*Tak jest.* That's right, admit it for once," echoed Dan.

"Fuck off the pair of you. You didn't warn me what Rodrigo would be like. He turned Jack into a dog. I mean, who the fuck can turn someone into a dog?"

Stan mumbled something unintelligible while Dan stared blankly at the wall.

"Now what we have to do is put a stop to all this pointing of fingers and concentrate on helping Jack. That means we need to get some fast cash and we need to find Rodrigo. Any ideas?"

"Well . . ."

"Erm . . ."

"Useless. Completely useless, the pair of you. Tonight we'll go out and ask some questions. You two go ask Ahmed and his lot what they know, and then ask Chinese Dave. He seems to know everyone."

"And what are you going to do?"

"I'm going to take Jack to Mama's," said Paddy, lowering his voice.

"What!" cried Dan.

"Do you really think that's a good idea?" asked Stan.

"Shhh! I'm worried," said Paddy, checking the room with a glance over his shoulder. "He's becoming more like a dog every day. I'm worried that soon something's going to happen so that Mama will never get to speak to him again."

"Like what?"

"Keep it down," urged Paddy, nodding towards the bedroom. "I don't want him to hear. I'm just worried is all."

"What will you tell her?"

"I don't know. I'll have to think of something."

As the door slammed behind the twins Jack appeared from the darkened bedroom, his tongue hanging from the side of his mouth like a slobbered-on slice of ham.

"Hungry?" asked Paddy.

Jack barked his assent.

Paddy felt a flush of concern pass through him like bad chicken. "Jack?"

"Yeah?"

"Nothing."

Paddy went to the kitchenette in the corner of the living room, opened a can of dog food and spooned it out into a bowl for his brother. For himself he retrieved the half an onion from the fridge. He gave Jack his dinner and bit into the onion. It was a good onion, but the gurgling lamentations of his stomach told him that it would be insufficient to satisfy his hunger. Jack thrust his muzzle into the mushy pile of brown and began scoffing noisily. He was clearly a little irritated when Paddy interrupted his meal.

"Why did you bark just then?"

"When?"

"When you barked instead of saying yes."

"I dunno. Felt like it, I guess."

Paddy went back into the kitchen as Jack continued his feeding frenzy. He was still too occupied with his guzzling to notice Paddy return and sit down on the floor right next to him, cross-legged, brandishing a fork.

"Move over."

"What the hell are you doing?" cried Jack.

"If it's good enough for my little brother, it's good enough for me. I'm starving."

Paddy loaded up a forkful and brought it slowly to his mouth, pausing to smell it. He braced himself, took a deep breath, opened wide and in it went. He chewed twice, three times, and then with great effort swallowed. He saw Jack staring at him.

"Well?"

"Let me try it again." Paddy took another mouthful. This time he chewed a little more, and swallowed with a little less effort. "It's not too bad," he said.

"Does that mean I have to share?"

"I'll open another can."

Paddy was still sitting cross-legged by Jack, leaning with his back against the side of an armchair, smoking a cigarette. In front of them lay the licked-clean bowl and the can of dog food, empty save for the fork protruding from it. Paddy had offered Jack a cigarette; Jack had politely declined.

"Paddy . . ."

"*Czego?* What's up?"

"Why do you think I'm getting worse?"

"What makes you say that?"

"I'm a dog. We have excellent hearing. I heard every word you said to Stan and Dan. I don't want to see Mama. I don't think I could bear it." His head dropped and he whimpered a little. His tail was tucked up between his buttocks.

"I think you should."

"Why?"

Paddy lit a cigarette with the end of the one he had just smoked and mulled over his words.

"You think I'm going to stay like this, don't you?"

Paddy said nothing.

"And you think I'm becoming more dog and less human every day."

"Well," exhaled Paddy, "you have started doing things you would've refused to do at first. You chase lights, you lick your own balls, you don't smoke, you drink from the toilet." Paddy watched Jack stare down at his crotch and inspect his testicles.

"I dunno. I guess they all just seem so . . . such . . . natural things to do now."

"That's the problem. It's all starting to seem a bit natural for you. And you're a dog now. I've no idea how he turned you into a dog, and I've no idea if he can turn you back. I've no idea where *he* even is, and I've no idea if we'll ever raise enough cash to pay him off. The only thing I *do* have an idea of is that I think you should see Mama before you're all dog."

Jack trotted through the open door into the hallway where there was a full-length mirror and began to watch his own reflection with great interest.

"What kind of dog am I? A golden retriever?"

"No, I don't think so. Your fur is the wrong colour. And it's too short. Oh, and your nose is too stubby."

"A Rottweiler then?"

"No, you don't look strong enough."

"A German shepherd?"

"You're way too small. No, I'm afraid you're a mongrel, my little brother."

He wished he could take back his words when he saw Jack turn away from the mirror, lie down and sink his head between his paws.

"Ah, you're still a handsome mutt. And everyone knows that mongrels are smarter and healthier than pedigree dogs."

"I'm not going."

"You have to."

"I won't see her."

"I'll make you." Paddy went to get the leash.

"Over my dead mongrel body you will."

"Oh really?" Paddy drew towards Jack with the leash.

"I won't speak to her. I'll just bark and she'll think that you've gone mad," Jack bristled back at him.

Paddy dropped the leash to the ground. He was defeated. Tired from the vodka, and from the way that the whole saga was grinding him down. Beaten by his brother's adamant stare. His well was dry. His throat was parched. All he needed right then was a seat and a drink and a moment's peace just to think things through.

"He's gone!"

Paddy burst into the twins' room.

"Jack is gone! I can't find him anywhere."

"Shit," said Stan, half asleep but waking fast. "Are you sure?"

"Of course I bloody am! He's disappeared. I found the front door open."

"What time is it?" asked Dan, still under his blanket, curled up in the foetal position.

"One. We'd better go and start looking for him right away."

Stan and Dan rolled out of their beds. Stan started pulling on his clothes. Dan had slept in his.

"Have you seen my jumper? The grey one?" asked Stan.

"Not likely," Paddy replied.

There were half-drunk cups of milky coffee fermenting on the windowsill. Patches of damp on the wallpaper, peeling and faded. A dog-eared poster of Pamela Anderson in her *Baywatch* swimsuit, peeling too. Crushed beer cans that had been called into service as ashtrays. Dirty clothes everywhere. And the rest of the flat wasn't much better. It wasn't fit for a dog to live in. Perhaps that was why Jack had left.

"Have we got anything for breakfast?" asked Stan.

"There's dog food," Paddy replied.

"I'll live."

"Did you get any leads last night on where we might find our Mr Rodrigo?"

"Nothing," said Stan. "No one knows anything about him. They haven't seen him around or heard from him or anything. It's like he doesn't even exist."

"Shit."

"Where shall we start looking?" asked Dan.

"Not the pub," said Paddy.

"Give us some credit," said Stan.

"Sorry. OK, why don't the two of you try looking around here. Look in the park and ask at the butcher's. They may be our best bets right now. I'll go to the copy shop and get as many posters printed up as I can. Have either of you got any cash?"

Dan and Stan turned out their pockets, and between lint and fluff managed to muster up five pounds twenty-three and a cough drop between them.

"That'll have to do, I suppose."

Paddy managed to put up around a hundred posters on lamp posts and telephone boxes. Since he had no photographs of the canine Jack they contained only a phone number and a simple description: "Lost – A small light-brown mongrel with big brown eyes and pointy ears. No collar. Answers to the name Jack. A much-loved family dog who is greatly missed." He worked all the way down Streatham High Street, past the ice rink and down to the Common, where he received sympathetic nods from people walking their dogs. He remembered the English reputation as a nation of dog lovers, and he found this thought comforting.

When he got home at six he was surprised to find the twins still out. He was even more surprised when they came home an hour later stone-cold sober.

"Any luck?"

"'Fraid not," said Stan.

"We must've walked for miles," added Dan.

"We only came home because it was getting too dark to see. We saw some of your posters on the way home, though. Nice work."

"Thanks."

"We managed to do something, too."

"What was that?"

"Well, when we went to ask Ahmed about Rodrigo yesterday, he said he couldn't help. But he did give us a tip. He said if we bet on horse number two in the five fifteen at Catterick today we couldn't lose. Then he winked at us. We managed to borrow fifty pounds from Chinese Dave and stopped off at the betting shop earlier while we were looking for Jack. You'll never guess what. The horse won! Ten to one!" He threw a crumpled wad of twenties on the table. "Five hundred pounds."

"*Ja pierdole!* Bloody hell, boys! We can eat!"

"And drink." Stan fished a bottle from inside his coat. "It won't make Jack come back, but then not a lot will."

Paddy sighed. "I guess a little drink wouldn't hurt. Why don't you grab one of the takeaway menus and we can order some food."

"What're we gonna do about Jack now, Paddy?" asked Dan.

"No idea. I guess we just keep looking until we find him."

"What if we don't find him?"

"We will."

"But what if we don't?"

"We will. But until then I guess I'm stuck with the pair of you mad bastards. Come here."

He wrapped the twins up in a fraternal bear hug. He wanted to say something but didn't. He didn't want to be labelled the big sister.

Paddy was woken at the indecent hour of ten in the morning three days later by the shrill nag of the telephone. Why had he agreed to have it in his room? That's right. Dan and his sex lines. He fumbled for the receiver and managed to hold it to his ear.

"Patrik? *To ty?* Is that you?"

"It's me Mama."

"Are Stanisław and Bogdan with you?"

"They're still sleeping."

"Were you sleeping?"

"Yes Mama."

"But it's ten o'clock."

"I know Mama."

"Why don't you get up and come over to mine?"

"Maybe in a bit Mama."

"Come soon. I want to show you something."

"OK Mama."

Paddy turned over and shut his eyes but further sleep eluded him. Mama was right. It was ten o'clock. No time to be in bed. He grudgingly crawled out from under the duvet and pulled on some clothes. He shouted the twins' names and banged on their bedroom door. No reply. He put his ear to the door and heard two strands of heavy snoring. He banged on the door harder and harder until it rattled in the frame and he finally got something approaching a response from within.

"I'm off to see Mama. Are you boys coming or what?"

Incoherent rumblings. Paddy threw the door open to be greeted by the sight of Stan and Dan in the contortions of hungover sleep, blankets twisted, the air foul with the stench of sweat and farts.

"This whole fucking flat is a complete pigsty. Do you hear me? I'm off to Mama's now, but when I get back I want this whole place tidied. Any questions? No, I thought not."

With that Paddy marched out of the room and grabbed his coat. He was about to leave when he caught sight of himself in the mirror. He stopped abruptly. "Bloody hell," he muttered, running a hand over his stubble and pulling the skin under his eyes. It was out of the question to let Mama see him in this state. He chucked his coat down and went to the bathroom, where he had a steaming hot shower and a shave.

It took Paddy twenty minutes to get to the estate by bus. He spent the time looking for some kind of good news to bring Mama, but could think of none. It had been so long since he had thought about anything other than Jack. For now Jack was in France, but there would be other questions. He decided he would ring Zbysiek later to see if that Irish builder had any more work going. Or maybe the agency. That way he could at least tell her there was work on the cards.

He took the lift to the tenth floor of her breeze-block tower. The

English government had been kind enough to give her a council flat near Forest Hill that provided her with a fine view of London. On a clear day she could see a panorama that still made her giddy with delight. It stretched from Canary Wharf in the east to the giant steel arch of the new Wembley to the west. When she had asked why a stadium needed such a big arch, Paddy had explained to her that it was like the new *bazylika* of English football. Her flat was easily recognisable by the neat little window boxes which seemed to be permanently in bloom. Paddy and the boys had sorted out some little shits who vandalised Mama's flowers once, and now it was well known that the flowers were to be left alone. When he knocked on the door he thought that he must still be asleep because he imagined that he heard a dog barking inside.

Mama opened the door. "Patrik! *Dziecko!* My baby!"

"It's Paddy now, Mama."

"Oh, what rubbish you boys talk with your English names. What's wrong with the good Polish names I gave you? And Patrik? That's the same in English anyway! Never mind, never mind! Quickly now, come inside before you freeze to death."

Paddy knew better than to argue. He leaned down to give Mama a kiss on the cheek, but she swiftly wiped her hands on her cooking apron and yanked Paddy's head into her considerable chest, planting kisses on his scalp.

"It's good to see you, Mama."

"Are you hungry? I can make you some food. I have eggs and bacon."

"Eggs and bacon would be great, Mama."

Paddy removed his shoes and hung his coat up on a peg. He breathed deeply, enjoying the sweet smell of cleanliness. It smelt of peaches. He wished that he could live somewhere that smelt of peaches.

"Come, come through to the kitchen."

Paddy let his Mama take him by the arm.

"So what did you want to show me?"

"It's in here," she said, pushing the door open.

Paddy stopped dead in his tracks.

"J-Jack?" Paddy could barely push the word out.

"No: Jacek. I told you. Polish names are perfectly good," said Mama.

The dog was lying under the table. Its big brown eyes stared inscrutably at Paddy. They betrayed nothing.

"But how did you know his name was Jacek?"

"I didn't, silly. That's what I decided to call him. What I want to know is how you knew his name. It's quite uncanny. It must be a sign that I've given him the right one," Mama said, clasping her hands together and smiling. "Yes, that must be it."

The dog's mouth opened wide in a cavernous yawn that culminated in a lazy lick of its lips.

"So he . . . he didn't tell you his name?"

"*Ale skont zie?* What are you talking about? Of course he didn't! What has gotten into you? I may be getting old, but I know perfectly well that dogs can't talk. I found him."

"But he said he didn't want to come here," muttered Paddy, more to himself than to Mama.

"Son, are you OK? Have you been smoking that horrible crack stuff? Please don't tell me you've touched that stuff. It's a terrible, terrible thing. I've seen it here. You mustn't be going anywhere near that stuff, it's –"

"I haven't been smoking crack, Mama. Sorry, I'm just tired and I thought that I recognised that dog, that's all."

"I first saw him a couple of days ago and then I realised that he was following me wherever I went. Every time I looked at him he tried to hide or turn away from me, but still, he'd always be waiting near the doors if I was at home. I decided to try and make friends with him, but he was very shy at first. Then I told him what a beautiful dog he was, how lovely, and he came closer to me. I think he just wanted a bit of kindness. So I offered him a piece of *kiełbasa* and he came right up and ate it out of my hand. And when I saw him up close, well I cried out to the Blessed Virgin saying if those big brown eyes of his aren't the spitting image of my Jacek's then I . . . well, I just don't know what. I thought of how I miss my Jacek now that he's run off to France with that harlot of his, and I thought that it must be a sign – that the Good

Lord has sent me this beautiful dog to keep me company while my Jacek is gone. He even watches the soap operas with me like Jacek used to. Only he can't tell me what's happening in them, like Jacek would, seeing as he can't speak English like Jacek could."

Paddy stared into those big brown eyes and tried to fathom their depths. Was his brother still there? He didn't know what to think. "Jacek. Here Jacek. Here boy."

The dog barked and wagged its tail.

BENEATH THE FIRE
Gul Y. Davis

that nurse, that young tart tara, doin that thing with the window in the door, turnin the key so they can goggle-eye in at you. bangin open the door, tellin me my room stinks
and to get out of bed and to go see this doctor
make out I'm asleep but she's yankin the duvet right off and my knickers 've ridden in and my top's all up showin it. an her face when she saw me. she doesn't mean to make that face. my insides all twisty lookin up at her starin. try cover myself with my hands
turns her back
"get yourself sorted out" she says, pulls open the curtain

tara swipes her card at lock an lets us off ward, swipes it at another lock, gets us on the stairs – I back away, pullin at my hair
"doctor amis said I should use the lift cause of my heart"
tara bitchin that my heart won't get no better if I'm just lazy in bed and stairs do me good. want so bad to tell her to fuck herself. stare at her, all that black eye make-up and red-lip
"come on" she says. "it's only stairs"
foldin my arms to stop em twitchin "– doctor amis said I gotto use the lift"
"it's only one flight of stairs –"

"I can't fuckin do it!"
"you're not that fat you foul-mouth bitch, no skin off my nose, take you back to ward if you carry on"
"– but I can't –"
"that's up to you then – that'll look good, won't co-operate to go see him. let me tell you. thought they're even considering letting you in a mile of your kid. makes me sick"
stood at bottom of the stairs, smile on her face like a half moon cut with her red lippy, watchin me holdin the rail, my arse an my legs and my sweat an all, makin my hair all wet with my breathin
I know what I look like
that smile on her face listenin to me strugglin
gonna get her I am

she's sweet as pie flutterin her lashes at the doctor as she lets me into the interview room
he smiles at her lookin at her titties
tells me to sit down
the chair's rubbish, his eyes, large like moles in his glasses, watchin me tryin to squeeze in
"hello miss morcomb, my name's richard jones" an independent somethin-or-other he says. "how do you prefer to be called? is miss morcomb ok?"
"alison." then think bout how I'm not scared, not of his mole eyes starin. "but if you're – well you just keep on miss morcomb if you're gonna be a bastard to me"
he smiles at this, warmlike. scratchin at his sideburn says, "that's understood"
puttin my hands on my lap to stop em fidgin
"I'm nothing to do with this place, alison. your solicitor, ged, asked me to come and do a report for the hearing next week" – watch his throat, like a bobbin apple bove his tie done up bad like a schoolboy's – "I don't work for anybody but myself and what I think I'll put down regardless of what anyone else says or thinks"
make myself look at the doctor. "ged says – he says he's gonna get

the court to let me see lucy –"

> my hand too heavy to move stop lucy itch-itch-itchin herself, nails pickin into her head. my eyelids too heavy to look shuttin so I don't see her greasy hair bunchin up, little trickles of blood. only shelly's little, sleepin breathin hot gainst my skin, tiny, tucked up, clingin into my side

"lucy's your child?"
"they're with my aunt – I mean, I mean" – wipe my mouth – "I mean it's so nice for lucy to be with my aunt in scotland –"
he's glancin at papers on the desk. "your aunt's looking after –?"
"cause" – my mouth loud – "when I was little I used to love stayin with aunty –"
"were they good, those times with your aunty?"
the varnish on the desk with that headache light smackin against it, and aunty stuffin parsley into pig-insides an goin yum-yum-yum haggis is made from brains, at dinin table makin a face that she's eatin brain till I squeal – an on the spot want to get out the doctor's room, like needin a pee only I don't need pee need to get out room right then
"are you in touch with your aunt often? – how's your daughter finding it? – when did you last hear from her?"

> the hairs in my nose singein – it's nosebleed burn but worse, my eyelashes alight and lucy screamin

an I am shoutin fuck off at the doctor, leave me alone, and he lowers his head. passes a tissue
he's not shoutin at me for swearin, not sayin right all your leaves off-ward are cancelled you hear
with my hands goin bad, blow my nose, stare into the tissue
he's scribblin on his paper
my breathin an the scratch-scratch of his pen
"– please, please don't put down me shoutin at you – please don't put it down, they'll never let me see, they'll never let me if you do, I'm sorry doctor I'm sorry, I won't do it again I'm so sorry doctor –"
he looks up, turns the piece of paper round for me to read only all I

can see is scribble, turnin pink I wipe my eyes again
"can you read?"
"it don't matter anyway" I say, and look at the unplugged computer restin in the corner of the room on a little trolley, an wonder if I knew how to work one what I'd be able to do on it
"I wrote" he says, readin his piece of paper, "miss morcomb became very distraught – which means upset – when we started to talk about her older child lucy"

> shelly screamin breakin nails on blackboard her screamin scrapin right down inside my bones – tuggin tug tug lucy won't stop pullin at me "mummy-mummy-mummy" whinin, pawin at my hair at my arm, pullin at my clothes, curled up on my bed pressin shelly against me her screamin gettin inside my brain, cuttin into the backs of my eyes, my tit oozin milk down side of her face, won't suck, screamin an screamin, press her into my belly – lucy screechin "mummy-mummy-mummy", shelly screamin, day an night day an night, won't stop both of them, can't make them – stop – stop

"is that fair enough, what I have written, would you say it's accurate?" – stare at furry hair on his knuckles – "I need your advice" – my stomach sicky, the walls of the room makin me all whitewashed in, linkin his hands on the desk, leanin forward pressin me in with the white walls starin – "to write this report, to do your circumstances justice, I need to talk to you, talk to you about what happened, but I know that must be a very upsetting thing for you" – everythin always white, like snow on the rottin bins to make em look all clean, all evil things always covered white so you don't know, you don't fight when they come get you – "so how do you suggest – how do you advise we do this?" – blinkin at me, his shirt, white. lumps all in my throat – "is it best we start by just getting some of the housekeeping out the way – you know, how long you've been here, how old you are?"

> chris raises an eyebrow at me, "what's it tonight then chick?" "pint of stella" I say, hoppin up on a stool.

"who's she?" "this is my missus." "you're old enough
to be her dad!" "fuck off – only fuckin two years older
than her!" his eyes all hurt

"never ask a woman her age" – dabbin at my mouth, sittin myself up
doctor smiles at that. "ok I won't –"
his eyes all crinkle an blink shut when he smiles, big behind his glasses, his mouth all loppy
"ok, how long have you been here?"
I study the pattern of the wood on the desk
"since the court"
"and before the court you were?"
I run my finger on the desk, the varnish trappin all the roughness beneath
"in burns unit in queens. then in the locker holloway, that's till they trialled me and the judge said to come here"
"why did the judge say that?"
"should ask him." pickin at my nail. my eyes feelin all squashed in my head
leanin his palms at me, "I'm not here to ask the judge –"
"– cause he thinks I'm a schizoid – don't he? cause doctor said I'm a schizoid and I should come here"
"and you think the doctor was right?" his elbow restin against my file
"I'm not schizoid"
"no?"
pink an blue paper fillin it fat with lies
"no. – there's lots of schizoids here – seein things and thinkin bin laden's out to get them and all that"
"and you don't?"
I stare at it, an he turns, looks down at the file
"I've been in this business a long time. long enough to listen to what is said rather than trust what's written down"
glance up, then stare at my hands goin, nails with all them white flecks in em. "bin laden's got better things to do than waste his time with someone like me"
"don't you feel there might be forces at work here that made this

happen? why do you think it went wrong?"
pickin at a sharp corner of thumbnail. try keep everythin down in my belly "– I shouldn't have had my second. it was different than with Lucy. different havin shelly than it was with lucy. with lucy he was there –"
"he?"
"chris"
"who's chris?"

> "food – is that all you think about? disgustin – why've you let yourself go? look how fat you've – how'm I supposed, how's any man supposed when you let yourself get –"
> "you don't need to think up no excuses – I don't give a shit if you sleep around"
> "I know you, know what you're doin" – puts his finger to his head – "your game, know that's why you keep sayin you're not in the mood" breathin into my face "keep puttin idea in my head don't you? deliberate. clever bitch. keep denyin me don't you? – kiss me"
> "no"
> his chest goin in an out "– fuckin with my head aren't you? get me frustrated so I go shag someone else then you can be all proven right about what a bastard I am, I know what you say about – I'm a good husband, do you hear?"
> "just you fuck off all right." I shove him, hard, away
> "don't you hit me" grabs me, pullin at my top, sour breath breakin against me, tears runnin down his face "– I know my rights, I'm your husband. you can't keep sayin no. I'm a man. you're my wife. kiss me"
> "no" – start workin myself free. shoves me back against the wall "why are you makin – why are you makin me" wettin my face with his face, tearin at my trousers "you're so hot chick so hot" his mouth pressin down so hard, can't breathe, alcohol, fags, perfume

"stop it" squirmin down wall "get away from – stop – *no*" my breath clenches out. his nails, forcin in. hurt. so bad, his fingers inside and lucy's screamin for me her little fingers grabbin at him tryin pull me free "go to your room or I'll fuckin tan you!" pressin against me he tries to kick her "why-does-nobody-obey-me?"
I hear my scream

the doctor's talkin but the sickness in my belly
"pardon?" can't look at him
"chris? who is he?"
"was his wife"
"had you separated by the time you had shelly?"
nod
"I see. and was there anybody else there to support you with your baby? your mother perhaps, a friend?"
shake my heavy head, look down
"I think. I think now I might understand. you feel things went wrong as having a second child without the support of your husband was too –"
"– with lucy. he wasn't. not support but –" hold everythin in my throat
"I'm sorry?" the doctor's eyes blink behind his glasses "weren't you saying having a second child with your husband having left you led to things breaking down?"
"yes"

huggin shelly against my breast tryin to warm her

"I'm sorry you've lost me"
"yes"
"yes? are you ok? I'm sorry, I know this is difficult –"
"yes"
"why don't we. shall we talk about something a little easier for a –"
"– least someone wanted me, before, when lucy was born. even he weren't there. with shelly with him an the police an –"

shelly's little lips and her little nose so soft under my palm can't stop the bubbles in my throat and my eyes are burnin and the doctor's eyes are all sad, and comin round my side the desk handin me a tissue, holdin my hand –

rap. rap. rap.

feel the doctor tighten, look round. "come in?" he says, stayin where he is holdin my hand, an I'm all twisted as tara stares at us, doctor in his suit leaned up against the desk holdin my hand, me all redness and blubber from cryin

"– well." she says

"is everything ok, can I help you?" he says

"well" she says. frumps herself up lookin down at us like she'd caught us bonkin or somethin. "I'm afraid it's medication time – alison needs her medication. we close the medication room at one thirty, and it's already twenty to two –"

"I'm sorry about this, but I'm sure it's ok for alison to take her medication late on this occasion?"

"nurse-in-charge is keeping medication room open especially and needs to know if you'll be –"

"I'm afraid we will need to complete the interview –"

"but I'm afraid we shut the medication room at one thirty –"

he breathes in. "forgive me. I am causing an inconvenience, I'm sorry. could it be at all possible to ask nurse-in-charge on just this one occasion to bear with me? I am ever so sorry about this. we'll be another thirty minutes"

"well, well I'll just have to tell nurse-in-charge what you –"

"I will be up onto the ward in any case to look at miss morcomb's medication chart and will apologise in person to – who did you say was in charge?"

"angie – staff nurse taylor, I'll ask nurse-in-charge and see what she –"

"I'll apologise to angie in person for the inconvenience I'm causing" an he smiles a thick-lipped charmin smile

"I'll tell staff nurse taylor that you'll be another thirty minutes so she can close the medication room. I'll tell her you'll be thirty minutes –" tara says as she bustles off

he puts his hands together on the desk again

"are you feeling any better now?"
I nod
"a couple of questions, do you mind? I'm sorry to put you under pressure but it does seem we'll have to keep half an eye on the time. I read that you don't get out of bed, you have problems washing, is that correct?"

> plates, cups sticky, spilt coffee brown an gummy all
> over lino an lucy diggin around all them dirty nappies,
> empty takeaway cartons on the floor, findin one half
> full pawin curry into her mouth her hands stainin
> dirty yellow. and the flies again all on my little shell,
> in corner of her eyes. no point chasin them, I'm tired.
> she's stopped cryin. they'll only fly back gain

I stare at doctor. badness. bad blood, feel it slow and black in my flesh. my chin heavy against my chest. spread my hands on my lap, watch my fingers twitterin
"I do wash. sometimes"
"sometimes. do you find it hard?"
nod. wipe my mouth again
"why is that?"
"dunno"
"some people find thinking of just one word to describe how they're feeling, it helps them communicate a sense of what they're experiencing? – if you could only use one word?"
I shrug
"maybe describe how you're feeling at the moment, is there one word that sums it –?"
diggin my chin into my chest
"wearin"
"wearing? I don't under–"
I stare up into the blue-white barlight. its throb-throb in my eyes. "like that, always on. under your eyelids wearin you out"
"I see. yes. that's a good way to describe – it really helps me to get a sense. and what medication are you on? do you know? anything to help you with that feeling of wearing out?"

"on dipixol." my eyes gettin wet
"anything else? nothing to help you with your mood?"
shake my head
"and for the side effects?"
"stuff for loo. and prostitutin –"
"you mean procicladin? does it help?"
I hold my hand out. he watches it jerkin and shakin, slowly his head tiltin to one side
"my mouth" – wet from my eyes hot an curlin behind my ears – "my mouth's full of spit. all time. it's disgustin"
liftin his glasses onto his forehead. rubs his temples. pushes over the box of tissues
wipe my eyes as he scribbles on his paper
"and why do you think you're on dipixol?"
"told you, think I'm schizoid, don't they? I tell em I never had heard voices. no difference needle every week in my bottom –"
"– I understand that you don't hear voices and" – his eyes go all bright an he smiles – "that you're fully aware bin laden's got far too many bomb factories to keep going than to bother with you –"
can feel my cheeks, look down at desk smilin
"– but I was led to understand, that you felt – that evil spirits had entered you around the time of the – do you feel you might be on the dipixol to help you with –?"
"no!" – pressin my hands against table "– never said that, never said that" – my face all hot "– that wasn't it, that – that doctor, wouldn't listen, she kept tryin at me, that, that wasn't it, that – with what I had – and the burns an prison I couldn't get my words but, it wasn't – said to her – said to her it's not like, that wasn't, but she kept pouncin that wasn't it, it wasn't –"
pushes the box of tissues closer. the chair all diggin and squeezin me, my back an all and the doctor all bug-eyed starin like I'm lyin, like I'm cheatin
"– that wasn't it, it wasn't like she said, doctor, weren't no spirit possessin, I don't know why I – I don't know why –" crossin, uncrossin my arms, salt wettin my mouth bitter like everythin inside me

"help me understand –"
"– no. you don't understand – you don't under–" pushin back the chair "– don't know why I – don't know why – I wasn't anywhere, my spirit like it left me like I was cold and far, watchin me gettin them all cleaned like I said to her –"
"getting them all clean?"

> shelly's little lips and her little nose so soft under the hard pressin down of my palm. bliss of her peaceful silence. I open my eyes. still for the first time in weeks an weeks so I can wipe her, clean her bum with wet wipes like she needs, and make her comfortable and hug lucy, standin quiet now too, and test the water with my elbow, weave my fingers through the smoothness of shelly's hair an soft scalp, latherin it up citrus and springtime ticklin at my nose from the shampoo and tiltin her sweet head back, rinsin the soap away, wispy like cotton her hair when it's dry, clean and baby smellin she is, and changin her properly, an puttin her in the nice little baby-pink suit with yellow flowers, and for first time since she came out of me she looks content an clean

hummin in my ears. the dark with my eyes closed
can feel my skin
slip my hand under my top. spread my fingers round my belly, lumpy, tight, tissue-crisp skin. scratch in with my rough, picked-sharp nails. pinch and dig my fingers in, let pain slow my breathin
"are you ok?"
nudgin me the box of tissues. can't look
"please help me understand. you felt like you were watching yourself?"

> her top alight, white flame, lucy screamin

"I'm sorry to push you – you felt you were watching yourself getting your children all cleaned up, had you already decided to do what you did?"

> combin. lucy tryin not to yell out as I work the comb

through the tangle knottin up her hair, her face all scrunchin up in ouches, an I love her so badly it's twistin up till it feels like my ribs are broke. lucy's wide eyes starin up as I separate her hair into two plaits, and with hairbands make her hair into ponies like she likes

"– both of them day an night – doctor, doctor –"

"mummy move" – lucy grabbin at me – "mummy" – tuggin at my arm – "move, move mummy" – can't move, can't shakin at me while I sob, shake-shakin at me till she's screamin face purple screamin, pullin at my hair, diggin – "mummy mummmmiiii"

"– couldn't feel nothin, doctor, couldn't see nothin, not even move myself to loo"

comfort-warm of wet, risin like a cuddle round my legs, steamy pissy sleepy smell –

"– nothin was like nothin – I don't know why I – I don't know why I – she's so upset, she's – doctor – I was dead weeks weeks was dead still them screamin screamin fillin my head –"

"it's ok"

lucy whimperin. her ribs, her ribs stickin out –

" – no she's so upset, all time, nothin was in me went good for nothin an – couldn't clean her, couldn't feed them – hungry all time hungry screamin, screamin, screamin both of them day an night – day an night –"

my wee coolin on my legs. pullin Lucy to me, her nails cuttin into me, her face buried in my stomach. blue, watchin it's like magic blue floatin bove chair growin, suckin, spreadin, lickin in rainbow orange, clawin out an blackenin walls, listenin to its breathin, like it's livin, snappin, poppin, crackin, smellin smoky-warm like mummy and bonfire – whiz an bang, glistenin silver on black sky night, candyfloss sticky holdin mummy's hand, guy fawkes alight, sky explodin an showerin –

takin off glasses. waitin
the suck of my breath. my face fizzin. can't open my eyes
"I'm so sorry to have to push you like this – it's just so important I understand what you're saying. I don't want to misunderstand – to put words in your mouth. please, if you can. let me know if I understood this right"
turnin way from him
"you found yourself unable to get out of bed, even to go to the toilet or take care of your children's basic needs – you felt like your body was dead?"
nod
"this deterioration – when did it begin? how long after the birth of your youngest daughter?"
pushin away. "you know what I done – you know what I –"
"I know how difficult this is. – please. just try and bear with me. it's important I understand. you said your spirit left you? what did you mean?"
sweat shinin on his forehead

> nappies, cartons, clothes, plates, rottin food – all of it, squirtin sprayin splashin it over everything. throw match. the suck like a breath. heat. lucy starin. bedtime. be good girl. we're all goin bed. pick her up

"I watched me. I watched me do it –" fold my chin gainst my chest, try an keep the noise in my throat as I shake
I open my eyes. he's still there. his glasses are folded up on the desk, his eyes shrunk in his face. head tilted as if he's feelin it all inside me. waitin. for breathin to slow. he's passin me tissues. my hands are goin. I blow my nose. clean up my face
he leans up against the desk, fixes his glasses back on his nose
"– like, like –" my mouth movin without me "– that picture, me in news, what they all wrote. I think. it true. am evil – what they all wrote bout me is true, every word of it –"
my belly pressin sicky into back of my mouth
"I'm not your doctor." lookin at me sad like I'm dyin. "but let me say this, in case it is useful. if a man kills his wife and the next day risks

his own life to save the lives of two drowning children – is it accurate to describe this man as good? is it accurate to describe him as evil? or is it that he is a man who has done good things and evil things and can do more good things in the future if he chooses? perhaps this would be useful for you to think about"
watch the pen, it wagglin in his hand as he writes

> smoke makin ghosts, curlin like cuddle, cradlin the bed wet with sweat, hazy and thick, sleepy like cloud – an shelly against my breast, cool against my skin cuddled to me sleepin, and lucy, chin diggin in between my breast an shoulder, her skin hot, sticky-soft, smellin of johnson and colgate –

"I am going to suggest that a diagnosis of post-natal depression is explored. there're several medications effective for this – it would seem to me to make more sense – particularly as I have not witnessed any symptoms typical of schizophrenia. the side-effects from your current medication regime are significant –"

> – fast little heart against my ribs, lucy, boom-boom-boom echoin inside me, like she did before she was born, her nails dig, scratch like she's tryin to claw inside me, break through this clammy skin of mine, this shell of meat an bone that's left her all alone since she came out of me

I choke again. the blood-noise pressin in my head "– they, they all think I didn't love them" the feel of his finger tips gainst the inside of my wrist –
rap. rap. rap.
"come in?"
"I'm sorry to interrupt. it's thirty minutes and nurse-in-charge sent –"
tara stops speakin. starin at the doctor holdin my hand again
"well." she says
"I'm sorry I kept alison so long. – but if you're feeling up to it –" lookin at me "we're ok to wrap up now? I'm sorry it's been so upsetting"
tryin to stop my blitherin, tryin dry, cleanin up my face with tissue

"well, it doesn't matter now does it? nurse-in-charge has sent me down with alison's tablets, nurse-in-charge thinks she can take her medication down here"

"that's fine – although I think we've covered all we need to have covered today –"

tara frumpin into room with my medication

my hot face. I grip doctor's hand, standin myself up I kiss him on the cheek. sandpaper-and-lynx skin prickles my lips

hear tara, I turn round, all my tablets on floor by her feet, water splashed up her leg, tots upside down, her mouth all open

"thank you doctor" I say

he steps back, shakin his head, smilin. "are you ok?" he says to tara, handin her the box of tissues

"fuck" she says her red lips all thin, dabbin at her legs. "all right thank you"

tryin to keep my breathin steady, watch her bendin down, her fat arse in the air, on her knees pickin up the tots and the spilt pills. glancin at doctor, I hold my hands together to stop em shakin, look back down at her. "nurse" I say "need to take my medication, please"

from her hands an knees, she looks up at me

UNDER WHITE LIGHT

Thea Bennett

For my mother Thetis the goddess of the silver feet tells me
I carry two sorts of destiny toward the day of my death. Either,
if I stay here and fight beside the city of the Trojans,
my return home is gone, but my glory shall be everlasting;
but if I return home to the beloved land of my fathers,
the excellence of my glory is gone, but there will be a long life
left for me, and my end in death will not come to me quickly.

Iliad 9.410-416

It is the hottest part of the day. There are still some tourists on the beach, mostly women, limping over the burning sand and crouching beneath beach umbrellas to suck on plastic bottles of warm water. In front of them the sea slowly unfurls and retracts, aquamarine in the sun, ink black and petrol green in the shadow of the cliff.

The waiter sits under the awning at the back of the terrace, tired knotted hands curled in his lap. He would not choose to be out of doors at mid-afternoon. Behind half-closed eyes he evokes the stuffy darkness of his room. Shutters closed. Gritty wool blanket under his cheek, hollowed mattress cradling his aching limbs. A thin line of sunlight moving across the bed as afternoon slides into night.

A paperback book lies on one of the metal chairs on the terrace, purple-and-black cover curling up in the heat. If one of the women comes to buy a Coke or a salad he will ask her if she knows whose it is. It is his job to keep the café tidy. But to move out of the shade now is to feel the sun's rays on his skin like a knife. Let the book stay. He waits, easing his stiff spine against the white stone wall of the café.

The ceiling fan sends a current of cool air over her body as she stands in front of the mirror. Square face, square short body, fair hair cut square to the chin. I am free, she breathes, licking her dry lips. This is the first day of my freedom. She reaches out and touches her cold reflected cheek.

Behind her on the bed she can see a suitcase. Very small, small enough to be hand luggage. It contains no suits, no high heels or control panties, no heavy reference books or folders of documents. Like jetsam, these things are drifting away in her wake.

Leaving her misty image she steps out, naked, onto the balcony. Heat sears her lungs and prickles over her skin. Across the bay, a mountain range shimmers, its bulk insubstantial in the glare, its slopes bleached to pale violet. Everything is turned to light. There is nowhere to hide.

The recent past is blanked out. Images swim up from further back, deeper in, and she hears again the soundtrack of childhood. Her mother's impatient Kensington voice: "Electra, stop being so miserable!"

How else could she be, with such a tragic title? Her mother, tall, dark, impressively cheekboned and eyebrowed, wanted a daughter in her own image. Called the girl Electra after an art-house Greek film she saw, with Irene Papas emoting, tearing her long black hair and rolling her eyes over her father's grave.

It must have been galling that little Electra took after her Welsh father: stocky, fair-haired. And that she grieved for him endlessly when he was ejected from the house and banished to occasional Sunday afternoons in tatty tea shops and at the zoo. But, being Electra, what else could she do but mourn? It didn't become her very well, a dumpy child hanging around in dark corners, whingeing and picking holes in the silk upholstery.

Sadness coagulates under her breastbone. She lifts her arms to the sun and stretches upwards and the heaviness dissipates like fine dust on the hot wind that is now blowing in off the sea. She needs to swim, immerse herself in the wide bay which glitters down below.

A van door crashes shut. The waiter comes back to consciousness and coughs at the stench of diesel exhaust. Costa is back from the farm. He is throwing wooden crates of aubergines and peppers onto the counter by the kitchen door.

"Uncle," he growls, "get down on the beach and sell some ice cream. Summer doesn't last for ever. No customers, no profit!"

Costa has missed the start of his siesta, the long and luxurious drift down into oblivion. He will lie next to his wife in the hot bedroom and struggle to sleep for the last precious hour of rest.

The waiter pulls himself up. He meanders slowly through the café, stepping round tables and chairs on his way to the freezer. The book is still lying in the same place. He picks it up. Most of the women who came to the café for lunch were German, but this is an English book. He recognises some of the words on the cover. "The Night" is written there. And above, in big silvery letters, the strange English word "Water", which always seemed to him so very foreign. Here on this book, an "s" has been added. This he knows must make a plural. "Waters". Why is this written here?

Leaning on the chipped metal lid of the old freezer, he opens the book and lets the pages flick over. "Oxford Street", he sees. He has been there. He saw the sign, high up on the buildings. He knows London. There are waters there. The wide river rising and falling, like a great animal breathing, twice every day as it slid over banks of mud to the sea. The weight of water that would never run dry, unlike the bed of stones and dry grass at the end of the beach.

The smell of water everywhere. The strong fresh smell of the river, pulling him back to stand on the concrete banks and watch it flowing past. Thin rain sifting down from the grey sky so that the dirty pavements smelled earthy and alive. His brother's sour-smelling bathroom in Finsbury Park, where the ice-cold water burst out of the taps with a force that shocked him when he first twisted the metal handle. Water that tasted flat and dead when you caught it in a glass to drink.

Metal chair legs scrape on the café floor. Women's voices, talking and laughing. He will not have to go down onto the sand with the coolbox hanging from his shoulder and a bag of loose change at his waist. He has customers.

This island, famous in antiquity as the refuge of the hero Achilles . . . White light on white paper dazzles. Electra lets the guidebook drop. It is a struggle to focus on the small print as she peers through the lenses of her big sunglasses, which are not prescription. Middle age, she thinks, lying face down and letting her turquoise-costumed belly spread over the towel on the hard, ribbed sand. It feels like a man's body under her. A lean, blond man with golden skin and sun-bleached hair. Was Achilles a blond? Brad Pitt-style, like the movie?

Dry wind riffles her hair and she pictures the hero striding over the violet mountains, thighs flashing under a short tunic, spear gripped in his lean hand. Not a big man. Slight, leaping over the bushes. She stops in mid-daydream. She is seeing him like Rory. Spare and fair and blue-eyed, Rory, dead for thirty years now, has lain dormant in her mind for almost as long. Her subconscious is unfolding under the magnifying glass of the sun, hidden memories illuminated by its burning lens.

Grief presses down on her, a heavy door shutting out the light she is bathing in, pushing her back into the moment of loss, shutting out her future, shutting out love.

She is drowning in agony in her mother's big bedroom, where everything is so beige, with heavy dull gold tassels on the curtains and thick gold frogging on the bedcover, and too much upholstery everywhere, which muffles the sound of her crying, stifles everything except the pain of knowing she will never see him again.

Electra rests her forehead on her arms, tries to pull back into the heat and light of the moment as the dark undertow of the past draws her down into herself.

Not that they saw each other that much. Not that it was an exclusive thing. But when they did meet, his smile, his blue eyes glowing – it was like a spotlight shining on her, making her centre stage. She felt she could do anything, be anything.

When his sister phoned to say she was going through his diary ringing all the numbers to tell them that he had come off the Moto Guzzi and died in the infirmary, Electra was alone in the house. She needed to go and sit somewhere, somewhere private and anonymous. A church. And she wanted to put on a black dress, but didn't have one. That was why she had gone into her mother's bedroom, to borrow her black Chanel minidress. On Electra, it was knee-length. But still Chanel. And it carried her through that long grey afternoon; picked her up off the floor and walked her out through the front door onto the rainy West London street.

She shivers, remembering the caress of the black velvet against her skin. That afternoon she discovered the sustaining power, the protection and comfort of expensive clothes. A carapace for the hurt and confused child within. A way of being that, except for one moment on that grey afternoon, she clung to.

Once she stepped inside that luxurious, protective shell, the world of money and status and designer clothes, Electra became detached, cool, analytical. As she walked into a glass-walled boardroom, or sat behind the polished wooden monolith of a desk, people looked up to her, were even afraid of her, despite her short stature, soft blond hair, tender complexion. They saw her as one of the best business brains around. And she made money. Money that worked for her and grew and multiplied until the moment when she found herself in the master suite of her new seven-bedroomed glass-and-steel box in Beaconsfield and realised it was all for nothing.

In front of the high empty window the interior designer was holding out a swatch of neutral fabrics for her to choose from. "You could have taupe," she was saying, red-painted lips popping the words out lasciviously, "or there is this lovely new shade, tallow. It's all about luxury." It's all beige to me, Electra thought, as the woman shook out a handful of glittering metallic strips. All beige, with gold highlights. I have come all this way, achieved so much, and I am just back in my mother's bedroom again.

The house was gone now, sold. A flood of capital released to set her afloat on her journey. She felt nothing for it. Only, perhaps, missed the scent and whisper of the three tall pine trees that grew in the big garden. Older than the house, tall enough to catch and rustle in the lightest of breezes.

Rolling over she sees three stunted pines growing above her on the cliff top. Weighed down by the sun, their branches are still and silent.

And love. Did she find love? Would love have breathed life into that empty, shiny, modern box of a house? Certainly she had many affairs. Sat opposite many suited, smiling men in many expensive restaurants, waiting for them to astonish her, make her laugh, make her forget her status and authority. Then gradually the faces opposite became younger, as the men of her own age sought girls who might have been her daughter, if she had had one. Now it was sharp and hungry young males who courted her, keen to pick up the bill (at least on the first date), keen to make inroads into her world, make a conquest of the sophisticated older woman.

Her body recoils from the thought and she springs up and runs to the water's edge, kicking off her flip-flops. There are two tiny rocky islands in the bay. She will swim out to them, get things back into perspective.

The waiter holds up the book and shows it to the group of young English women. They giggle and shake their heads. They are only interested in cold beer and almond cakes. Their legs, spread on the metal chairs, show patches of vivid fuchsia where they have caught the sun. His own arm, holding out the tray of glasses, looks almost black beside their pale skins. They are not meant for this intense light. It bleaches out their subtle skin tones and then stamps them with a colour too strong. The waiter has seen it before, summer after summer, and still finds it unpleasant. As unpleasant as he finds their cravings for sugar and alcohol in the middle of the afternoon. Today he has eaten only bread dipped in salt, and a handful of bitter black olives.

He retreats to his corner by the back wall and lets the book fall open, struggling to remember the different alphabet, the words he used to know. He wants to revisit the great grey city again, smell the damp air, walk the streets of tall buildings. He can only pick out a few words, but he reads them hungrily.

They were lying together in the bath. That he understands. He remembers the cold white shell in his brother's bathroom, stains dribbling down the enamel beneath the taps. Plenty of room for two. He never used it. And there is no bath here, just the ancient showerhead with its crusted porcelain tray.

"Look how dark your skin is . . . Really, you're as swarthy as a Greek." He catches his breath. Who is this Greek person? What is "swarthy", a word he has never seen before? He can find only what he thinks are women's names. Helen. Julia. Two women in a bath? What is happening? He cannot make it out. *Pink*, he reads, *stomach . . . leg . . . foot . . . tail . . . gold.*

Two women, in a bath, in London. Two English women. He looks up, then closes the book, blanks out the raucous, sunburned girls swigging beer in the café and steps back in time again, lets the wet London afternoon wash over him. That time just after he arrived, when his brother let him go early from the Kebab Palace and he walked and walked into the heart of the rainy city, dreaming of riches and success, and found the river and looked for a place to shelter.

Safe at last on the island, Electra rubs her legs, grazed from crawling up onto the rocks. She is out of breath. There are strong currents in the bay, and she has not swum for a long time. Four teenage boys are also on the island, tinkering with snorkels and a metal trident. They watch her and whisper to each other. Their lean brown bodies are delicately muscled, dark hair curls over their smooth necks and foreheads. They look like brothers or cousins.

Perhaps they are seventeen or eighteen years old, thinks Electra. If this was the Gambia, which she has read about, one of them would come over and speak to her. Ask if he could be her boyfriend. Make her feel special and important as he helps her to spend her money. As it is, she feels uncomfortable, like a fat child with scraped knees. They are so beautiful, so physically perfect, like young heroes. Won't last though. A few more years and they will be thick and hairy like the taxi-driver who brought her to the hotel, sweating and smelling of garlic and cheap cigarettes.

The boy she slept with on the day she heard the news about Rory must have been a bit older than them. But he was still beautiful. Thin, sensitive lips and big dark eyes, like the velvet inside flesh of a black olive. He stared and stared at her. Asked her name, but couldn't say anything else. And blushed dark red when she told him.

She could feel the heat from his body when he came to sit beside her in the church, even though they weren't touching. It was the first time she had felt warm all day. He stayed there until she left St Mary's, and then she just let him follow her home. She took him into her mother's room, with its huge glossy bed. He kept on staring at her. She wanted him. She wanted it quick and rough and hot before she closed down for ever. When she pulled the Chanel dress over her head and threw it on the floor he shouted something and she saw he had come already, all over the satin counterpane.

Then she locked the door and took off the rest of her clothes. She opened the windows and let the fresh air blow in. She lay on the bed with him and stroked him and held his hand and after a bit he opened his black-olive eyes and stared at her again and they kissed and it was OK.

Her mother was due back that night, so when it started getting dark, she made him tell her where he lived (playing charades to make him understand what she wanted) and he told her "Finsbury Park". She called him a taxi and sent him off into the night. She never saw him again. She hung up the dress in the wardrobe, but she left the sticky stain on the counterpane.

The boys have left the island and their dark heads are bobbing around in the water near the rocks. Electra waits until they move further away before she swims back to the beach. Her body is stretched and loose from the long swim and she lies heavily on her towel on the hard sand. The memory of sex has released her from the dark currents of the past and she sleeps dreamlessly under the sun.

It was Sunday. Rain was soaking into the flat squared pavements. There were no people on the street, and no cars except for one that went by and made a great wave of dirty water which almost hit him. On Sundays at home, he would go to church. So that is what he did when he was too wet and cold to walk any more. He pushed open the door of the big white building and saw a man in dark clothes speaking to a small group of women who sat right at the front. The church was bare inside. No gold, no candles. No saints' eyes watching him from the walls. He did not want to go in. But there was one spot of light in the gloomy building. It was a woman's golden hair. She was sitting at the back.

He went and sat beside her on a grey plastic chair. The monks at home would not have allowed such a thing in their church. Her head was hanging down so he could not see her face. Fine, soft hair, falling forward in silky pale strands. He could not understand anything the priest at the front was saying, so he kept on looking at her.

Her small hands were folded in her lap. His own broad hands were very dark brown next to them. Then she looked up and he saw her sea-blue eyes and her wet face. Her face, soft pink, a flower that could only thrive in rain and mist, under grey skies. She stood up. She was, strangely for so young a woman, wearing a black dress. She was not very tall. When she was older, she would have a body like his mother's.

She was looking for a way to dodge past him, to get away. He had to stop her leaving. "*Ti einai to onoma sou?*" he said, and then tried again in English, the only phrase he knew properly: "What is your name?"

"Electra," she said. And she did not run away.

A hot hand touches his shoulder and the waiter leaps into wakefulness. A damp, scarlet female face looms over him. "Hey, love, can we pay?" The girls are leaving, belching and shoving the metal chairs back. He gropes for the leather money bag. Six beers and six cakes. Not much of a profit for a long afternoon. He should think about trying to sell a few ice creams before Costa wakes up.

As the crimson-faced girl scatters a few small coins on the table in front of him he remembers the crisp notes Electra put into his hand in the great gold-trimmed bedroom before she took him down to the taxi. Crisp, clean, beautiful paper money.

He had gone to London to make money. There was so much there. You could see it through the golden-lighted windows of the big houses. In the crystal and glitter of the shop windows. There was not much of it in Finsbury Park, though, and certainly not in the Kebab Palace. He worked every day and long into the night, but his brother's business did not prosper.

He had gone back to the big white house where Electra lived many times, but he could not find her there. A tall woman with long dark grey-streaked hair and bony legs under a short red coat shouted at him to go away when she found him standing in the front garden. He should have stood up to her, demanded to go in and speak to Electra, but his English was not good enough. He should have broken the small window behind the bushes at the back of the house, and climbed in and gone up the stairs to the big golden bedroom and found her, pink-cheeked under the silken sheets, and taken her again. But he didn't. Eventually he stopped going back. He gave himself up to the Kebab Palace, until his brother told him he couldn't afford to pay him any more. And then he went to some of the restaurants in the centre of the city and asked them for a job, but he wasn't family, and they would only offer him casual dishwashing. He could have tried harder, but he didn't.

And so he had come home, not much richer, and not much of a prospect for the local girls; and single and childless, without a family of his own, he had continued to work. On the farm in the winters and then through the long summers in the café, every day and long into the night.

He scrapes up the coins from the table. No tip. He goes to the freezer to fill up the coolbox. The sun is beginning to drop in the sky, but it is still worth a try.

Electra wakes and stretches. The skin is tight on her back where she has lain too long in the sun, but her mind is clear and refreshed. She picks up the guidebook. *The most famous of the Greek heroes of the Trojan war, Achilles had two choices: long life and obscurity, or an early death and great fame . . .* And of course, he chose the latter. She sighs.

Will she miss the world she has left behind? The challenge, the mental exertion, the uncertainty, and then the great rush of adrenalin when she has pulled off another deal. Will she just fall apart now that she has stepped away from all of that, let go of her protective shell?

Anxiously she feels for her compact in her bag, and opens it up to look at her face. Is this what obscurity looks like? Flat and colourless, without lipstick or mascara or rouge, she looks her age. A sallow small-featured fifty-year-old, with pale lashes and dry, bleached hair. Is this what she really wants? Should she have stayed and fought her corner one more time? Maybe looked for another, more congenial, glass palace to hide in? She drops the compact back into her bag.

Someone is walking slowly up the beach towards her, hugging the shadows under the cliff. An old man. "Young lady!" he calls. "Hey, you miss lunch? You want ice cream?" He is carrying a grubby blue plastic box, hanging from his shoulder by a long strap.

Go away, she says under her breath. Just fuck off, old man. Don't spoil my afternoon. She looks away, but he is still approaching. He comes closer, squats on the sand a few feet away.

He is holding something out to her in his dirty gnarled hand. "You like cigarette?"

She has not smoked for twenty years, but suddenly she wants one. She takes it and he lights it for her with a disposable lighter. Cheap Greek cigarette, she thinks, but it is very good. Acrid as the white hot sky and the silver sea and the darkening lavender mountains.

And now, just go away, old man.

But he is moving closer, his face scored and collapsed into deep lines, punched in by toil and disappointment. "Who are you, lady? From England?" The whites of his eyes are yellow and dull; the pupils, dark as black-olive flesh, are ringed with the blue-grey beginning of cataracts. She cannot look away. Encouraged, he smiles, revealing stained and gappy teeth.

"My name is Achilles," he says.

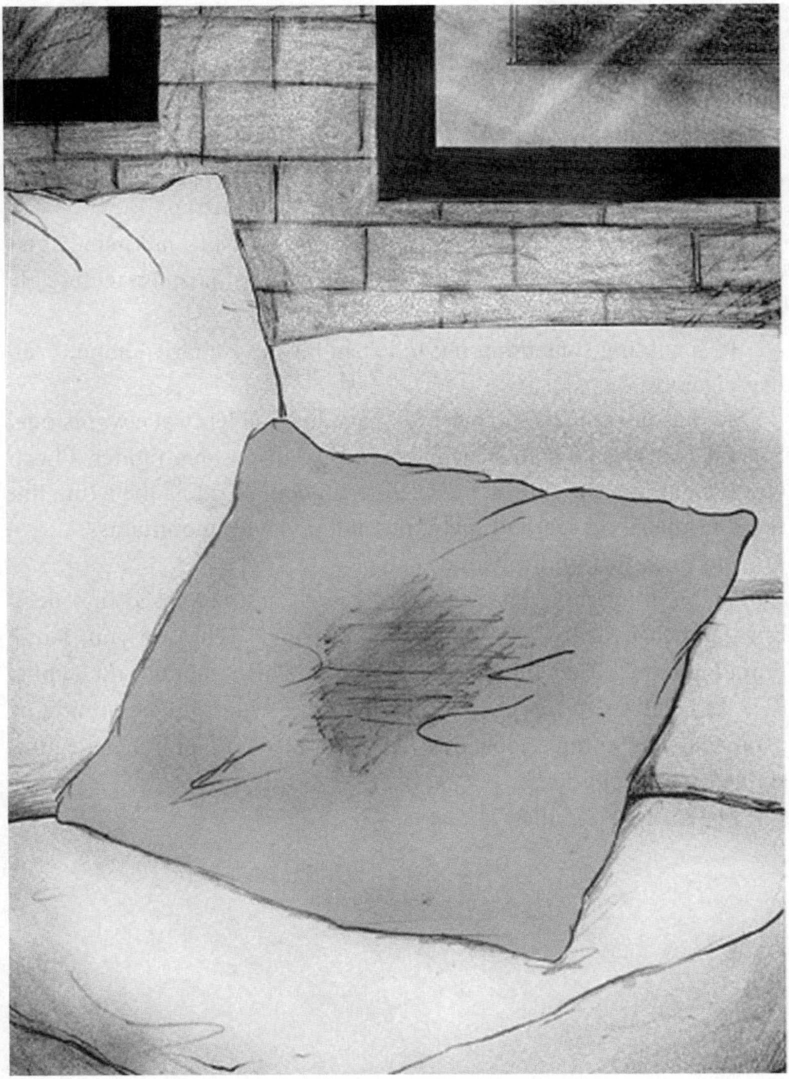

RIDICULE
Pippa Griffin

She circles, poised, balanced on a single silver blade, one leg stretched in an arc behind her back. Her tiny skirt flutters over taut cheeks. She glides backwards on the ice, hands held out in front as if to reach and hold. I catch her leg, draw it towards me, fold her petalled skirt across her back like a leaf, pull her on.

I lie on the sofa, beer knocked to the floor, spilt, head spinning, cheeks hot, body tingling like never before. Lucy will be back in ten minutes. Stop. Eject disc. Throw it away. Must have set the wrong channel. No, keep it, record something else. Head shaking. Tuck disc behind the stack of coffee-table books on the floor. No, not there, in the kitchen, slip it inside the cereal box, push it down. She doesn't like cornflakes anyway.

Lucy arrives. Says, you look rosy. Been to the gym, I say. Came out easier than I was expecting. She kisses me, says it's nice to be home. Nod.

That night, I take her. Face pushed into the pillow, focused on her back, *my flat-chested Russian.* Next morning, she raises her eyebrow, says, you were a bit rough last night, had you been drinking. No, I say, busy day, stressed, sorry. On the way home I buy a bunch of flowers. She laughs, says there must be something wrong.

We met through work. She was shooting new portraits of the partners, for the reception area. Black and white, reportage. Tough call when you sit at a desk all day. I'd brought her tea and biscuits. Said, you must be exhausted trying to make us look good. Some need more help than others, she said. Then, I didn't mean. It's OK, I said, I never look my best on Tuesdays. She laughed, said, why's that, are you busy Monday nights. We made plans. Dinner. We were engaged within six months. That's quick, they said, you hardly know each other.

She moved in the following month. Nothing to hide back then, just a pile of dirty boxers and a bad-taste cufflinks collection. Even now, the only real porn I own is a pack of topless playing cards that sit at the back of my bedside drawer. Not exactly hard core. Yet here I am again, the lights dimmed, the TV on standby, ready to unzip because I'm too hard not to.

Arms stretched above her head, hands clasped. A tulip, unopened. No point trying to hide it from yourself. Never works. *Wrists flick and dance, perfect nails.* The more you try to think of something else, the bigger it grows. The more you want it, the bigger the pay-off. *Slender fingers, wrapped around me, warming.* Like some kid discovering his dad's porno mags for the first time and promising he'll never take another look. *She starts to turn. Faster, faster.*

She filled the apartment with her black-and-white photos, said she liked the contrast against the exposed red brickwork. Said she loved these shots, real, spontaneous, people being true to themselves. Friends, she said. So many friends, I said. There, she said, feels like home now.

My favourite photo is stuck to the fridge, one of those disposables. Me and Lucy on the slopes. Me holding the camera, arm in view. Both of us grinning, new, in love, Lucy's hat sliding over blue eyes. Not bad, she said, despite the glare. *Ice white, pure, sparkling.*

I try not to think about it. Start meeting Lucy from work or going to the gym so we arrive home together. Says, she's never met someone so attentive, her Prince Charming, then giggles as she tells me how she used to kiss her Adam Ant posters, pretend he was in her bedroom. I squeeze her hand, ask her if she'd like me to don stripes, sing Ridicule is nothing to be scared of. No way, she says, it's just a fantasy. That's all right then.

From a distance she is almost naked, neckline open to her navel. Costume so tight you can see her stomach muscles.

At my desk I watch numbers move up and down, not linking what I see with what I am supposed to do. Come to the bar, they say. No, sorry. Finish my coffee, type in Romanova, close it before the pictures download. Wait, where are you going.

Not exactly something you talk to your peers about is it. By the way, did you see the figure skating last night, wasn't it brilliant, anyone else get off on that. No, thought not.

Another drink. OK, conversation's back to football. Then Charles says, hey, had a dream last night, took it in turns, new receptionist. Others compare notes, Cindy Crawford, Jennifer Aniston, debate about whether she'd be dirty enough, girl next door and all that. Laughs all round. What about you Jules? I shrug, drain my pint, say, go for the quiet ones, it's always the quiet ones, and head for the door. Behind me the quiet ones are no doubt debated, ranked. Walk home trying not to hurry.

Jewels cover tiny rosebuds. I pluck the sequins one by one.

Next morning Lucy leaves early for a flight, Madrid, three days. When I wake the flat is empty, her side of the bed already cooled. Brew coffee, turn on the news. Snow in the Midlands. Ice. Stare at the TV screen, blizzard across my eyes. Move into the kitchen, craving cornflakes.

Spinning slows, quickens, slows again. Body lowers to the floor, one leg outstretched. Stops in front of me, face waist-high. I pull the flower from her hair. Dark eyes look up, lipstick mouth falls open, hair unravels down her back as I hold her head firm.

We used to love our reunions. The time I went to Geneva. We were still new, still exploring. Four days away, four days catching up. We only left the house for milk, champagne and bacon sandwiches. Still hard to prepare food on that worktop even now.

Hi gorgeous, lovely to have you home. Arms around my neck, her perfume faded with the day's travelling, breath like honey.

Later, Lucy on top of me, holding on to the headboard, tits pushing in my face. Lovely Lucy, just like it's always been. I shut my eyes. *Romanova circling.* Lucy's rhythm thrust-ing push-ing *left, right, left, one foot crossing the other, gathering speed, tiny ankles balanced on those blades.* Lucy grinding harder against me, reach to hold her hips, hold her steady, *pull her onto me, push through the satin and the silk, opening.* Lucy groaning. Shhh shhh. Lucy says my name, says, coming, harder. Her voice, wrong accent. Lose it just as her face breaks. Crying then, didn't you miss me. Sorry, sorry.

Next night she lies beside me, her hand stroking the line of hairs below my belly. It tickles too much, so I push her lower and she cups my balls before moving upwards again, hand wrapping around me, softer than she's expecting. Is it me. She starts to pull away, retreat. No, no, you're lovely. Turn to nuzzle in her neck. Her hand starts to rub again, slow, uncertain. *Romanova kneels before me, lipstick mouth, opening.*

Lucy smiling, handing me a tissue. I hold it to my belly, swing my legs off the bed, clean up in the bathroom, lights off. I brush my teeth without looking up, splash my face with cold water, hold the towel against my eyes.

In the middle of the night I wake for a pee and a glass of water. Lucy stirs. You'd tell me, wouldn't you, if there was someone else. There's no one. Kiss her head, say go back to sleep. Stare into the dark until the grey dawn evaporates the shadows.

Ask my mother if she ever took us ice-skating. No why, she says, stirring gravy, you thinking of a career change, smiling as the wooden spoon circles in figures of eight. We used to watch your sister at ballet, she says.

I remember. Plump little cherubs chanting good toes naughty toes, short stocky legs clad in white tights and pink shoes, teacher counting up two three and down two three. Sister grinning at us there on the balcony, forgetting to keep her head still when she turned so she always lost her balance. Said she was going to make grade six, points.

That's when your toes bleed and your nails fall off, she said. Didn't make it of course. Discovered boys, satin pumps thrown to the back of the shoe cupboard, ribbons trailing to my trainers below. Didn't I have anything better to do. No, she says, you gave up karate, cried you weren't as strong as the other boys. You preferred watching the girls anyway, used to have to tell you off for trying to guess whose boobies would sprout first. It was your sister's I seem to remember. I close my knife and fork, push the plate away.

Lucy rings, says, what time are you meeting me from work. Not tonight I say, leaving early, paperwork, see you at home. OK she says. Change into my running kit. Pace hard, pound feet, count rhythm. Lucy's studio on the next corner. Look there's Jules, she'll say, hey you, she'll say, stay for a bit, let's have coffee. Only she doesn't because at the last minute I turn left, eyes focused on the tarmac.

Arrive home, warm, blood pumping. Double-lock the front door, draw curtains, dim lights, silence the mobile, mute the answerphone. Feel the rise as I retrieve the disc. Look in the bedroom, double-check there's no one there, glimpse her open drawer full of knickers and nylons, hands shaking as I pluck a flesh-coloured stocking *legs wrapping around me.* Quick to the sofa, pushing at my shorts even more than usual. Take hold.

Tiny ankles, round swells push at Lycra. Stretches out her limbs ready to begin. Girl-woman.

Did you get it all finished. Lucy, head on one side. What, yes, much easier working at home, probably do it again, that OK with you. Sure, why wouldn't it be.

Surrounded by files and pieces of paper. Scribble PRODUCTIVITY = DEADLINES + REWARDS. Cross it out, retrieve the stocking from my running-shorts pocket, move to the sofa. Hit Play.

Romanova circling, speeding, building to the triple axel.

The telephone rings, beeps, then, hi darling. Fuck. It's me, she says. Softening. Missed the answerphone, fucking answerphone. Wondered if you'd meet me from the station, so much shopping, I'll be there in ten minutes, beeps.

Fifteen minutes later and the screen has turned to black and I am just staring, tingling. Clean up, shower, push the stocking to the bottom of her laundry bag, pull on an old jumper that smells of Lucy. Key in the lock. Thanks a lot, she says, dumps the bags at my feet, walks into the bedroom, slams the door. Sorry, really sorry. I start to put away and make dinner, but the onion mist stings my eyes and I can't see to slice.

Who's Romanova? Lucy looking at me, hair pulled back from her face, pale, tired. You said the name in your sleep, thought you were having a nightmare, tossing, turning. Don't remember, I say and turn away to pour another glass of wine. Does it matter. Lucy's eyes filling, says, OK sorry.

We watch a film, the story of a young woman who makes friends with an older man. Pervert, says Lucy, he only wants to screw her. Who wouldn't, I say, it's Scarlett Johansson. Thought you preferred older women. I do, I say and chuck a cushion at her. She grabs it, bats me back. I pull another out from under me. Lucy laughing. Don't laugh at me. That smile, turning up in one corner, like she knows. What are you saying. Cushions fly. Pervert. What did you call me. Still that smile. She holds a cushion against her chest, moves it up to protect her face as I take aim. Say that again. Pervert. Don't you ever. Giggling. Don't you ever. She starts singing, Ridicule is. You want Adam huh. More giggles. I hold the cushion over her face and she mumbles the rest. Fingers freeing the buttons on her shirt, then lifting her arms, stretching, *tiny wrists reaching overhead, holding on to the corners of the sofa. Fuck me, whispers Romanova beneath me.* I hold the cushion against her mouth, run my hand up her skirt, pull her knickers down. I hold the cushion firm, pull open my jeans, move on top of her. Skirt rides up around her hips. Push her legs open with my thighs, *girl-woman opening for the first time, warm and tight inside.* I hold the cushion down, *blades cutting deep into the ice, grating, carving, spelling out the word PERVERT. Romanova, stronger than I was expecting. Don't you ever. Ever. Ever. Feel her back arch against me as I push. Good toes naughty toes says Scarlett, grinning at me from the TV screen. Get the fuck off me screams Romanova.* I lift the cushion. Lucy red, black smears on her cheeks. Sorry, sorry. What the fuck, I couldn't breathe. Runs into the bathroom, locks the door. Scarlett laughing, let's never come here again because it will never be as much fun.

Lucy, I. Sorry. Don't know what, sorry. I thought you. Lucy crying in the bathroom. Sit outside staring at the floor. Go away. I love you. PERVERT.

She starts to run a bath, turns the lights out, candle shadows flicker underneath the door. I have retreated to the sofa by the time she unlocks. Wait I say, but she runs to the bedroom, throws me a blanket and a pillow then goes back inside, furniture scraping across the boards.

Four a.m. Pins and needles in my right hand from leaning into the crevasse of the sofa. *Romanova circling, says here let me, hand wraps around me, says it's all right, it's all right. Angles me to her mouth* as the numb hand rubs. Pins and needles subside just as the heat hits. Pull the blanket over my head. Bedroom door clicks.

Front door bangs. Lucy, gone already. I peer into the bedroom. A pile of tissues on the floor, duvet crumpled at the end of the bed. I lie down, burying my face in her pillow, her perfume wrapped around me. When I wake, there is a message on the answerphone. Jules, it's Charles, you OK, Lucy rang, says you're sick. Press Delete, watch the red light pulsing until the beeps flatline. Run myself a bath although there is not enough hot water, so it's only as deep as my shins. The water is cool and it makes my heart pulse faster. I submerge my ears and listen to it slowing as I shrink with the chill. I stay, grateful, until my fingers are wrinkled and the jagged quicks of my nails are white and swollen. I shave at the mirror, reluctant to look, but I still see more than I want to.

I pick up the phone to ring in, but decide to email instead. Type, thanks for the call, yes, fucking sick, sick in the head, sick in the groin, can't stop being sick, don't understand this sick, never sick, unless I've always been sick just never realised, Lucy sick of me, me sick of me. Delete it all. Retype, thanks Charles, see you soon. About to close, then click the blue E for a glimpse of the world outside. Type E-B-A-Y. But I have everything. Search, just look. But I have everything. Not these. Groin pushes underneath the laptop, hold it steady with my left hand, click to enlarge the image. *Romanova preparing, criss-crossing laces like a corset, pulled in tight. I tie knots around the blades and secure each leg.* Click Buy It Now, work delivery. Close the laptop, *push her open.* Run to the kitchen sink, bile rising. Sit with my back against the cereal cupboard for the rest of the afternoon.

Lucy comes home later than normal, says she went for a quick drink, did I have a problem with that. No, of course not. I made dinner. Already eaten, sorry. Could have called. Yes, sorry, I didn't feel like hurrying home. I know. Jules, do you want to talk about it. I count the blocks in the parquet floor. She is wearing the shoes I bought her in Italy, they are brown and green like a mint humbug, with a bright-purple heel and sole. Like your shoes, remember when we. Jules, don't. Sorry. I eat the casserole alone as she makes a call from the bedroom. The wedding, she says when she comes out, maybe wait for a bit.

When she goes to bed she leaves the bedroom door open, turns off the lights. I clear up in the kitchen, tiptoe in beside her. I lean to kiss her cheek, but as the bed moves under me, she turns to face the wall. Goodnight, she says. Goodnight.

Sister comes round, says, you all right, says, it's just that, Lucy called. So damn smug now she's married, kid on the way, thinks she knows how to fix everything. All different now. Not like then, sitting on the kitchen worktop, cotton-wool balls dipped in a clear bowl of warm water, saying aye yi yi yi, as she wipes my knees.

Welcome back Jules, feeling better. Nod, thank you. Turn to my desk. Cardboard box, a thin strip of Sellotape running across the middle, red security stamp ticked in the corner. THIS WAY UP. Stomach lurches, hands tremble as I reach for the delivery note lying open on top. Charles smirking over the desk divider, looks interesting. Present for Lucy, I say, surprise, it's her birthday. Flicker of his eyebrow, good to see you anyway. Turns back to his office, makes a phone call. Couple of the lads across the way erupt in laughter. Ask Jules, they say, he knows all about that.

At lunchtime, I lock the box in my desk and go for a walk to clear my head. Pass a car showroom, stop for a moment, stare at silver stars and leaping cats, chrome wings ready to soar. *Tiny body turning in the air.* My focus shortens, the man in the reflection does not smile, his eyes are fixed and he stares back at me, a furrow between his brows.

Charles comes up behind me. All right old boy, expecting a hefty bonus huh, pointing to the cars inside. No, thinking of selling. Lost your va-va-voom have you. I wish. Lucy keeping you busy huh. Something like that. Should have told me it was her birthday, I would have bought her something. She didn't want a fuss. Did she not. Charles walking off, a spring in his step, whistling. I wrap my scarf around my face, walk towards the river with my head down, counting cracks in the pavement.

It is gone eight by the time everyone leaves the office. Catching up I say to Charles, but he doesn't answer, just waves as he heads to the door, mobile held to his ear saying, couldn't help myself, you're worth it.

I lift the box onto my desk, peel back the Sellotape. The smell of leather hits, even before I open wide. Angel boots buried in polystyrene snow, blades glinting. I take them out, one then the other, cupping each boot to my nose and mouth, *kiss me.* Run the blades across my palms until the grooves redden, raw, stop before I stain the ivory hide. Repack them in my gym-kit rucksack, computer off, coat on, fists squeezed tight. Hurry.

Walk through the City, feel the blades banging, *Romanova on my back, wiggling,* scarf tickling my ears, *whispering.* Turn through lanes and narrow streets, weaving my way home, focused on the headlights where the roads are still busy. See the dirty spire of a church and for a moment I want to take refuge, sit for a while, gather my thoughts, but she does the thinking for me. *Wouldn't it help to know.* The scarf has tightened around my neck, *flesh-coloured stockings pulling at my windpipe, head lightening,* I tug at it to loosen, to lessen her control, but *she pulls the ends tighter from behind, riding on my back, blades knocking on my kidneys.* I put my hands in my pockets, hold myself as I walk, *left, right, left. Feet crossing over tiny ankles, turning me this way and that* until the streets are less familiar but the destination certain. Once, only once before, me, Charles, a gentlemen's agreement, not to be broken. *Blades cutting, grating, carving out a bruise on my back, Romanova rubbing on it, turning on the pain. You have to know.* Doors with buzzers labelled Senorita, Suzy. Buzz in. *Blades knocking, bruise rising.* Joss sticks burning over stale sweat, pinky-orange carpet detached from its gripper, rumpled in the corners, black at frayed edges. Bare bulbs hang in the hallway, stare into the light as I climb the stairs, *pearly glow, reflections from the ice, sparkles in the corners of my eyes, this way.* She shows me in, says no funny business. One thing. Open the bag. Please. She shrugs. £40. Shut my eyes. *Blades strike the ice to raise the jump, lands toe pointing backwards, leg outstretched. Pull her onto me. She traces a serpentine down my chest. The blade is sharp, cold. She stops just above, holds the pressure while she rocks against me. Dizzy with spinning. Run my finger along the blade as she takes me in her mouth, saliva like warm blood trickling.*

She was heavier than Romanova, too busty, tall. No magic in her eyes, no ice shine, no youthful hope, no innocence. But the voice is silent, my insides warm and still.

Back on Commercial Street I turn on the mobile to find eleven missed calls, handful of messages. Just wondered. How long. Where the hell. Not funny now. Please, please.

She opens the door as soon as my keys start to turn in the lock. Hugs me, then, it's past midnight, where the hell. Screaming. I know, I know. Rucksack heavy on my shoulders, lean against the wall to steady, balance. Wince with the deepening bruise, push against it, harder. What is going on. On every wall, gorgeous people stare at me with black-and-white grins. Almost hear their glasses clinking, laughing, cheers. A voice rising above the chatter of the crowd. Tell me.

She cries for hours, asks all the questions I have no answers for, tells me things about myself I know already. Sick. Can you stop, she asks. I've tried. Notice a vase on the sideboard. White roses. *Stems thrown onto the ice.* A card, Happy Birthday.

End of the week and the MD calls me in, the HR sitting in the corner, already making notes. Jules, he says, your bonus. Says, I've been skating through the figures. Page rustling behind me. You're on thin ice. Says, you're not scoring top points at the moment, maybe time to leave the arena. Go back to my desk. A picture of Torvill and Dean stuck to my screen, my face superimposed on his. Charles grinning, shame about you and Lucy, he says, mind if I have a crack?

HOT STEPPAH
J. D. Keith

The air in the street was stifling and syrupy thick. Smoke rose from the tarmac and fumes from stationary exhausts choked the sweat-greased crowd that was beginning to gather. The music had stopped and the singing was over, but Pastor MacDonald's voice was still audible from outside, even through the heavy Sunday-afternoon traffic, now being diverted away from the cordoned-off Plaza.

The microphone settings had been specifically adjusted to project his voice out into the world, towards the seething mass of unbelievers that passed along the road every week on their way to the cinema, the bookmaker's, and even the Methodist church, because broad is the way that leadeth to destruction. The building wasn't designed to keep noise in.

Pastor MacDonald first knew the place as a butcher's back in the 1960s. He enjoyed recounting to anyone who would listen how it became a temple for God and, even though he was not one to embellish a story, every time he told it the church's history became increasingly laden with signs and miracles.

His wife, Constance – respectfully called Mother MacDonald by church members – had several memories of the butcher's. Pastor, leaning against the pulpit, was standing where the counter used to be, where he would send her to beg for scraps of meat at the end of the day, back when they had no other family on what she called "this wretched island". She was in her mid-thirties then and her belly had begun to stretch with Joshua, her firstborn. (And now, every day, she prayed for him, repeating the same words: "'Elp 'im, Lawd, cos yu did say hif yu train up a chil' in de way him should go . . .")

The heathen butcher needed God more than most. She had hated going in there, stooping her neck, sensing his crocodile smile but refusing to look into his eyes. She was older now and vowed never to be humiliated like that again, unless it was for Jesus' sake, because blessèd are ye, when men (an' women too, hmmph!) shall revile yu, an' persecute yu, an' shall say hall manner o' heevil against yu . . . She still felt guilty about the pleasure she derived, years later, from hearing the butcher had died suddenly. He had choked on a steak, if rumours were to be believed. And that was how Wimpy's bought the building.

After only a few years, the Wimpy's closed too and it was left derelict. Squatters came in and the council did nothing until the church applied to take it over, holding several twenty-four-hour vigils outside the imposing brick structure of Brent Town Hall, marching up and down the steps as if expecting it to collapse at any moment, like the walls of Jericho. A sympathetic councillor agreed the building should be put to good use and, eventually, it became the True Word Centre.

Over the following months, the congregation took to the streets after every service, collecting money for the building renovations. With a small budget, they began trying to erase the evidence of the restaurant. A sealed corridor now led to the toilets at the back, but they still had the Wimpy's red doors and round windows in the middle. At the end of the corridor was the side entrance and, next to it, running along the left side of the building, was the Sunday-school room, which had once been the kitchen. The raised platform on the right, on which some of the congregation sat, betrayed where the restaurant's seating area used to be. The spotlights were unchanged here but, on the other side, there was strip lighting and a higher ceiling, left over from the butcher's.

It was an unspoken rule, but only the more attention-seeking members of the congregation would come straight through the main glass door at the end of the aisle after service had started. Latecomers and curious outsiders, drawn to the music, would come in through the more discreet side door and peer in through the window at the end of the corridor. So when the main door opened suddenly that afternoon, everyone was surprised.

Mother MacDonald was among those in the eighty-strong congregation fanning themselves with their Bibles; the hot, stale air had baked everyone to feverish distraction. Pastor MacDonald strongly disapproved and would have used the moment to throw himself into a righteous fury about using the Word of God as a fan. He could have talked about how the scribes and Pharisees defiled the Word of God too, but instead he stood in silence for a while. He could not remember what he had just said, so he lifted up his head from the passage he was reading and took a sip of water.

His co-pastor had nodded off to the lilt of his voice and only the faithful few were spurring him on with sporadic "Amen"s – Mother Dawkins, right at the back, the Bailey sisters in the middle, Sister Ogilvie and the little preacher boy, aptly named Samuel, both to Pastor's left in the front row. Their positions rarely changed week to week.

Mother MacDonald was in the second row desperately trying to keep her husband in focus, but he kept splitting into two. She was seated behind some of the disruptive children she'd deliberately placed at the front – "children" meaning anyone under twenty. Sarah, Reuben, Obadiah, Nathan, Daniel and Natasha: all were joined together in their unruliness despite being a decade apart oldest to youngest. She removed her glasses and breathed on them, then bent down to look for a tissue to wipe them with. She nudged Sister Davies next to her, a large, alert woman with bright-blue slippers and matching tights. Sister Davies was ready for her and there was no need to say anything: out came her expensive-looking leather handbag, which her son had bought her with his large wages. She offered Mother MacDonald a packet of Kleenex, Polo mints, Olbas oil.

Mother MacDonald snatched the Kleenex and wiped her glasses.

She then wiped down her neck and the sweaty cleavage that always seemed to end up rising up and into the open, announcing itself as she danced, singing to the congregation. (No dress can hol' dem down. No blouse, no coat, no gown, amen! No tomb, no too-oo-omb, no tomb couldda hol' Him down.)

The chairs' wooden slats were beginning to take their toll on everybody's buttocks; most people had begun fidgeting. Mother MacDonald looked to the right and studied Sister Ogilvie's back; she was sitting up on the platform as always. They were both wearing the same hat: black felt covered with tiny silver sequins that sent light sparkling off in all directions every time they moved their heads. Sister Ogilvie and Mother MacDonald were kindred spirits, separated by just half a decade and about a hundred pounds in weight. Mother MacDonald marvelled how that skinny old woman could cope with the slats digging into her bones for four hours. She wondered whether, if the congregation paid its tithes more honestly, they could have bought proper chairs, not the cheap garden ones most people were sitting on. "Brudder Davies could have feed da five t'ousand an' den some with what dey tell me him get pay," Sister Ogilvie had once told her over the phone. And as she returned to that thought, she adjusted herself and straightened her flower-print dress, while her husband kicked back into gear.

"An' dere shall be weeping-ah . . . an' a wailing-ah . . . an' gnashing of teet-ah. And again I say-ah . . . dere shall be weeping-ah! I said-ah *weeeping . . .*" Pastor sang the last note in a falsetto voice and the keyboard kicked in with the organ effect. "And way-ay-ay-ling . . ." he added and, again, the keyboard player riffed over him, always attentive, always looking up at the preacher or casting sideways glances towards the congregation.

The children in front were elbowing each other. They were anxious to get outside, waiting for the sermon to end so they could step out into a world that promised not eternal damnation but ice cream and much-needed fresh air. Mother MacDonald resisted the urge to reach over and scold them and instead found herself shouting aloud, "Preach!"

The atmosphere was starting to warm up. Samuel was crying

loudly – his mind full of conjured images of hell – and some of the congregation were shifting about in their seats. The restless bodies were becoming more alert, more aware of something that was happening. Mother MacDonald sensed a stirring in her spirit, and she started trying to tune into what the Lord might be telling her. Some of the teenage girls at the back felt the noise from outside getting louder, and they too had recognised a new buzz in the air.

Marsha – acne-ridden and usually truculent – was sitting in the middle of the back row as usual, her shiny face bursting from holding in her breath. She was trying not to laugh out loud at the cartoon she had been passed, drawn on a scrap of paper torn from a hymn book, of the child crying at the front. Right at that moment, the noise level from outside rose even higher. Someone was entering the main door. Her whole row turned.

Pastor MacDonald stopped mid-flow. Sister Ogilvie's body swivelled around instinctively, her head following. Sister Davies, who always kept an eye on Sister Ogilvie, copied her and then nudged Mother MacDonald. The rest of the congregation waited for the split second that the door banged against the wall then, as one, turned to see who had entered.

It was Sovereign.

He didn't mean to open the door so rough but it had swung back the whole way. He'd practically run in, his breath heavy, his forehead itching with sweat and his hands shaking. His entrance must have been loud because a whole sea of eyes turned to greet him. He almost backtracked. Maybe he should have gone into the Methodist church opposite.

There was a host of women in shoulder pads, men in dark suits, walls covered with blue curtain. He'd seen it all before – he'd been dragged into holes like this as a child by his grandma – but this time was different. He was a big boy now.

He realised his head hurt.

A woman with a doily on her head pointed to a spare seat near the back, up on the raised bit. She walked him towards it. She had a badge that said Usher, which he'd always thought was a guy's name. He clocked a pair of eyes staring back at him. Marsha, from school. She turned away in what looked like wide-eyed horror and folded into the chair. He left Usher pointing, went to the other side and sat down at the end of a row just in front. The pinstripe-suit guy sitting beside him almost seemed not to have noticed he was there. He'd picked up the large Bible on the seat next to him and put it on the floor, allowing Sovereign to sit down, and that was that. Didn't even look at him.

The preacher seemed to be waiting. He'd removed his big round glasses carefully to wipe the sweat from his shiny head, which reflected the bright light from above. He replaced the glasses, putting them as far down the end of his nose as he could, and the sweat poured down to his beard, yea, even Aaron's beard: that went down to the skirt of his garments. Resting his left arm on the pulpit and leaning over, leaning right up close to the microphone, his slightly crossed eyes rested on his audience and then he began to speak.

"I have," he started, in a low echoing voice, "a revelation right now-ah." He paused again and there were a few mumbles in the background: "Speak, Laawd. Yes!"

"Dis is-ah," he continued, "the time-ah to repent-ah. Dis may be your last opportunity right now-ah."

The eyes that had stared at Sovereign began darting about. Several old women, in assorted large hats that swallowed their faces, looked round and stared past him to his left, where Marsha and her friends were. The lethal, half-squint accusations coming from those watery, yellow eyes were enough to freak anyone. He tutted and smiled to himself. Looks like everyone knew what she was like.

He looked over at her row again. Several pairs of batted eyelashes and dipping eyelids, no hint of make-up. Apart from Jezebel herself, they were all fixed on him. Every time he crooked his neck a little, he could sense the eyes bearing down, following his every movement.

He checked out the row directly behind him and caught one girl square in the face. Four of them sitting together, all acting like they weren't checking him, but she'd looked away too late. She had the soft, round cheeks of an innocent church girl but he could see from the way she held his look before turning away slowly that she was one of *them* ones. One of those beenies that want to mess with you. The kind who will giggle and go on all shy if you chat to her around her friends, but when you get her alone, you get the other side.

Intelligent. Probably stayed on for Year 12. She leaves home for school with her socks rolled up tight, skirt below the knees, copper face shiny and smelling of coconut lotion, greased-down hair in pigtails, even. She turns the corner and pulls down the socks, pulls out the hairbands, pulls up the skirt and unbuttons the blouse till she's got some decent cleavage going. Then on go the clip-on earrings and the lipstick. He knows.

Marsha was just like that at school. And she'd go on like a real sket, but here she was every Sunday shaking her booty in the name of Jesus . . . And Jag told him some *things* about her recently. Well, maybe he said that just because she darked him. You never know. And the first and last time he'd jonesed that girl was five whole years ago. He'd been nearly fourteen and it was his first time. He'd tried to lie, act like he'd been doing it ever since he could get it up. Those were the days.

He felt all the eyes up and down the rows looking at him looking at this other girl. The preacher was yelling "Repent!" He'd repeated that for the second time. The girl bit her lip. The friend next to her gave a nudge. It was Shantelle's sister, Ruth. What, like half his class had family here – this was *unreal.* After Ruth nudged her, the corner of the girl's mouth went up and her body spasmed. She put her hands to her face styling it out like she was sneezing. Blatant with a capital B.

A few guys had started looking over too. One of the only other guys around his age was sitting just in front, yellow shirt, red tie, an out-of-date Afro with a parting. Shameful. This guy practically swivelled his head around 180 degrees just to cut his eye at him. Must be digging the girl as well. Too bad. I've done been with church girls and I ain't about that right now. He gulped, and for the first time since he'd sat down he thought about how he came to be there. He let the beads of sweat trickle down his head and looked around again at the other eyes.

Mr Pimpstripe next to him had his closed tight shut. Just as well because, from the looks of it, my man here spend the whole weekend with a wavecap on. Now that gives you *real* headache, worse than what I got now.

Sovereign thought about closing his own eyes but his mind had begun racing. He wondered what might be going on outside. He became aware that his body was aching as well as his head and his thoughts were moving too quickly from one place to the other. When he blinked, flashbacks clung to the back of his eyelids, spoke to his brain. "Repent! For the time is at hand-ah." His mouth was dry, and his hands were now unwilling to unclench themselves from the taut fists he'd created on his lap. He tried to focus his attentions instead at the wave of women surrounding him.

Two sequinned hats looked across at each other and twisted their lips in his direction. Sequin Hat Number One bellowed out a powerful "Amen" that seemed to shake the foundations of the building. She was just a small old woman, didn't look like she had it in her. Meanwhile, Number Two peeled herself from off her seat and ambled towards the back. She was hench – bingo wings, mafia boss's mother type. Her expression was resolute, her eyes constantly shifting through the rows of chairs to meet other eyes and her cheeks puffed out like she was on the cud. Her boulder-like breasts hung down in her flower dress like ammunition in a sling (and David say, "'Ow dare you defy my Laawd de Gawd of Hisrael?" And 'im did swing him sling and Goliat' did faall). He would not have liked to get on the wrong side of those babylons. He thought he recognised her face from somewhere, but couldn't quite place it.

"Dere is-ah no coincidences with Gaawd-ah. You are not here by coincidence-ah. You may heven have just stepped off the street-ah and your life may be out of control-ah, but Jesus is calling you now-ah. *Jeeesus*-ah . . . is calling-ah . . . you . . ."

The older eyes refocused their attentions from the pretty little eyes sitting in the front and the back. Everyone was looking at him. He met the first few stares and then looked instead at the floor, then at his dirty trainers, his ripped jeans, his baggy string vest, hugely different to the suits and ties and neat polished shoes that didn't seem to fit with the weather. Not only was it baking outside, but the clammy bodies pushed together in this strange place had produced a hellish heat and a heavy odour. Sweat mixed with strong perfume . . . and stale cheese. Worse still, the main door and the windows were closed, but he could still hear the noise of the High Street traffic. He picked his red baseball cap up from the floor and began to fan himself with it. Hot Steppah, it said on the front.

"How will you antsah this day-ah? I said how-ah will you ants-ah?"

Sequin Hat Two with the bazookas stood by the glass door at the corridor entrance. She swatted off a little boy who tried to push through to get to the bathroom. As she bent over, the little butterfly on her dress wobbled. Her face and neck were glowing with sweat.

He wondered how they managed to put up with the stifling heat. When he'd gone to America, all the shops had air conditioning, even the dollar stores. They were better at things over there. Then again, even if air conditioning got big in this country, it wouldn't end up in a converted shop like this one, here in Harlesden, the place even God had forgotten.

"Are you dat prodigal son-ah? Today-ah He is telling you to come-ah. Dis may be your las' chance-ah, for we know not the day nor the hour-ah. Will you come back to the fold this day-ah? I said will-ah . . ."

He kept his eyes down for a while, stretching out his legs and crossing one foot over the other. He thought of America, the tall buildings, all those nice cars and that don't-give-a-shit attitude. He wanted to go back there, get away from his crew, the Terror Boys; get away from the chicken shop and all the trouble that came out of that place. In America they didn't have to hang out in holes like that. They had Fifth Avenue. They had bigger guns and better drugs. What's more, they had style to go with it.

He breathed in deeply, unclenched his fists. He felt inside his deep left pocket. The weighty metal was warm. Although you could see the bulge in his jeans, it wasn't that noticeable. He wanted to readjust himself and put it inside his waistband. He breathed out. Shit! He must have said this aloud because the man next to him made a kind of "Hmph!" noise.

He felt his heart thud and decided to concentrate on something else. He continued looking at his faded Nike trainers. $45 from the flea market and better than the real thing. A couple of times, when he first came back with them, he got stopped in the street and asked where he bought them. And then he remembered how once, some boy stepped on his foot and he flipped. Him and a couple of the crew, Shortie G and Slicer, they dragged the boy out of the chicken shop, his arms flailing, cursing at the top of his voice. Slicer got all hyper as usual, shouting out in his squeaky voice, "Let's mash him up, mash him good." They kept dragging him through the High Street and past Headlines, where Big Jeff got out waving a razor and said, "You better leave that bwoy alone." Shortie G, always practical, was like, "You guys are on a long ting. Just kick the bwoy down and let's go back." So, with a crowd starting to form, they put him down outside Headlines and got a few kicks in. A siren went off somewhere. Everyone walked off nicely. Just how it should be. He wasn't concerned about people chatting his business and getting him into it. Not like now. Shit.

"The Spirit is telling mee-ah that there is a soul here today-ah. A soul-ah that is lost-ah. A soul-ah that is wrestling-ah. Wrestling in their mind-ah. And the Bible says-ah that we wrestle not-ah against flesh and blood-ah, but against principalities-ah and powers-ah."

Sovereign tried to switch off completely, think about where he was now instead, but he didn't want to look up. He studied the floor. Both feet were now firmly in the middle of one of the brown carpet tiles that went up to the pulpit area. He followed the pattern of squares for a while and the places where they had lifted slightly. He looked across the aisle, noting by their relation to the squares how uneven the nine rows of chairs were. His eyes skimmed over the things people kept under their chairs: Bibles, hymn books, tambourines, handbags, handkerchiefs and, under a few, high heels. So that was the cheesy smell. Old-people feet. He scrunched up his nose then looked over towards the walls, covered with a thick royal-blue curtain. Most of the light came through the shop-window entrance and the strip lighting. There was nothing else to decorate the room, just a large banner at the front saying "Victory in Jesus '92". They must have reused it three years running.

"Are you wrestling this day-ah?"

He checked his breathing. His pulse was still racing but he felt back to normal. In fact, so normal he was thinking about risking it and leaving Pastor to see to the rest of his flock again. As much "fun" as it was being here, there was still business to deal with. He needed to work out what had gone down, how bad things were, whether he should lie low for a bit. Maybe go up to Wolverhampton for a while and stay with some family.

He looked behind him to the entrance and thought about ducking out but Number Two fixed him an iron stare. That's when he recognised her. Constance MacDonald – Jag's aunt. Jag was one of the Terror Boys, always mouthing it off, saying how his older cousin was the baddest thing going; he was in for ten years or something after he peeled up this guy who juiced one of his girls. So when Shortie G said he's got to be one fool doing that for a girl who probably smelt like fish, "because that gally's been round the block twice, better believe dat one," Jag went, "Yeah, you chatting Biggie now? You just watch. He can even get you from inside, trust." And so Shortie got all scared. Sovereign had kept quiet. Not worth getting involved.

He wondered if Constance recognised him. He'd only been round there once, when him and Jag were still in school, like more than two years ago now.

The preacher lowered his voice almost to a whisper over the microphone and spoke the last words of the sermon. "Today-ah, your soul-ah may be required of thee-ah."

Sovereign groaned. Oh, God. That was the punch line. He cut his eyes at Constance, moving his head back round to face the preacher, whose bulging eyes were fixed on him. He met the preacher's gaze and wiped his mouth, still stinging from the sharp right hook that had caught him square less than a half hour ago. He looked down at his hand and jumped when he saw how much blood stuck to it. He must look real bad.

The preacher let out a huge cry which made him jump again. No one else seemed surprised. His eyes again hooked on to the preacher's, daring him to outstare him, knowing he would have to look away soon and address the rest of the congregation, who were starting to get noisier with "Amen"s and "Preach!" and other exhortations to continue. Sovereign didn't look away as he began to hear sirens outside. There were only a few but they echoed in his head, getting louder each time and forcing the congregation to crescendo in turn in some twisted battle. Wrestling against the powers. His mouth went dry.

He felt his eyes widen as the sirens blazed on, whirring, whooping, hollering, rising against the sounds of the congregation, which was being charged up by some strange energy, bubbling up with no limit, no control. An old woman led the stampede – squealing loudly, she leapt from her seat as if it had struck her and danced to the front. She must have been at least seventy, but her stooped heavy frame glided across the floor, weightless, effortless.

As she got up, she knocked the head of the young girl next to her, almost removing her black beret, which was stuck down with a hairpin. The girl, who could have been no more than twelve, convulsed in her chair like she'd been given a jolt of electricity, then fell forwards muttering and then back again, stretching out her hands and screeching. The chair rocked back and forth and a couple of women from the row behind grabbed on to it to steady her.

The dancing caught on like a Mexican wave and soon nearly half the congregation were shouting and shimmying their way to the front, whilst the others were righting upturned chairs, limiting the damage.

At this point, Sovereign felt a hand on his shoulder as Constance leant over him, breasts level with his eyes, grip firm and unapologetic.

"Come to de haltar," she commanded, not waiting for him to look up at her.

He could still hear the sirens, but they seemed stationary now. Loud whoops that made him dizzy. Definitely more than one and probably a whole legion of cars and vans surrounding the place. He gulped.

She repeated herself. His legs moved of their own accord – his will was giving way. Eyes welling up with angry tears, ears filled with nothing but the cars outside. He found himself pleading for a miracle that would clear up the stupid mess he was in. If he hadn't been there that morning, it wouldn't have happened. If Jag hadn't given him the piece, then it wouldn't have happened. If those damn boys hadn't wanted to start something, and if *that* one especially hadn't got feisty, it definitely wouldn't have happened. He wanted to scream.

"Come," she said, and pushed him up roughly. He staggered towards the front, steering his body around the limbs of the crowd, which had begun to sing. His ears could not focus on the words and his eyes were now clouded over. The bodies blurred around him, multiplying until he was standing among a myriad of spirits.

Constance shoved him further forward until he was standing right by the pulpit. She touched his head and he felt himself falling to his knees. Weak and heavy, dry-throated and naked in front of the thickening crowd. He was hotter than before, almost dizzy with fever, and his sweat poured down around him. He closed his eyes.

Constance was kneeling behind him, but her voice seemed to surround him completely. She was transformed, swallowing him, increasing as he decreased. She pressed his head down until it was almost level with his knees and now all he could hear was her voice. A voice that spoke words he couldn't understand. That seemed to be scolding him and comforting him at the same time. A voice that went on and on, barely pausing for breath.

And now the sirens stop, the yelling and the crying and the singing around him cease. In the silence, his spirit lifts itself, up through the congregation, through the glass door, through the police cars parked outside, through the High Street and upwards, upwards, upwards. His spirit is giddy, slicing through clouds and surging forwards. It begins to spiral downwards, swirling towards the chicken shop, where he can see a large circle of curious bodies stretching over a police cordon. He doesn't have time to wonder if they managed to hide all the stuff that was under the counter because it continues floating onwards and, just as he thinks his spirit is running home to safety, to a third-floor flat on the Stonebridge Estate where the police won't find him, it turns back towards the car park in the Plaza. It hovers over the blocked traffic, where the noise of horns fills his ears like sweet gospel music and joins with the hum of the choir back in the church, still weighed down with the notes of *Sinner Come Home*. It skates through the police barriers, cuts through the whirring of sirens and lowers itself slowly into the corner, just by Blockbuster Video. The air out here is stifling and choking smoke rises from the tarmac and his spirit twists with the rhythm of Pastor Macdonald's voice, echoing louder, stronger, deeper, above all of the other sounds. The car park is unfamiliar: almost no cars, no people running into the shops screaming, just a heavy atmosphere of uniformed men standing watch while an ambulance approaches. His spirit hovers over the boy lying in a pool of blood, the still conductor in this orchestra of sirens and choirs and weeping and hollering.

Constance knocks him backwards and his body feels light. His spirit is melting. Its weightless world merges with the carpet tiles on the floor and the sound of the preacher talking over him and the woman with the sequinned hat chanting over him and now his own words, which surprise him. He shouts out to Jesus, shouts out for salvation, shouts out for something or anything that will rescue him, take him somewhere else, make him new and clean and safe. He remembers chunks of the Bible he learnt as a child and his shouts become screams become noises become whispers. "Let this cup pass, let this cup pass, please let this cup pass . . ."

And then she's on his left-hand side and she's pressing her body into him. He can hear that they've entered. Hear the tension in the air because the music's stopped and the singing's stopped and there's a voice telling him to freeze and put his hands in the air and everyone else better back away. Suddenly it gets a lot noisier again and he doesn't know what's going on because it all seems like a dream and his heart has gone into his mouth. But Constance has been holding on to him, squeezing his leg and now she lets go. The preacher's saying something. He's talking to them, saying, "How dare ye gentiles defile de House of de Lawd! 'Ow dare ye enter into dis sacred ground! You come here under whose name? Under whose right?"

The police have grabbed him roughly, wrenched his wrists behind his back and clicked on the handcuffs. He's hardly moved because he suddenly needs to pee and now he can't see much because his eyes are blurry and he wants to close them again and not open them until he wakes up from this nightmare.

All he notices through the blur is that the congregation is moving towards the front, singing at full strength, and that the pigs have got bullet-proofs on. They're saying, "Stand back, stand back, we are dealing with an armed murderer," and the preacher is saying, "De only authority you must respeck right now in dis place his de autority of de Lawd." He's at the pulpit, his voice still coming through the speakers. And the congregation has begun a new chorus of *We Shall Not Be Moved*. This has got to be a dream. His arm feels weird up against his back and the cold metal cuffs are digging into his hands. He's still talking to himself, still asking God to help him and the police are patting him down. "Where's your weapon?" they're asking him and they're going into his pockets and pulling out money and keys and cigarettes and rolling papers and nothing else. "Where's your weapon?" they keep saying, and the chorus has gathered pace, quickening, louder, fuller, angrier. More police have trickled through to the altar and one of them is on his radio calling for backup and they're shouting at the congregation, "Stand back."

Through all the commotion he can hear them: "I'm arresting you, Christian Wilson, for the murder of . . ." and then "Just like a tree that's planted by the wa-a-ters" and then "Anything you do say may be given as evidence" and then another pig's threatening the preacher saying, "Quiet down or we'll arrest you and all for obstructing the course –" and suddenly the preacher's struck the cop and he's been handcuffed too. But he's still trying to talk into the microphone, saying, "Brethren, let us render unto Caesar dat what pertainet unto Caesar – but dey shalt be struck down if hany 'arm shall come upon dis boy." And he hears the preacher saying, "Lawd, I deliver us into your hands," but he's not on the microphone any more.

Then he feels himself being dragged up the aisle and the congregation parting like the Red Sea, still singing, right? Only it's something else he can't quite catch the words to. He can't stand properly because he's weak. And then Pastor is right behind him, saying, "I know ye scribes and Pharisees. I do know all your hungodly ways. I know what you did to my Joshua." And he's wondering who's Joshua, and he's wondering what happened to the gun, knowing now for certain what happened to the boy. And then he's wondering where he is because his mind goes funny. Then he feels his wrists again and the arms squeezing his elbows and he panics and wonders where Shortie is and where Slicer is and where the rest of them all is. And then his head is being pushed down into one of the many police cars. And when he looks out onto the street and sees Constance standing among the crowd that has rushed out with him, he knows he doesn't have to wonder what happened to the gun any more. She just looks at him through the glass as they speed off to the chorus of sirens.

A GAP OF SKY
Anna Hope

It is dark, but the wrong dark. Something is wrong with the dark. Ellie reaches a hand out from under the duvet and flails for water; there is only an empty pint glass. Fuck. She retreats, rests her swollen cheek against her palm, but her need is too great. She takes the glass, stumbles towards the little sink, fills it and gulps the water down. It tastes chemical. She has to pee. She thinks of the hall toilet, at the other end of a chilly, uncarpeted corridor, and, thinking better of it, hoists herself over the sink, turns on the tap, and lets rip a glorious steamy stream of relief. Better. She clambers down and checks out her reflection with one gummy eye. One gummy eye stares warily back at her. There are clumps of black in the corner of her eyes, clumps of yellow lacing her lashes, like frost, like thick yellow eyefrost that came in the night. "Blaaaaargh," she breathes; sticks her tongue out. Jesus. She burrows back into bed. Her chest hurts. The room is cold. It is warm under the duvet though, and meaty smelling. Ellie bashes the pillow gently with the side of her face and curls up into it. Traces of her dream waft towards her like wisps of smoke from underworld fires. What was it? A man, and a woman – a scary woman with tiny nipples on her eyeballs – and then she was near the sea, standing looking down at the sea from a beautiful hilltop. Fuuuuuck . . . She shoots up from under the duvet, scrabbles for her phone, finds it beside the pillow. 16:29. Oh *shit* oh shit oh shit oh shit.

Monday. It is Monday. Essay there is an essay due, *important*, due for Tuesday morning. *Virginia Woolf. And the . . .* What was the title? *Something Oyster of Perceptiveness.* Fuck. How the *fuck* did she manage to sleep for so long? She sits on the bed, brings her legs up under her chin, rummages for what she can remember from the night before. She was with Toby, and some girl; she remembers the club finishing and then a house, somewhere near Spitalfields – of course, that friend of Toby's, something in music. She remembers the face of the girl, the sloping angles of her as she leaned in to light her cigarettes from Ellie's lighter. She remembers going out for booze. Did she get booze? Cans, some cans of lager, and then more coke arriving and – K, didn't they do some K? They must have done, because Ellie remembers the light, the morning light on the ceiling, and looking up at it and thinking she was in a barn somewhere, a beautiful spacious light-filled barn and not actually in London at all, and then getting up and saying, "Virginia Woolf!" very loudly in the middle of the room. And everyone laughing, everyone pissing themselves like it was the funniest thing ever. And then leaving, and getting the tube, getting the fucking *rush-hour* tube home. That must have been at about eight this morning. Nine ten *eleventwelveonetwothreefour* – eight hours sleep. OK. OK.

Ellie takes the kettle, fills it from the sink. She finds her tracksuit bottoms under a pile of clothes on her chair and pulls them on; T-shirt, hoody. Boots up the computer. She's going to have to work through the night, but it's fine. This is fine. Coke. Does she have any left? Find the wrap, in the bra. The bra, in a tender little pile on the floor, curled around her knickers. *Yessssss!* Clever Ellie. Little bump just to get things started. Nice, now. Coffee. Swill out cafetière, fill it. Computer. Is. On. Fags . . . Student shop. She could always score some more, too; see if Jez is about. Good plan. Good, this was good, fine. Coffee plunged, poured, slurped; hot, fuck that's hot. Anything else? Of course: printer, printer's out of ink. Student shop too. Fine. Time? Ten minutes to get there. Shit. Should she do the essay first, print it in the morning? No. No time. Needs to be handed in at nine. She's already had her extension. She remembers the letter, the stomach-lurching letter: "If this lack of application continues we will have no choice but to reconsider your place on the course." Toby! Maybe Toby has some ink. She dials his number. No reply. Unsurprising. Fuck it. She'll get the ink. The fresh air will be a good thing. Room is a state. Ellie's eye ranges over the bed, the single bed. She thinks of Rob, in the bed, Rob with his face all creased from sleep on the weekend he came to visit, and waking up beside him like it was some kind of miracle, and laughing, both of them, laughing. She hates the bed, hasn't had a single bed since she was ten. Fucking students. Fucking halls. Fucking student halls. She grabs her hat and shoves it on. It's a grey alpaca hat that Rob gave her. One of the flaps is all loose and unravelling; makes her look like a hippy but she likes it. She remembers him giving it to her, last birthday. It was sunny and warm and they were sitting out in the park and he gave her the hat and she said what are you giving me a woolly hat for and he said because I won't be with you in the winter and kissed her but what Ellie remembers is this little kid getting tangled up in a kite and screaming for its mum and watching it happen over Rob's shoulder and the kite winding more and more into the little boy's wrists and not the kiss really, not the kiss at all. Ellie pockets her wallet, pulls on her coat and rattles on through the corridor and out onto Maple Street.

The air is cold, makes her gasp, cold and hurting on her ragged lungs. The light is bright, searing light from the sun. Setting sun. Ellie pulls her hat down and shoulders her way over towards Gower Street. Crosses Tottenham Court Road, over to the big UCL quad. She sprints across towards the far corner, through the doors and down to the basement shop. Closed. Damn. Sweat trickles down her back. She can smell the sharp smell of her rising up through her sweater. There is someone in there, stacking shelves at the back, the young Asian guy who works there on weekdays. Ellie bangs on the door to get his attention, but he ignores her. *Fuck.* She checks her mobile – 17:02 – climbs the steps up onto Gordon Street. There is a boy there, smoking. "'Scuse me, could I blag a . . . ? Thanks mate." Straights. Marlboro Lights. Ellie doesn't like straight fags, but needs must and all that. She walks down the road, towards Gordon Square, heads through the iron railings, sits on a bench. The square is darkening, and in the darkening Ellie's heart is beating, beating fast. The coffee was a mistake. The coffee and the running and the bump of coke and now the cigarette. What if she has a heart attack? Has a heart attack right here in the middle of this square. The park-keeper might come and lock the gate, and nobody might find her until the morning. All frozen. The cigarette is lovely though. Ellie takes big deep needy drags, letting the smoke out slowly through her nose. It mixes with the catarrh and the last night smells that remain there, the booze and the coffee, and she feels comforted and alive. So. The shop is closed. She needs to get some printer ink, if she's going to do this essay. And if not? Will they really kick her off the course? Or will she have to repeat the year? She thinks of this past year, of university, and it feels like sludge, like thick dark sludge in her brain: Brontës and Dickens and Gaskell and the social-problem novel and blah blah blah. Shudders. No way. She's got to get this essay in. And she's all right, actually. Virginia Woolf. Better than Elizabeth bloody *Gaskell.* It's only five still. She can get to Tottenham Court Road in time. Plenty of shops there. She'll go there. They won't close till sixish. It will all be fine. There will be time for everything: time to get ink, to get cigarettes; maybe even to get a bit more coke.

There is a tree, a blackened tree at the centre of the square and, on a sudden whim, Ellie walks towards it, tosses her cigarette butt into the moist leaves fallen at its feet and, reaching out, touches its bark. She sees that the blackness is not city blackness, not pollution, but its real colour. It is like hide, looks like hide, feels full and tight and pulsing with something. Ellie pulls her hand away. Laughs. Twat. Purple beech says the sign. She thinks of the tree's roots, going down into the black of the earth, and the other roots down there, the latticed network of life, reaching down down down towards . . . What? There is a rustle in the leaves at her feet. Ellie jumps. An animal of some sort. When was the last time she even saw an animal? She can't remember. Pigeons. Of course, *pigeons.* She sees them every day. Probably.

Ellie looks up, at the houses that ring the square. They are tall and elegant; five storeys high, with those big blue and red doors. They seem full of purpose, sure of their meaning somehow. Ellie can see a sprinkling of those blue plaques on their fronts: So-and-so lived here. So-and-so who did such-and-such and yadayada blarghblarghblargh. There is something comforting about them there, those houses, as though they were standing watch, standing watch over an idea of London, a London of learning, of elegance, and achievement, but gentle somehow, like this square and the life within it and beneath it.

Ellie turns on her heel and marches out of the park, turns right, past the golden-stoned church on the corner and left towards Senate House. If she has to go to Tottenham Court Road she'll walk the back way. It is good to be outside, actually, to be out on the street. There is a clarity to the air, a quickening; it is the time of the day, the time of the year. There are people, moving together, here, in this part of London, moving with purpose, with *meaning*, and Ellie is one of them. There is a large tree in front of Senate House, and a large moon appearing behind it, behind its Gotham frontage rearing into the night. Ellie loves Senate House – the outside; she hasn't been inside yet. She imagines rows and rows of students, but all dressed in 1930s' costumes, like they were in a musical about New York and about to break into song. Or women, on telephones, sexy women telephone operators in pencil skirts in rows like in the war with red lipstick. Didn't Hitler want it for his headquarters when he conquered London?

At Russell Square she stops, leans against an iron railing. Every fifth spike or so is topped by an urn-looking thing, like funeral urns. They remind her of the urn her grandfather's ashes were kept in; of taking it down to the quiet country churchyard and standing there with her cousins while her mum and aunty dipped their hands inside and put the ashes into the earth. Her eye runs down the rail, where her gaze stops on an object, a dark object. She walks slowly towards it. It is a glove, a black leather glove, rammed down over the top of one of the spikes, its middle finger raised up to the sky in glorious salute. Ellie giggles. She touches the middle finger. A volt of naughtiness passes through her. Life seems, suddenly, filled with possibility, with giddy possibility, with irreverence, with delight, for what, really, was there to be reverent to? To whom? To what? To why? To God? To *Mum*? To *Dad*? Not them, *especially* not them. It was *their* fault she was doing this bloody course in the first place. The glove was a sign, for sure it was a sign; she was nineteen, and in London, and she needed to get some printer ink before the shop closed, and she should write an essay, but, really, she was free. She was totally and absolutely free, and last night she smoked a crack pipe and danced on a rooftop in East London and everything was grey and misty but beautiful still, and she didn't want the night to end, but it did, and she was alone, and that was fine, and now she could go and do anything that she liked. There is a rattle behind her and two trolleys full of coffee and sandwiches pass her, wheeled by two South American-looking men. They are heading for the back entrance of the British Museum, and so Ellie follows them. Fuck Virginia Woolf. She's never been in there before, and so, why not?

Inside the museums, Infinity goes up on trial goes the song in Ellie's head. She can't remember where it's from – it might have been one of the ones that Rob played to her – but it rolls on and on as she walks into a large hall. She recognises one of those big figures, those Easter Island figures at the far end; it has its back to her. It looks strange, its posture resigned, its shoulder blades jutting out slightly like the beginning of wings. It reminds her of a child's back, slightly hunched, like you wanted to pat it, or touch the smooth skin between the shoulders. "There there." Would be funny if it could talk. Must be shit, holed up in here, looking out over gaggles of tourists, camera phones aloft, instead of out over the sea . . . Where? Pacific? Atlantic? Whatever. Better than here. Better than looking out over the fucking *shop*. The length of the room is taken up with a low case, full of pills; it's an exhibition of some sort. Lots of pills. Headache pills and anti-depression pills and pills for everything under the sun. Ellie becomes aware of a throbbing in her skull. A horrible throbbing, metallic and insistent and wrong. She takes off the hat and puts her hand to her head. The pain is intensifying; feels as though it is in that place where the drugs have gone, snorted up and into her brain. "Living and Dying" reads the plaque on the wall of the hall. "How different cultures cope with the realities of Life and Death." Ellie's not sure she's ready to cope with death. There are four enormous papier-mâché figures above her head: a red horse with bared teeth, a locust and a vulture and a skull, all grinning manically down at her. They must be the Four Horsemen or something. *The ghost of electricity howls in the bones of her face, howls in the bones of her face . . .*

Ellie's head is throbbing and her skull feels as though it might split open and she really feels as though she might die. And what will happen to her, if she dies? Will she meet someone like the figures reared up above her now? She wheels around the room, but there is no comfort here. No. Death was terror, was grotesque, was horrible. And if she dies, who, in all this city, who would care if she disappeared? There's her mum and dad and brother in Somerset, but they wouldn't be able to get here for hours. There's Toby, but he is fast asleep somewhere, and Rob, but Rob was halfway across the world up some Andean mountain or something and he didn't really give a fuck about Ellie anyway or he wouldn't have gone away for a year would he? She knows there is a hospital nearby, she goes past its back entrance all the time on the way to lectures, sees people, yellowed people, sucking on cigarettes, their faces parched with worry. Would she die there? And would they stare at her? A doctor, maybe not much older than herself, shaking her head and writing on her clipboard and letting out a hissing sigh: "All that potential and then . . . thisssssss." Ellie sees herself, stretched out on a . . . a . . . gurney? Was that what they were called? Her body. Her *corpse*. Would someone wash it? Would someone wash her corpse, and would it be tender, or harsh? A stressed nurse washing her corpse while thinking about going outside for a *fag*?

Ellie needs to get outside. She stumbles across the hall with its great vaulted ceiling, and the diffuse light falling on the floor, past the crowds queuing for tickets and out onto the steps. Down the steps Ellie hurries and onto the street. In the lighted dark of the street, in the bustle, Ellie feels afraid. *Nasty, brutish and short* say the lines in Ellie's head, *nasty, brutish and short*. Ellie doesn't want to go to a shop now, couldn't go into a shop now, doesn't want any bloody *ink, can't* write an essay, no matter *what*, no matter what it matters, doesn't want any more coke, *ever again*. She wants to be outside, to stay outside, to walk and walk and walk.

She dodges her way through the traffic, clotted like blood in the arteries nearing the heart of the city. She turns left, onto Shaftesbury Avenue, and as she turns there is a gap of sky to her right, an emptiness, a vacancy that she doesn't remember seeing before, something destroyed, or being built; diggers move inside it with insectoid malevolence, and as Ellie stares one rears up before her, sizing her up, finding her wanting. She turns away, away, and hurries down through Covent Garden, Seven Dials; she doesn't know where she is going, maybe the river, yes, the river is what she needs, to look at the wide river, to see the wide river and wash this feeling clean.

On St Martin's Lane her pace slows and she stops to catch her breath. She can see the tip of Nelson above the roofs and the lacy ball of the Coliseum ahead of her. She knows the way to the river, she has only to carry on, to carry on past Trafalgar Square and down and she will reach it. To her right is a little street, a side street she has never seen before. It is prettily lit, old-fashioned looking, with tables of books and what look like postcards and pictures laid out in front of the shops. It looks warm, inviting. Surely she can get to the river this way, too? She turns, and walks up the street, fingers a book from a stall. It is a children's book, hard backed and gently stained with age, and there is something calming, something earthing about the touching of it. Ellie begins to feel a little better. She will not die, after all. So silly! Not yet. Not for a long time. She is only nineteen, only living, and if that was sometimes a little extreme, well, how should life be lived? That was the way she wished it, has always wished it, to dig, to the core, to get the . . . pith? Was it pith? *To suck the pith from life . . .* Ahead of Ellie someone opens the door to a shop. Light is thrown onto the street and Ellie steps up it and follows the person inside.

Something chimes above her head as the door closes. The shop smells of something; incense, but not unpleasantly. Its tables and shelves are loaded with New Agey-sounding titles. There is a chart in front of Ellie, a bestseller list, something called *Cosmic Ordering* is number one. Great. Who the *fuck* buys this shit? There is a young earnest-looking man at the till and two women browsing the shelves; both look to be in their thirties. The one nearest to Ellie looks pretty normal. Ellie peeks at the title she is holding: *Soulmates: Finding the One*. Fuck. The other woman is wearing a purple skirt, and a top with Indian lettering on it. She is up a step, in a section called Earth Mysteries. *God*. There is something depressing about this shop, about these women, something coming off them in waves. *So obvious*, so vulnerable in their reaching, their needing. She would never, could never end up like them, washed up here, in this little bookshop, their yearning so transparent, giving themselves away, giving themselves away and trying to find themselves again in this rubbish.

There is a wide window ledge, big enough to sit on, and Ellie throws her bones down onto it. The guy at the till flicks her a nervous little look. She feels rancid, as though the tide of her being has retreated and left her on the shore surrounded by plastic bottles and used sanitary towels and syringes and rusty cans. In front of her is a table, filled with pots of little stones. If she leans forward she can look over it without having to move from her seat. There are orange stones and blue stones and purple stones, stones for everything under the sun. Ellie takes one, holds it in her palm. It is a deep orangey-red. Red jasper says the sign. It is light, almost weightless. With a jolt, Ellie remembers her mother giving her a stone like this. *Of course*, when she went away last summer, with Rob; it was to give her protection or something daft like that. She had just shoved it into her rucksack somewhere. Probably still there. The stone feels pleasant in Ellie's hand. She thinks of that trip, of the time in Morocco, when they were cornered by two men – late, both of them stoned, a little lost – and how terrified she'd been. One of the men had pulled a knife, and then – what? Someone had come along, just come along and walked down the street and the guys had disappeared. She remembers the relief, the great shaking relief of it. What if, thinks Ellie suddenly, what if that little stone that her mum had given her *had* brought her protection, had kept her and Rob safe. Whatever, it was still an expression of something, a distilled expression of something, of her mother, of her love, and Ellie had just shoved it away, taken it for granted.

Her mother appears before her mind's view; she is wearing the faded cheesecloth blouse Ellie loves best, those favourite jeans of hers. Ellie turns this picture of her mother round in her head. Thinks of the moment that her mother must have picked those jeans out, trying them on in the shop, looking at herself in the mirror, alone in a changing room with herself. What did her mother think when she looked in the mirror? What did she see? What other lives might she have wanted to lead? Her name, she says her mother's name: "Hilary". She always thought it was a stupid name, when she was at school. She tastes it now, on her tongue, savours the syllables. It's a pretty name, actually; it feels on her tongue like the stone feels on her palm. Sitting there, on the windowsill in the bookshop, Ellie conjures her mother before her and says her name and in saying it she honours it and gives it back to her. Realises this is something she can do. Ellie feels lighter suddenly, but filled with something fizzing and alive and beautiful. Feels as though everyone must be able to see this substance she has inside her, wants people to see it. She looks over at the man at the till, but he is oblivious, engaged in serving one of the women. But she looks, and she sees: *he has it too*. He is filled with the *exact* same thing that Ellie has inside her. The woman, buying her book, she too has the thing inside her! The woman looks up and straight at Ellie. Ellie smiles, and the woman smiles back. In a flash, in a moment, Ellie sees that it will be all right. That the woman is absolutely and utterly all right, that she has all the love she needs and that she knows this, too. Ellie laughs, and it is a bubbling laugh that feels as though it could carry on and on like a stream from the earth at the top of the mountains that just is, and, as though floating, Ellie walks out of the shop and onto the street. It is filled with people, and everyone, *everyone* Ellie sees has the same substance within them, around them, connecting them, looping between them in great bonds of love.

She skirts Trafalgar Square and turns left onto the Strand. There is a clock hanging above one of the buildings. Ellie giggles. It looks funny. What a strange and funny thing it is, slicing the day, serving it up; five forty it says. Five forty. She needs to buy some ink, *yes*, remembers where there is a shop, a computer shop, at the far corner of the Strand and Kingsway, but, glimpsing the river – the *river*! – through a gap in the buildings she walks down to a terrace where she can look out and over towards it. Below her she can see gardens and the road, and then Cleopatra's Needle, all lit and beautiful in the London night, and she remembers sitting there, with Rob, in the summer, sitting between the great arms of the sphinx to the left of the Needle, the pair of them, her holding Rob, she being held by him, sharing a bottle of wine. Ellie blesses herself, that self who was there then and the self that is here now, and blesses Rob, the Rob that was there then and the Rob that is now, wherever he is. He is himself.

Ellie tips her head back. She wants to receive this night and its great dark pulsing, this beauty, this moment; she is nineteen and in London and she has an essay to write and she needs to buy some printer ink, but there is a shop that she knows will be open at the end of the Strand and she will buy her ink and write her essay for the morning. She will write her essay and that will be a good thing. A good thing and the right thing to do.

PADDY AND HENRY
Toby Litt

Paddy was with Henry in the pub.

Henry had just bought a third round. Paddy was on Guinness, because it was Agatha's turn to get up with Max the next morning; Henry was on bitter, London Pride, with a whiskey chaser, Bushmills, because he no longer gave a fuck – or wanted to give the impression he no longer gave a fuck.

"We're getting divorced," he said. "May and I – of course May and I, how stupid! Who else could I say that about? We're getting divorced, and it's my fault. I'm the one, if you're looking for the one. It's because I *want* to. We shouldn't be getting divorced – the kids – we still love each other, as far as that goes. But I'm insisting we get divorced – I'm following through – as a necessity, as a matter of urgency."

Outside, the late August afternoon, Saturday, was beautifully, reliably warm – it had been hot for two weeks, and everyone was acclimatised. The country, particularly the seaside, had done its mood swing: women were sexier; men were stronger; children were more easily entertained. England was semi-Californian, at least in its clammy dreams.

"So you had an affair and May found out?"

"Yes, but that has nothing to do with it." Henry picked up the whiskey and downed the top half.

"Does May think it has nothing to do with it?"

"No," said Henry, blinking. "She would stick with me, despite that. So it *is* irrelevant because it's not the reason I want out. I wanted out a long time before I met Philippa."

"Do we know Philippa?"

"From work. No, you don't. She's not relevant."

"How old is she?"

"What does that matter?" asked Henry, looking at Paddy for the first time since saying the word *divorced.*

"She's not forty, is she?"

"No. Of course not."

"So, she's – what? – twenty-nine?"

"Four. Twenty-four." There was part of a smile.

"That would be why May thinks it's relevant, then."

"Look, I expect you to give me a hard time – don't think I don't."

"This isn't a hard time. What Agatha will give you is a hard time."

"Philippa being young wasn't the reason I had an affair with her."

"But if she hadn't been young you wouldn't have had an affair with her."

Paddy, inevitably, was thinking of his own recent temptation, Kavita – although that wouldn't have been an affair, and he hadn't ever seriously considered a divorce.

"Look, we're getting off the point. I have something very specific to say. Philosophical, almost – not to want to trespass on your territory, being merely an humble journalist." Paddy was bored with dealing with Henry's professional insecurities, and had, a while ago, stopped responding to negative set-ups like this. Henry, who had been expecting the politeness of an interruption, found his rhythm off-put. "What it is is, we've looked up, our generation, up and back, and seen all those divorces among our parents' generation, and we're so determined not to repeat their failures – repeat their crapness – that we're killing ourselves, literally killing ourselves. With suppressed desire, as you ask. Those poor kids, we think – meaning us in the seventies, but also meaning our own kids, in anticipation. So we never grow up. We avoid pursuing our desires. And I can't help but feel this is going to hurt our kids even more. All this coveredness. Because we're going to blame them and secretly hate them, without being able to admit we hate them. It's unnatural to be perfect parents. It's unnatural to *want* to be perfect parents. Our kids will see that, and they'll be traumatized by it."

Paddy took a moment to sip his pint; it was an obvious prop, but it gave him the time he needed – a cigarette would have been better.

"I don't think," he said, "there's any danger of me being perfect."

"And me, too, you mean."

"Were you trying to be perfect?"

"Yes, I think I was. I think I've always tried to be something inhuman, even though I knew it was impossible. I loved robots, when I was growing up. Loved doing robotic dancing. I always wanted to be a robot – even in *Star Wars*."

"R2-D2 or C-3PO?"

"R2-D2, of course. I'm not that much of a freak."

"Of course," said Paddy.

"Kids need to be secure about their mother and their father. They need a good home. But they also need to be able at some point to see round them, see beyond them – see through them, I suppose. Otherwise they're – we're gods they'll never be able to bring down. Not without a catastrophic loss of faith. Is that what you want to set Max up for?"

"Max doesn't believe in God. He told me that the other day – out of nowhere. I didn't bring it up."

"What does he believe in?"

"Firemanland. It's a place. He made it up when he was about three. I think it's a little like heaven but without God – just lots of firemen."

"No fires, then."

"Oh, lots of fires. But they're all put out before anyone gets harmed. Max puts them out. He's the Fire Chief. It says so on his yellow hat. That's important to him."

"Did your parents get divorced?"

Paddy shook his head.

"Didn't think so."

"I wanted them to," said Paddy. "At times, I even prayed for it. All my friends' parents were getting divorced. And my friends got two of everything – two bedrooms, two bikes. They could get more of whatever they wanted. I liked the girlfriends better than the mothers. It seemed ideal."

Paddy wore flip-flops, blue cotton trousers and a white T-shirt. He was aware of his belly, but it wasn't embarrassingly big; his height disguised it. Henry was in blue-and-white deck shoes, khaki shorts and a pink polo shirt, brand new.

"I don't like us, as a generation," said Henry, returning to his theme. "We've got computers – they define us – but we haven't gone far enough with them. They just break down all the time, and we spend all our time dealing with that. We haven't gone far enough with them to be able to reject them, when we need to. We're still madly incorporating them into every aspect of our lives."

"R2-D2 speaking?"

"I don't like digital. All this copying – one-to-one faithful copies, copies the same as the original, but no soul. No soul at all. A digital generation. Compressed. Repressed. Unoriginal. We're not allowing ourselves – we're not letting ourselves live. We need the freedom of moments when we're not in control."

"I'm never in control."

"Aesthetically in control."

"What about raves? All that drug-communal stuff that was meant to last. We got out of it *en masse*."

"Perhaps," said Henry, who was nostalgic for ecstasy, and had dropped it a couple of times with Philippa, who had been losing interest in it. "Did you do all that?"

"No," said Paddy. "Or only once. Somewhere in Oxfordshire. I was too worried about messing up my brain. Agatha was more keen. She loves dancing."

Without announcing it, Henry left for the loos. Paddy drank up then looked around. He felt comfortable in this pub; its demographic was his own. He wasn't a regular, but the bar staff smiled at him whenever he came in. It didn't matter if they recognised him; they recognised and accepted his type. At the stage of life he was at, that seemed to be enough. Henry was demanding more: he was talking as if it still all mattered, and could be altered. Paddy felt disturbed by this. He wondered how much of what Henry was saying he really disagreed with. Little.

Henry returned, with drinks. He had switched to lager, but the chaser remained.

"You can get the next lot," he said. "And the lot after that."

"OK," said Paddy.

"The story of my childhood is the story of a divorce. Not my parents' divorce. That, fortunately – for the most part fortunately – never happened. No, it was the divorce of my best friend's parents. She was a witch, you know. A proper one. Wiccan. I only learnt that recently. White robes at midnight, kind of thing. She was having an affair with my uncle Ian, who was living with us, and that's why my best friend from when I was five moved away, aged fourteen, and I hardly saw him after that. And before that we'd been like that."

Having hit a wall of *that*s, Henry paused to look around him. Paddy decided that a silence was better than a response.

"I never understood that until now," said Henry. "My father mentioned it at Christmas – as if it were something I already knew. He was talking about my best friend's mother, Penny. She still lives in their village. He was saying he wondered how anyone would go for her. I could see exactly. She had that witchy thing. May doesn't have enough of it. I think that's why she bores me. In bed, she bores me. In conversation. I don't like her any more. I blame her for being who she is, which is unfair."

"It is," said Paddy. "You knew who she was when you got married."

"I did. And I haven't found out any more. I think that's it. I expected some revelation – as if wives were made of different stuff than other women."

"They are, I think."

"Really?"

"They're more solid."

"They become more solid, yes – after children."

"No. They have more density. They exist in a more certain way."

"I feel the opposite. May has evaporated. She's gone – all that's left is kids and clothes."

"She works."

"Kids, clothes and bitching about the local education authority. It's not much."

Henry drank for a while, and Paddy watched to see how he was doing it – to see how good at it he was. There was a lot of acting, still. Bravado of consumption. All drunks had that, though. Paddy felt he might need to start being responsible, which would alienate Henry instantly.

"Have you slept with anyone but Agatha?"

"No," said Paddy, immediately.

"Have you wanted to?"

"Yes," said Paddy, as immediately as he could.

"At least you're honest," said Henry, and returned to drinking.

"Don't you want to ask me any more?" Paddy said.

"No," said Henry. "If you'd slept with someone I would. But otherwise it's just more digital repression." He looked at Paddy with a woozy intensity, as if from six inches underwater. "We're a generation that hasn't made any mistakes, and *that's* our mistake."

Paddy nodded, smiled. "I think you might be right."

"Do you think I'm fucking right or not?"

"It's a good working hypothesis."

"Is it true?"

"We're careful for a reason. We're trying not to hurt things."

"If you don't hurt things, you don't respect them – because you don't really acknowledge their existence."

"And that's why you want to hurt May, to acknowledge her existence?"

"No – to make her exist. To make her sweaty and alive – force her back into analogue and the seventies. It can always be the seventies. We can reinvent it."

"That doesn't really make any sense."

"Fleetwood Mac, *Rumours*. You know exactly what I mean. Cocaine. California. Misery. Sunshine. Misery in the sunshine. Great tunes. Sweat. Divorce. Real women with real armpits." Henry lifted his glass and, for a moment, Paddy thought he was about to propose a toast, loudly. There were quite a few other people around.

"Is Philippa real?" Paddy asked.

"Of course not. She never existed."

"You mean you made her up?"

"I might as well have. It didn't matter that it was Philippa rather than Rachel or Natascha or God help me Belinda. She had no real existence. She was too young."

"Did you hurt her?"

"I tried to. She wouldn't let me. That generation are very tough. They don't allow it. They just tell you to fuck off, and they mean it. She wrote a blog about me, which caused a whole lot of trouble before my boss persuaded her to take it down. Everyone had read it by then. Everyone had read it within the afternoon. That's how May found out."

"Did she read it?"

"A fucking blog."

"Did she?"

"No. She confronted me with her knowledge of the fact of its existence."

"So, you didn't tell her any of this until you were forced to."

"I wanted to get caught. Can't you see? I chose Philippa because she's the world's least discreet woman. She's all celebrity culture. Nothing but. If it isn't public, it doesn't exist."

"When did this happen?"

"A month ago."

"Before or after you came round for dinner?"

"Day before. We were barely speaking, otherwise."

"You put on a good act."

"Oh, we're very good. The best."

"I don't think Agatha noticed anything. She didn't say she did."

"I like Agatha. Agatha exists."

"She does."

Henry finished both drinks, working up to: "I wish I were married to Agatha, not May."

"No, you don't."

"Maybe not. May is better, now she's miserable. I can feel things happening inside her, developments – it's exciting. A bit like when she was pregnant, the first time."

Paddy was sure he didn't want to know this. He would have to decide how much to tell Agatha. It would be a relief if Henry asked him not to say anything. There was no sign of that; the opposite.

Outside, it was still light and still warm.

"Are you seeking my approval?" asked Paddy. "I think that kind of cruelty is disgusting and immature."

"Don't go all formal on me."

"It's not original. You're not innovating. The same argument could be made for wife-beating."

"I've thought about it."

"What have you thought?"

"I think it might help, with communication."

"Henry, you're not that stupid."

"I am."

Paddy knew he had to be responsible.

"Let's go home."

"You owe me two drinks – four drinks."

"Another time."

"Excuse me," said a young woman who'd been sitting with another young woman at the next table. "Is that all you're going to say?"

Paddy realised after a moment that she was talking to him and not Henry.

"You're not just going to leave it at that, after he said what he fucking said?"

"Which part?" asked Paddy, who wasn't sure when they'd started listening.

"The part," said the other young woman, "about wanting to hit his wife."

"What a wanker," said the first woman.

Paddy knew this meant him.

"Why are you attacking me?" he asked.

"Look, this one's just a cunt, but you're a fucking wanker. Why are you still even friends with him?"

Both the young women had long straight hair, patterned tops, short skirts, bare brown legs. Paddy was finding it hard to tell them apart. They were in their mid-twenties.

"Let's go," he said to Henry.

"No," Henry replied. "I'm staying."

Paddy was aware that many people in the pub were listening. He'd stood up, at some point, and his height had drawn further attention.

"OK," he said. "I'll see you later."

"See you, mate," said Henry, and held out his hand. "Thanks for listening."

Paddy shook hands.

"I can't believe that," said one of the young women. "I can't believe he's just leaving."

"I'm just leaving," said Paddy. "Goodbye."

Walking home, he decided not to mention the divorce to Agatha – not until he'd had another chance to talk to Henry. On the phone, preferably.

"How was he?" Agatha asked, in the kitchen.

"Fine," said Paddy. "Work's a bit manic, you know."

"How's May?"

"She's fine."

"What did you talk about?"

"His job. Politics. My work."

Agatha seemed satisfied.

"How was Max, going to bed?" asked Paddy.

At ten o'clock, Paddy received a text from Henry: "I went to her place and fucked her. The fit one. Amazing fuck. Don't tell Agatha."

Paddy had *Rumours* on vinyl. He eased it out of his alphabetized record collection, put it on.

"Why are you playing that?" asked Agatha, coming into the living room.

"Henry mentioned it. I wanted to hear it again."

Agatha smiled and said, "I love this album."

A HOME FOR BOBBY MACINTOSH

Anupama Kumari Gohel

The distance from Jaipur to New Delhi is 270 kilometres. I know because when I was married, Arjun and I used to drive from our isolated farmhouse in Jaipur to the capital once in a while. Actually, it was more like once every four months. But because the journeys were so rare they were inestimably valued from my perspective. I savoured the transformation in scenery along the side of the highway from the camel carts and mustard fields to the noisy juggernauts, the factories and lit-up motels.

The journey I'm making now, from Delhi to Jaipur, is not one I relish at all. It has been two years since I left India. But, having received my decree absolute, I thought it was the right time to return for my things, before Arjun's mother decides to throw them out.

I don't need the driver from the car-hire company to tell me that we have almost reached the winding pebbly track that leads from the highway to the farmhouse. Through the window I see the huge bottle-green board on the side of the road that says "Welcome to Jaipur", first in English and then underneath in Hindi. A familiar but disconcerting unease begins to gnaw at me. The driver changes gear as we climb the stretch of dust and stone that is more suitable for wild buffaloes or the wheels of a jeep.

I run a brush through my hair. My faded denims and blue shirt are heavily creased from the four-hour drive, and I struggle in vain to tidy myself up. Should I meet Arjun's mother or sister-in-law, I don't want to look a dishevelled mess. His immaculately dressed mother, with her Jackie Onassis sunglasses and French-chiffon saris, has never seen me in jeans before. And although it shouldn't matter any more, I can picture her eyes narrowing in disapproval.

I spoke to Arjun a week ago when I bought my airline ticket. I just wanted a few personal items from the cottage – clothes, photographs, the jewellery my family gave me when we got married. And also, of course, Bobby.

"Take whatever you want," he said. "I'll make sure I'm not there. And I'll let one of the servants know to expect you."

When I left Jaipur, I had intended to go away for only two weeks, to attend my brother's graduation ceremony in London, and then fly back to India in time for Christmas. I didn't cancel the Hindi class I had with my tutor straight after the New Year. I left a pile of saris on the chair in our bedroom, ready to send to the dry-cleaner's when I came back. I told the carpenter to complete the wooden cabinet to house our music system.

In London, after the graduation, I changed my departure date twice. Whenever I came away from India I was filled with anxiety about returning. On that occasion the unsettling feeling consuming me was stronger than it had ever been, and I was unable to nudge it aside as in the past. I hoped Arjun would reach out to me in an attempt to rescue our marriage. The months passed. He did not come. My parents sensed my unhappiness. "You don't have to go back," my father said. "This marriage has been a mistake."

I knew he was right. The wide-eyed girl with chubby cheeks had disappeared. A woman with sharp contours to her features and white strands intertwined with her black hair stood in her place.

It was then I cancelled my ticket altogether. I would not be going back.

More than simply to carry away my personal possessions, the most important reason for returning is to take Bobby MacIntosh back with me. I got him on a visit to my family in London during the second year of my marriage, and brought him to India as a five-month-old puppy. I had been concerned over how a West Highland White Terrier would adjust to a hot humid country. However, within weeks he was lapping up chappatis with milk, chasing peacocks, and barking at monkeys that sat in the trees raining berries down on his head. When the sun shone too brightly he swam in the pond with the lily pads and fish, and rolled around joyfully on the emerald-green grass. He squared up to poisonous monitor lizards, was fiercely protective when strangers approached me, and replaced my loneliness with affection and companionship.

In my world, where I was dependent on my in-laws and my husband for everything, Bobby was the only one who was dependent on me. Together, we were strangers in that place. But, whereas the farm seemed to become home to Bobby, for me it never became more than solitary confinement in a gilded cage.

A few weeks before my wedding, my parents had phoned Arjun's mother in India. "We have been growing concerned about her going so far away," they said.

"Anjali will become our daughter. You need not worry about a thing," my then future mother-in-law had said. "She will be free to live her life in Jaipur in the same way that she has done in London."

Arjun had been in touch with me throughout the engagement. He called to enthuse about a bathroom extension to his bedroom, and said he wished I had been there to choose the tiles. He told me that he had shown my photograph to his friends, and that he was counting down the days to the wedding.

I looked forward to being married. I practised what would be my new signature, and on a trip to Oxford Street, nagged my mother to buy me evening bags and make-up – items I thought necessary to being a married woman. I daydreamed about having children, chose their names, imagined taking them to school.

On our wedding night, in the honeymoon suite of the hotel where the ceremony took place, Arjun and I sat side by side on a burgundy-coloured sofa. I felt nervous. Not the confident poised woman I thought I would magically transform into the instant I became a wife. To my surprise a group of Arjun's friends appeared at the door. Soon the men lay sprawled on the sofas, their feet up on the coffee tables. Empty beer bottles and discarded peanut shells littered the carpet. Their wives in sequinned saris stood in a huddle, gawking at me. I made out the face of my sister-in-law whom I had met once before. I sought her eyes, hoping she would come and put her arms around me, welcome me to the family. She remained where she was. A plump woman beside her muttered, "Why so long removing her veil? Perhaps Arjun has got himself an ugly duckling." A smirk crossed my sister-in-law's face. I slumped into my seat, tired.

The surface is smoother as we approach the farm and the driver speeds up. Outside the large black gate he sounds the horn. The watchman appears, running out from his small shack with a steel ladle that is dripping liquid. He must have been in the middle of cooking his lunch. He peers through the bars at the car and the driver. Then the rattling wrought-iron gate swings and clangs back loudly on its hinges. I don't recognise him. He glances curiously at me. I pray silently that he will not ask who I am. To my relief, he steps aside and lets the car pass.

Both sides of the track are crammed with *shishum* and *khejri* trees, whose thick branches reach upwards and sideways in shades of green. I am reminded of the sunny morning I was brought here after my wedding night. I had sat in the back of the car with Arjun. His two laughing cousins were in the front, the ends of their rainbow-coloured turbans trailing across the backs of their seats. Supertramp played loudly in the cassette player. With my henna-painted hand I moved aside the magenta *odhna* covering my face to gaze in bewilderment at the big house where I was to live.

The music was soon drowned out by the trumpets and drums of a brass band. Five hundred guests waited to lift my veil, and press red envelopes filled with a token amount of money into my hand. As a mark of respect I had to bend down and touch the feet of each family member. I'd felt a sense of panic wondering how I would distinguish between family and friends. It was like my first day at school: dressed up in my smart uniform and straw boater with a wide green ribbon, my heart had thumped against my chest. About to enter a whole new world, all I wanted was the comforting presence of my mother, but Arjun had pointed out that according to tradition the bride's relatives do not accompany her to the marital home.

I ask the driver to pass the pink sandstone mansion with its marble porch and fancy white pillars. There are two cars parked in the driveway. I sit up stiffly, holding my breath until the house is behind us. But nobody pokes their head out of the front door.

When we reach the lawn leading to Arjun's cottage I ask the driver to stop. I hear Bobby barking as I get out of the car. There hasn't been a single day in the last two years when I haven't thought about him. First Zorro, the yellow Lab Arjun told me he bought a year ago, launches himself at me. Following a few steps behind is my Bobby, who catches my scent and begins yelping, and tries desperately to reach me, but Zorro pushes him back with repeated shoves from his well-padded bottom. I bend down, sitting on my heels to cuddle them both, reaching for Bobby as he struggles. Rather than weeping for having missed him, I can't help but laugh at his antics. I give him a big hug, feeling the velvety softness of his ears against my cheek, breathing in his doggy smell. "I missed you," I whisper into his neck.

Mohan, the devoted retainer of two generations, approaches as I give the dogs treats from my bag. He folds his hands in greeting, and I mirror the gesture. He looks embarrassed. Divorce is not something he understands.

I ask him in Rajasthani how he is – first forming the words in English in my head and then translating and speaking them in the local dialect. I enquire about his wife, Radha. He tells me she is fine. That is his standard response. When she stepped barefoot on a scorpion and it stung her, she was fine. When she miscarried after four months she was fine then too. In his world women do not question unhappiness.

"I like your shirt," I say.

He blushes. "You only gifted it to me. You don't remember? Before you went back to your village."

I smile. "Yes, I remember," I say, touched by Mohan's gesture of wearing his best "going-into-town" shirt for me.

There is an awkward pause between us. He's waiting for me to speak.

"I think I'll go up to the cottage now." My statement sounds like a question.

I navigate the rotating water sprinklers in the middle of the lawn, and slowly climb the steps that I've raced up with Bobby in the past. Small nervous flutters invade the pit of my stomach, as my shoes clap noisily – inappropriately loudly – against the sandstone. Flame of the forest trees, with their crooked trunks and rough grey bark, form a cascade of orange and vermilion flowers over my head. In my dreams I have pictured myself returning to the cottage, hesitating outside with my hand resting on the brass door handle. But the door is already wide open. The wafting fragrance of cinnamon and spicy kidney beans cooking on the stove greets me, and I step inside.

Arjun and I moved into the cottage four years into our marriage. I had grown weary of living with his parents and brother and sister-in-law in the big house. The food I cooked was too hot, too salty, too bland. The flowers I arranged in the silver vase in the lobby were not cut to the correct length. How dare I refer to my husband by his name? Why didn't I pray every day? Was I remembering to sleep on the right-hand side of the bed every night? His mother's encroachment into my bedroom, to organise my books in alphabetical order, was more than I could endure.

"Next she'll be rifling through my underwear and colour co-ordinating everything," I complained to Arjun. "I feel suffocated."

"I'll ask them if we can move into the guest cottage," he said, growing tired of our nightly arguments. "It's small, though. Tiny compared to this house."

"It doesn't matter," I said. "At least it will be ours."

Still it was a year before his family begrudgingly agreed to us moving out. Our marriage was not two people but twenty.

The cottage lacked the Baccarat crystal, Lladró figurines and cut-glass chandeliers of the big house. We did not have a grand dining room, priceless miniature paintings and expensive Persian carpets. Instead we had block-printed floor cushions and paintings of village scenes by local Jaipuri artists hung upon lemon-yellow walls. Arjun's family continued to impose their demands on a daily basis, but at least we didn't have to lock our bedroom door any more.

I stand at the threshold. The rustic furniture and bright hand-woven *dhurries* remain the same, but the coffee table with books on textiles and Indian palaces is now littered with Formula One magazines. A lotus-shaped marble bowl that once held water and floating candles now cradles grimy golf balls.

I stroll through the rooms, touching the backs of chairs, running my fingers across the television set my grandparents gave us when we moved out of the big house. The remote control, bandaged with Sellotape, sits by its side. I smile wryly remembering how I had hurled it at Arjun during an argument. Bobby took my side, nipping at Arjun's ankles before urinating on his trousers.

In the bedroom, I open the cabinet that holds my bangles. There are bright ones with coloured stones for weddings, red and white ones for the festival of Holi, blue for Diwali. There are plain ones for everyday wear, and a stack of hand-painted ones in varying sizes, with gold running through them, which I wore as a bride.

When I came to Arjun's family's house, I was told that a married woman could never be seen without bangles adorning her wrists. It would be inauspicious for my husband, the old women whispered with pursed lips and shaking heads. Arjun's grandmother said that the wedding *kadas* – twenty on each arm, graduated in size from wrist to shoulder – had to be worn for a full month after the wedding, even while bathing and sleeping. They were cumbersome and heavy, and it was impossible to rest in any position other than lying stiffly on my back. Furtively I began to remove them at night. Then early the next morning before anyone saw me, I would spend twenty minutes stacking them in the correct order back onto my arms again.

I open the wardrobes where my saris hang. The shelves are scattered with *neem* leaves and black pepper kernels to keep away moths and silverfish. My fingertips brush the crêpes, georgettes, cottons, silks, chiffons. "Bright colours for the first year," my mother-in-law had said. "It's auspicious for the marriage." For eight months I tried my best to do the right thing. Day after day I draped myself in the watermelon pinks, the sunset oranges, the sherbet yellows. Then one day I woke up feeling queasy looking at those bright colours. I went to a local textiles exhibition and picked up an indigo-blue *salwaar kameez.* At home I admired my simple baggy trousers and long fitted *kurta* in the mirror. For the first time in months I felt like the twenty-year-old girl I was. Arjun's mother told me that people would criticise her for being a bad mother-in-law. I softly suggested she simply say she had a bad daughter-in-law.

"Your sister-in-law was right about you. You're a foreigner with no values," had been her acidic response.

Finally, I turn to face the bed. The floral duvet cover has been replaced with a blue hand-woven quilt. I touch the corner lightly. Soon after our marriage Arjun's family began to whisper that I couldn't conceive. Eventually the doctors discovered that it was Arjun who was infertile. In this place where nothing was mine, where nothing responded to my attempts to love, children had been my last hope. Devastated that I would never know life growing inside me I withdrew further into myself. For a while after we'd received the diagnosis, Arjun came home earlier after his nightly drinking session with friends, sometimes with a DVD for us to watch. I tried to find comfort in his presence but invariably, thirty minutes into the film, the story was punctuated by his snoring. I wanted to grab one of the pillows and thump him, but instead I began using it to divide the space between us at night.

I wonder where Bobby is, listen for the sounds of his paws on the porch, but there is only a distant yip as he tumbles with Zorro or chases after a peacock.

Once, Arjun and I went into town for dinner. We talked about his day for a few minutes, and then gradually fell silent. I looked around at the people sitting on adjacent tables, laughing and sharing stories. I wondered if it would not have been a better idea to have the food packed, and eat at home. I turned to him in the car on our way back to the farm. "Why did you marry me?" I asked.

He shrugged. "Because that's what people do."

Biting my bottom lip, I looked at my lap and fiddled with my wedding ring. "Before our marriage you showed interest in me and our future."

"Romantic hazes don't last for ever."

"But our romantic haze never even began."

He took his eyes off the road to glance at me. "What is it that you want, Anjali?"

For you to love me, I thought. Instead I said, "Your time. Some affection." I placed my hand on his shoulder.

Arjun sighed. "Why can't you be like the other wives, and do your own thing? Go out with them for coffee or to see a movie."

I took my hand away. "You know they ignore me, and gossip viciously. When I attended my grandfather's cremation in London last year, they said I had gone because I was having an affair. They have sawdust for brains."

"What about my sister-in-law?"

"She snubs me, and has told all the others that I think I am too good for them, that I am a snob and will only talk to people who have lived in London. I would rather spend time with Bobby."

We had reached the farm. Arjun stopped the car.

"Then sit here and talk to your dog. You married into my family. It is for you to adjust."

I got out, closing the door, expecting Arjun to turn off the ignition. Instead, he pulled away, and sped back out of the gate.

Occasionally Arjun would take me to a dinner party in Delhi. "Please meet my wife, Anjali," he would say. "She has lived her whole life in London. She used to horse-ride there in the park. She speaks French and Spanish and can play the piano. Anjali flew her dog here all the way from England." His tone was not one of loving pride. It sounded like boasting. I was an object on parade.

I began to spend my days mulling over a painful question. Is this as good as it will ever get, waking up every morning with the long day stretching endlessly ahead? I bathed Bobby, pulling out ticks, combing through his matted hair. I scattered maize kernels on the lawns for pigeons and doves. I took my Walkman outside, and aimlessly circled the pond listening to love songs. Sometimes, when the servants disappeared to their shacks, and the farmhands were far away, I felt like the only person alive. Was there a world that existed beyond these surrounding hills and wide open fields? Turning on the television to the news channel, or hearing the faint blaring of a lone truck a kilometre away, reminded me life was going on, but I was not part of it.

I hear Bobby's paws on the marble as he enters the bedroom. He pads over to me, his rear end wiggling. After receiving a cuddle and licking my toes through my sandals, he sniffs at the items I've pulled out and left on the floor. I know what he will do next, and I watch him as he plods over to a floor cushion and flops down flat on his stomach.

Bobby always had an uncanny instinct for knowing when I was feeling low. Whether I was missing my family in London, or spending another evening eating dinner on my own waiting for Arjun to return from his club, Bobby would lift his paws onto my knee and place his head on them, offering comfort. When my sister-in-law took her children into town I took Bobby. He sat on my lap with his head sticking out of the window, and barked at every camel, cow, donkey and elephant that we passed. Passers-by, more used to the mangy mongrels on the roadside, would point and stare in fascination at his little face, with the snowy-white hair billowing wildly about his head. I used to think all he needed was a pair of aviator sunglasses to complete the look.

The day before I left India I phoned my sister-in-law in the big house. I have frequently wondered why I chose that particular day to confront her, but I think I already knew I would not be returning.

I had subscribed to a couple of UK magazines, which I eagerly awaited each month. They were a reminder of home, and my once carefree life. I would leaf through them until they were worn out and still not throw them away. For some time they hadn't arrived, and I assumed they had been lost in the post. One morning a servant arrived at the cottage carrying a stack of them. From my sister-in-law, he'd said. The magazines were badly creased, the corners were dog-eared and several pages had been ripped out.

When she answered the telephone, I took a deep breath and let out the feelings I had been holding back for years. I told her she was "a selfish, conniving, gossiping witch – or perhaps bitch." My head was dizzy and my limbs tingled with the thrill of escaped rage.

There were a few seconds of stunned silence. I could picture her with her mouth agape, her manicured fingernails holding the cordless phone. And those eyes of hers that could never make or maintain contact with anyone, darting around like little fish inside her head.

"You're unhinged. You've gone mad," she finally spat.

"Maybe," I replied, feeling my breathing grow shallow. "All these years I've kept quiet and shown you respect, when what I should have given you was a smart slap across that vain little face of yours."

I put down the receiver. My cheeks were on fire. For the first time, I felt in control.

I take a bunch of jangling keys from my handbag to unlock a heavy steel cupboard. For a moment I stare at possessions I forgot I owned. Purple notepads filled with my shaky Hindi writing, stained folded-up table mats, broken soap dishes, candles for power cuts, and tins of out-of-date SMA milk powder couriered to me by my father when he discovered my dislike of farm milk. Underneath, I see a roll of black silk that was meant to be given to the tailor to stitch into a Nehru jacket for Arjun. On the bottom shelf are my books, bought in London due to the lack of variety available here. Now they will make the long journey back home again with me. I pull out scallop-edged photographs of my grandparents as shy newly-weds, and ones of Bobby, spread-eagled on an air conditioner in the middle of summer trying to cool his stomach.

I open the locker fixed to the back wall of the cupboard. My eyes moisten as I gaze at the small red boxes and velvet pouches. My grandparents were not well off like other members of my family. For years my grandmother had done without new shoes, a kettle, a winter coat, in order to put away a tiny amount of the housekeeping money every month. On a rare trip out to India, instead of visiting her five sisters scattered about the country, she spent her days with goldsmiths discussing designs and stone settings in painstaking detail. While all the jewellery from my family is of emotional value, the gold anklets, the toe rings, and the dangling earrings given by my grandparents hold the greatest sentiment.

I pull an empty leather holdall from one of the shelves and begin to pack. I will have no need for the saris and bangles in London, nor for the paintings, the brass candlesticks, or the colourful glass vases that Arjun now uses to hold paper clips. These things have a place here. They will not fit in my small flat back home.

Outside, the sun has gone in and it's getting chilly. I walk to the back of the cottage, to the small terrace. The water sprinklers have been turned off, and a rusty lawnmower lies abandoned by a bougainvillea tree. Mohan approaches me holding a plate piled with food. I thank him, realising how hungry I am. I ask him if he could put my packed bag into the boot of the waiting car.

Looking out over the garden I watch Bobby and Zorro while I eat. They dig up Arjun's mother's precious lawn with scrabbling paws, burying their faces deep into the earth. After several minutes, they lift their heads back out and sneeze, their muzzles caked with thick brown mud.

I think of the white igloo bed and the food bowl I have already bought for Bobby in London. It occurs to me that after his six-month quarantine at Heathrow, Bobby will wait in the dark until I come home from work, much as I used to wait for Arjun. It will be no easy task to get him accustomed to a collar and leash. He will be lonely without Zorro. This farm, kilometres away from civilisation, where one aches to hear the sound of voices, where there are power cuts every day, and where one has to plan a day in advance to make a trip into town, is the only life Bobby has known. This is his home. A realisation creeps up on me softly but, just like when I was a child and my tiny fingers would get caught inside a drawer, the pain only arrives seconds later. All at once it is as if there is a clamp on my heart, squeezing and tightening.

I don't know how long I've been sitting here but it is almost dark. My tears have dried in streaks down my face. I feel something brush against my legs. It is Bobby. I bend down and stroke his silky head, looking into those dark eyes, so intelligent and intuitive. I scoop him up into my arms, while he shifts around making tiny grunting sounds to show he's not entirely comfortable. Hugging him to me, I know with gut-wrenching certainty that I cannot take him away from here. And as I place him back down, I am forced to finally admit to myself that he has aged in the two years I have been away. He has put on weight, his black nose has changed colour. The brightness in his eyes has dimmed.

I push his fringe back from his face. "You and Zorro remind me of Tom and Jerry. And you would hate me for taking you away from him and the farm, wouldn't you, Bobby?" I ask, trying to keep my voice steady. The mention of his partner in crime instantly has his body tense and his ears pricked. Zorro barks in the distance, and off Bobby races.

I go back into the cottage. In the bedroom I take out a stick of sunblock that was tucked between some beige cotton hats. I look around for somewhere to sit down. But there is only the bed. I perch gingerly on its edge. Then taking out a notepad and pen from my bag, I think carefully before writing:

> Dear Arjun,
> Thank you for giving me time here today. I've taken a few items that were mine. You can do whatever you like with the things I'm leaving behind. I'm not taking Bobby. He'll be happier here. And I know you will take good care of him. I'm leaving the sunblock. Please, please make sure you apply it to the insides of his ears once it starts getting hot.
> Love,
> Anjali

I cringe that I've written "love". But then I tell myself it doesn't matter. It's just a word. For a split second I picture a girl circling the marriage fire seven times, her hand bound with her husband's in saffron-coloured cloth. The image fades. The flicker of hope was extinguished long ago. I mainly feel numb towards Arjun now. Some sadness but, surprisingly, no anger.

I walk out of the cottage, closing the front door behind me. There is a smattering of stars in the evening sky. Peacocks that were earlier pecking for insects in the grass take off like huge winged beasts into the trees for the night. Bells from the family temple begin to ring, their tinkling sound breaking the still air. In a moment the priest will arrive, lines of marigold orange painted on his forehead and incense sticks burning from his hand. He will place one in the grass by the big house and the other by the cottage. Bobby will probably sniff and scent mark around the farm, barking in response to a howling jackal somewhere in the distance. In years past he would have come and scratched at the door, trying to get my attention. But now I think he will stay out with Zorro until Arjun returns home.

I crane my neck looking for Bobby, but I cannot see or hear him. Part of me wants to reach the waiting car as soon as possible, and the other part wants to slow my footsteps down. I hear a rustling sound and swing around. "Bobby?" But it is not him, only the wind rustling the leaves on the *rohira* bushes. Perhaps it is better I do not see him.

From inside the car I hear crickets hum and catch the faint fragrance of sandalwood in the breeze. As I turn around, I can just make out the shadowy figure of the priest in his distinctive white clothing walking up the steps to the cottage.

The driver starts the engine and we slowly drive back past the big house. The porch lights have been turned on, and moon moths mesmerised by the glow flutter in clusters by the windows.

The short distance to the gate seems endless. I feel a lump in my throat as Bobby runs after the car. Zorro chases for a while and then comes to a standstill staring after him.

The driver asks if I want to get out. I tell him no, just keep going.

At the same time my hand reaches for the door handle as I see Bobby panting, straining to keep up. I open my mouth to tell the driver to stop but the words don't come out.

My eyes follow Bobby and then flick towards the gate, which has already been opened for the departing car. When I brought him here as a puppy I spent weeks trying to train him to stay within the confines of the property. Now the car passes through the gate. I've shifted my position in the seat to see what he does. The dirt on the broken track is disturbed by the car's wheels and floats upwards, hovering like a cloud. The driver accelerates, and as the dust settles back down I can see Bobby has stayed within the compound. There is uncertainty on his face as he sniffs at the air and his ears move backwards. I force my gaze away, and turn around to face the road ahead.

POTASSIUM MAN
Sarah Salway

Thomas likes to get to the swimming pool at least five minutes before the children's session ends. He's not sure why he needs to see how they get more hectic as the time closes in, splash more, shout more, as if there's a whole lot of playing left inside. Perhaps it's the way they have to let it out otherwise something terrible might happen that interests him so much.

Today he watches a small thin boy carefully swim to the side long before the final bell is rung. He notices how this boy goes straight to a towel that is neatly hung up, not strewn around on the ground like the others, and how he doesn't splash in the shower or turn the water cold to make friends scream. You might not even notice the boy is there unless you find something about him strangely familiar, as Thomas does. Of course, Thomas thinks, this is the terrible thing that might happen. They are all terrified of disappearing into the nothingness of this boy.

Thomas eases himself into the pool. He likes to feel that some of the children's boisterousness is left behind in the water. Sometimes he even, so secretly he barely admits it to himself, opens his mouth to swallow great gulps of it. Then he'll kick out his legs, splashing, although he knows this will upset the other swimmer coming up behind him, the one he sees most days because she shares the same strict routine as him, and who he hears counting after each length – one, two, three. She'll get out after thirty, he knows, doing neither one length too little or too many. The truth is he likes to splash her. What he'd really like to do is to go underwater and suddenly appear behind her, beside her, surprise her, do something – anything – so unexpected that he makes her scream. But he doesn't, and even his occasional splashes seem too much.

He lets his mouth fall open as if by accident to swallow some water now. And that's when he sees it. A flash of orange, and then another. He blinks behind his goggles and when he opens his eyes the water is blue again.

When he opened the classroom door that time twenty years ago, he was supposed to be coming to his science teacher's rescue. He'd heard Mr Jones shouting from down the corridor, and thought that maybe the teacher – like Thomas – was being bullied and that Thomas could be the rescuer. The person he prayed every night to have for himself.

Now he sees a golden flash again, and this time his jaw really does drop. He takes in so much water that he thinks he might have to go to the side for stability.

Mr Jones had looked up when Thomas came in the classroom but not with gratitude. Instead, it was as if Thomas was someone to be wary of. The other boys didn't notice him; they were too busy crowding round, watching the pool of water in the bowl on the desk, the nugget of potassium the teacher held in his hand.

Thomas treads water. He isn't dreaming. There are four, no, five goldfish swimming round. The woman swimmer crashes into him, but as Thomas points speechlessly at the goldfish, she starts to laugh.

Thomas had wanted to shout at the teacher to stop, to point out how dangerous it was, that there was bound to be an explosion, but if the other boys watched the teacher's hands, Mr Jones had stared at

Thomas. "You're not one of us," he seemed to be saying as the potassium slowly dropped from his fingers and down into the water. "You never will be. But now at least I will."

Thomas is terrified. What if, by accident, he'd swallowed one of the fish when he was drinking the pool water? Immediately, he feels his stomach cramp, as the woman laughs harder and harder, clapping her hands now. The movement of her fingers echoes the flapping inside his stomach.

As the chemical hit the bowl of water, there was a bang louder than he had ever heard before. The whole classroom erupted, and, through the smoke, it was hard to tell whether the screams were from pleasure or pain.

The woman grabs his arm. It's difficult not to notice how naked she is next to him, only their swimming costumes hiding their bodies. They are in a goldfish bowl. He wants to call the teenage lifeguard for help but the boy is on the other side of the pool, texting on his mobile phone.

"They won't survive," Thomas says. "Not in this chlorine."

"But they're alive now," she replies. "And look how beautiful they are."

The teacher's face had been pink and excited when it finally emerged from the cloud that surrounded him. Even with the lines of ash on his face, he looked reborn.

"You're a legend, sir," shouted one of the boys. Others pretended to genuflect to the teacher, who was not looking in Thomas's direction any more. It was as if Thomas no longer existed.

As Mr Jones raised his arms up, god-like, Thomas shut the door. He ran down the corridor heading straight for the headmaster's study.

Thomas looks at the water. It must have been the children. This was why they were splashing particularly hard here, to hide the fish.

Just then a flash of gold darts by him. He puts a hand out to catch it but feels it brush against his skin as it passes. It is less a caress than a burn.

"You shouldn't have told anyone," one of the boys said in the aftermath. When the repercussions of what they were all calling The Potassium Incident were still sending ripples throughout the school.

Thomas didn't say anything.

He carried on not saying anything for the rest of his schooldays. The teacher left soon after, but his myth grew. Whenever classes got static, the boys would call out for something to happen. "Mr Jones set the classroom on fire," they would say, and Thomas would try hard not to catch the eye of whatever teacher they were taunting. They didn't want him to be on their side any more than he wanted them on his.

Instead he played safe, and learned how to keep quiet. He withdrew into the shadows, waiting for that moment his mother kept promising would come. When he could leave them all behind and step into his own spotlight.

He was still waiting.

The woman is pointing out more and more fish, here, there, oh and over there. There can only be ten but to Thomas it feels as if the pool has become a boiling cauldron. As if the fish are multiplying by the second. He puts his hands on his stomach because the ones he might have swallowed are thrashing inside him now, thrashing both inside and out. He is under attack.

He sees his towel hung up on the side. He wants to get out. To get dry and leave before anything happens. To remain alive. Invisible, disappeared, but alive.

At a dinner party, years after he left school, the conversation turned to childish misdemeanours.

"I bet you were a good boy," the woman Thomas brought with him had said. She laughed, and he suddenly noticed that her teeth were too big. It was as if they didn't fit her mouth. He knew then he wouldn't have sex with her ever again.

So, with nothing to lose, he told the story of the science teacher's experiment. This time he forced himself not to leave the classroom, and, as he watched the faces round the table turn to him, lit up by the candles, he got a glimpse of what Mr Jones must have felt. Perhaps it was this that made Thomas take over the story with a confidence he still finds unsettling.

"Mr Jones handed the chunk of potassium to me," he said. "I deliberated only a second before I let it drop into the water."

"But didn't you all know how dangerous it was?" a fellow guest asked.

Thomas smiled. "Of course," he said. "That was the whole point."

"My reckless hero," said the woman he brought with him, and as she winked at him, her top lip covered her teeth and he thought, well, OK, maybe just once more.

"We should report this to someone," Thomas tells the woman. Part of him wants to hand the tale-telling over. He still feels the silence of those school years somewhere deep inside his body, perhaps in the place where the fish are burrowing now. It worries him that he can't remember making a decision in the classroom about what to do; it wasn't just a case of being reckless or of being safe.

"Why?" she asks.

Can it be that simple? None of the other swimmers seems to have noticed the fish, although Thomas sees they all have their mouths firmly and sensibly shut tight.

Over the years, he forgot the teacher and became the sole protagonist of The Potassium Incident. Friends he'd made through his work as a lighting designer called for the story more than he admitted he liked. Potassium Man, they called him. What he enjoyed most about telling it now was how he remembered precisely how the sparks flew up when the chemical hit the water, the acrid smell of smoke and the way the noise was so loud it seemed to run through his veins. He was right in the middle of the explosion, so close to the fire, so amazed by its power and its beauty that he didn't even hear the door shut as an invisible boy ran for help.

"Why?"

When he looks back at the woman, he sees her staring at him and her face seems so alive that he knows this is it. The moment he can choose whether to leave the room, or to stay and experience what might happen. He's surprised he isn't more nervous. He remembers how the science teacher's hands shook. They'd even fluttered slightly as the chemical had dropped from his fingers. He'd still done it though and Thomas sees now it must have been worth it. What had really happened wasn't something that could be enjoyed secondhand.

He takes the woman's hand, forgets for one moment that they barely know each other.

"Let's chase the fish," he says, and he takes the kick of her legs as a yes.

They set off – Thomas keeping his mouth shut, he's not completely stupid – and head straight into the middle of the goldfish storm. Despite the stares from the other swimmers, both of them splash wildly as they go, whooping with joy. It is as if they want to let out all the playing that's been stuck inside them. As if, in that moment, they are living. They have become everything that could ever happen.

THE CONFIDENCE TRICK
Melissa de Villiers

Charnay woke with a start, and with the uneasy feeling that some greyish, hooded creature had just brushed past her. The plane was warm, and many of her fellow passengers were still asleep. But the man in the window seat was snoring loudly, a thick, rasping sound that soared upwards, then fell away in a hiss like a tiny balloon. Through her irritation, she made a note of the noise. It reminded her of somebody. Could she remember everyone she'd ever slept with, just by the way they'd snored? Like an audio ID parade? She could try to list them that way, in her head. It might calm her down till they got to Jo'burg.

"Michelle, Michelle, *'skuustog.*" Her neighbour on the aisle side – Pieter? – was touching her shoulder. "Excuse me, sorry about this, hey."

She'd lied to him that she was Michelle, an exchange student coming home from six months at a São Paulo language school.

She slid a hand under the aircraft blanket onto the hard globe of her stomach and left it there. Don't use the toilet. And stay cool.

Pieter was speaking again.

"You talk in your sleep, Michelle, did you know that?"

Middle-aged, with brandy on his breath. He'd said he was a doctor, but he didn't look the type. He looked like a good old *boykie*, the pick-up-truck-driving, Klippies-and-Coke-drinking sort who hung around the bars of Vanderbijlpark, dreaming of undressing girls like her in some failed motel at the end of the night. Telling racist jokes in a cloud of cigarette smoke. One of those types who – depending on the audience – could also switch on a spiel about the evils of apartheid and the bad old days. How they'd had no clue what was being kept from them, how they'd been so much in the dark. Nowadays, everyone appreciated the value of a good cover story.

Pieter's fleshy fingers were squeezing the mermaid tattoo on his forearm, kneading it rhythmically. The sleeve of his blazer was crumpled; Charnay could see how strained the cheap material was across the shoulders, and how his jeans bit into his thighs. A lace trailed from the shoe cocked on his knee. She wondered uneasily why this badly wrapped parcel of a man was so tense, why he hadn't tilted his seat back to sleep. She needed to calm down. But he was checking her out, his small, sharp eyes unblinking.

"*Ja*, you were getting *woes*, helluva angry. You sounded like you were calling somebody some very bad names."

"Sorry to keep you from sleeping, er, Pieter."

Charnay stroked her stomach gingerly. *Jirre*, man. She needed the bathroom.

"And you haven't eaten the whole flight. A young lady in your condition, with a baby on the way?"

His voice was soft, persistent. *Fokall* to do with you, my condition.

Now Pieter was taking the TAP in-flight magazine out of its pocket and holding it up theatrically to the overhead light. "*Eu penso que voce é muito estúpido,*" he said, slowly, as if he was reading her a bedtime story. "*Voce compreende uma palavra que eu estou dizendo?*" Then he turned to her as if he had just remembered something. "*Ja*, and you also sounded so sad, Michelle. A nice blonde girlie like you, on her way home from language college. Now tell me, Michelle, what have you got to cry about?"

The cabin gave a sudden lurch. The air rushing through the jet engines rang more shrilly now as the plane began to struggle gamely with unseen assailants, out there in the mist. An alarm bell rang. Stupid bloody fool! How had she let them persuade her into this? As the captain's voice came over the intercom, talking cheerily about turbulence, Charnay could hear people around her shifting about and sighing. Seat belts were clinking, with a sound like marbles pouring slowly into a sack. A child wailed. Wiping her sweaty palms distractedly on her jeans, she turned away from the man beside her and peered out at the sky.

Outside, long fingers of rain were stroking the window. She wondered if it would be raining on the farm: fat drops bouncing on warm red soil, darkening the thornbushes and the striped pelts of springbok. Funny how she still thought of that old plot near Kimberley as home, although no Delports lived there now.

She'd been seven when they left, skinny and gap-toothed, and the only girl in her class with a giant leopard tortoise for a pet. Skillie had been her grandfather's, too – his own father had found her in the bush and drilled a hole in her shell so she could pull the Delport babies around on a little sledge. But by the time Charnay had grown too big for the sledge, the Delports' farming days were numbered. Years of drought had sucked the life out of everything. Even the grass by the dam was brown. So once the government started cutting subsidies on farms like theirs, the bank had just taken it all back.

Petrus, the farm manager, had helped them load up the truck and the old blue Fiat. Watching from the car's back window, she'd seen her grandfather raise a hand towards Petrus as if to pat him on the shoulder, but then he'd dropped it again, and just stood there without saying anything. Charnay remembered Petrus's brown face, as stiff as Oupa's white one. She had watched Petrus out of the window as their little convoy crunched down the drive for the last time, seeing how he got smaller and smaller until he was only a tiny dot by the windpump. Or perhaps it was they who had looked small to him?

She was pierced by a grief for Skillie she had thought long gone.

"What's wrong, Michelle?" It was Pieter again. He was craning towards her, pretending to look out through the window with her. The plane was descending now, and would soon be coming in to land. She could see the spray of dandruff on his shoulders.

Make him shut up.

"Sorry, Pieter. Tired, you know?" She tried to smile but she knew it would have come out pinched and small.

"You're sorry. *Ja*, I'm sorry too. And I've got plenty to cry about. These days you have to learn to survive with less than four-fifths of five-eighths of *fokall*. *Ja-nee*, but what can you do, hey? Tell me, Michelle, you ever had an older boyfriend?"

This time Charnay slumped down in her seat, saying nothing. She thought of Ma. She would be waking up about now, shuffling off to the sink to wash before the other squatters got there first. The twenty other homeless Afrikaners, as Ma preferred to call them, who also lived stuffed into shacks and tents in that filthy patch of soil behind the main house. Ma would probably be planning to go to the church soup kitchen today, but you had to get there early for best pick of their secondhand clothes. Whereas, she, Charnay Delport, had just had a week's paid holiday lying by a pool in the sun, like some *blerrie* film star. She slid a finger up the bridge of her nose, where her sunglasses had sat.

"You know, I think I know you from somewhere . . ."

Jesus, this guy! He was really starting to freak her out. Charnay turned to him, noticing the way his hands were shaking slightly. *Ah, hy's gesuip*. Just another horny drunk. All those brandies, before and after dinner. What else might he have seen?

She was still turning it all over in her head as they bumped down onto South African soil. Get ready. Across the façade of the terminal, distorted in the convex window of the plane, she could see that three of the letters spelling out the airport's name were missing. The dilapidation was a crumb of comfort, somehow – slack might be part of the way things worked round here. She watched as a baggage truck, orange lights blinking, sped across the tarmac to the spot where their plane was heading to park. Behind it, two yellow vehicles. Police. Looking for illegal immigrants. Terrorists, even.

Or a girl with a stomach stuffed with cocaine.

The first shock had been that the promised beach-front hotel never materialised. But the big house they brought her to instead was so beautiful, Charnay hadn't cared. She'd caught a glimpse of São Paulo, anyway, when the tall guy with the cowboy boots, Zé, picked her up from the airport. Patches of colour flying past like hallucinations. A giant, winking, blue-neon Christ on a billboard, arms outstretched. Jacarandas, plumbago and hibiscus everywhere, just like home. Police with guns, too. Even a big shanty town, right near the rich neighbourhood where the villa was.

After the initial thrill of being there, the days had passed almost in a blur, each one feeling as though it were a part of the one before that, all connected by her restless dreams. With nothing to do but wait, she'd spent most of her time by the pool, eating prego rolls in her sunglasses and staring up at the hot blue January sky. Ringing for takeout, whatever she wanted: pizza with steak toppings, stir-fried chicken and spring rolls. The hardest decision had been how to blow the money they'd given her upfront, if they weren't going to let her out through the spiked gates that slid back electronically. In the end, she'd told Zé what she wanted and he'd gone out and bought it for her: a leather jacket from a big department store, something she'd spotted in *Vogue Brasil.* Champagne-coloured, like her hair. With the buttons done up, you could hardly see her bump.

She wondered where Zé was right now. Zé, with his woolly knitted cap perched on his soft black hair, and his eyes like licked caramels. Charnay had seen him checking her out as she emerged from the pool and stalked self-consciously back to her sunlounger, more aware than ever of how the soft swell of her belly made her hips sway. She was glad she was still so small, even now, with twenty-nine weeks gone. At night, Zé had stuck around to watch the soaps with her, laughing at the *telenovela* he liked best, at the complicated things that happened to Tião, the rodeo cowboy, and Creuza, the lustful woman who pretended to be shy and virginal. Despite not knowing the language, she had understood everything that was going on between them. But in the end, Zé had never so much as touched her hand.

The second shock had come on the fifth day, yesterday. Zé had arrived with a laptop and a big-breasted, hard-faced woman called Maria. She'd chopped out some lines on the dog-eared TV guide, looking faintly surprised when Charnay refused. Then she'd got down to business, spreading the contents of the laptop case out on her blue floral bedspread. The pill to swallow so Charnay wouldn't go to the toilet on the plane. The Chloraseptic spray, to loosen up her throat. Finally, the coke, half a kilogram in twenty-eight condom-wrapped pellets the size of her thumb. "Swallow, no chew, see?" Maria had explained, throwing her head back and demonstrating, her throat supple and brown against the whiteness of her T-shirt. "Two, yes? Every twenty minutes. Take your time, easy, nice."

Simply the thought of that stuff near the baby, swimming in its own clean sac, made her feel faint and sick. She'd stammered that there'd been a mistake, a big one. That the Jo'burg people had told her she'd be bringing a package home in the lining of a suitcase. There'd been a nasty moment of silence. Zé had stopped shifting the match he'd been chewing from one side of his mouth to the other, his face suddenly very still and alert. Then Maria had forced a smile. "*Mama pequena*, little momma," she'd cooed in a voice bright as a broken bottle. "No one will suspect a pregnant woman! Much safer than inside a suitcase." Then she'd pushed her mouth up close to Charnay's ear, tickling it with the heat of her breath. "Otherwise we keep you here and you don't go home," she'd said. "You want your money, white girl? Then work for it. Does anyone at your house even know where the fuck you are?"

They'd sat with her, then, for the next five hours, while she swallowed. Feeding her sips of water from a toothbrush glass. About halfway through, when her dry-retching wouldn't stop, Maria had rummaged in her bag for a half-full bottle of massage oil, and she'd shut her eyes and pretended it was medicine. They'd explained again how the rest of it would work, too. How when she got to Jo'burg, someone would be waiting for her at the airport. She'd go to a hotel, take another pill, wait for it all to come out. It could take a couple of days, they'd said. And after that, she'd get paid.

And now there were police at the airport, before the plane had even come to a halt. How could she have trusted Zé, not seen that he and Maria would lie to her? Of course there'd be another girl in the villa this week, wide-eyed and wondering at the easy luxury of it all, at the satellite TV and the surround-sound stereo system. Were they punishing her, perhaps, for being unco-operative? Could they have called the police? Maybe her arrest would cause a nice distraction, so some other stupid fool with a bigger haul could get through unnoticed. Or was she just letting her lack of confidence take over again?

Ma. Charnay had a sudden, desperate longing to see her mother's face. When was the last time she had seen Ma laugh – really laugh, slapping her hands on her knees the way she used to? Probably before Bertus lost his job washing cars and they'd had to move again. Before Charnay found work in the bar. The night before she left for Brazil, full of lies about spending a week with her friend Cornelle in Springs, they'd had a bad time with Bertus. Drunk and ranting about respect, grabbing Ma's greying plait, pushing his red face with its starbursts of broken blood vessels up close to her worn one. But she'd still been up at six, same as usual, to see Charnay on her way. She'd stroked her daughter's belly and even joked about how her unborn grandchild was already becoming a real traveller. Charnay had smiled back, but she couldn't look Ma in the eye. She couldn't face the intensity of that frightened, watery gaze, those eyes diluted with a sadness that seeped into her very bones.

She and Ma, she knew, would not meet again for a long while, not after this. For Ma, clinging to the old days, recognising nothing in what the politicians called the rainbow nation, would never understand where all the money had come from. Or how far Charnay had fallen. That there was nothing she would not now do, including begging a black man for help, to lift herself beyond the limits of Vanderbijlpark and seize her place in the larger world. How inside she was aching and hot and always empty. A farm overrun by the forest. Her fields were all on fire. The air was filled with smoke, and nobody seemed to see.

Fool, *blerrie* fool. But Charnay, you are something special, Zé had comforted her. What you have on your side is not just that you are so young, but your hair – your beautiful yellow hair – and your baby. Not at all what the police will be looking for. These things, Zé had said, would see her clear through the airport and help her come out the other side. But those waiting police vans were making a nonsense of all that. The game was up, and she was not prepared for it. Something had gone wrong.

"Let us in, man! We're good South Africans. We all like rugby and we all drink beer." A big guy in sunglasses and a green dashiki shirt was joking with an immigration official at the passport booth up ahead. A public-sector strike – another one – was in full swing, and only a skeleton staff was on duty that day. Police had been drafted in, a hoarse voice had announced over the public address system, so that security at the airport "would not be compromised". But everything was moving at an agonisingly slow pace.

"Just be patient, sir, and we'll try and get this sorted for you as quickly as we can."

Now, at the head of the queue, a woman in a long gown and a scarf wrapped turban-style around her head was arguing over a piece of paper. Soon it would be Charnay's turn. It had taken almost an hour, and finally she had come to the front of the line. But after this she'd also have to wait the Lord knew how long for the luggage. And before this queue had even started moving, she'd felt it – a pang of heat running through her body, the upwelling of a small, red pain.

She'd tried to ignore it. Zé had told her these were good-quality condoms, but you had to look after them, he'd said. Don't eat or drink on the plane. And be cool. Otherwise, acid from the stomach can melt the plastic and then . . . He'd shaken his head. Big trouble. Someone he'd known once, a Rio woman, had got an overdose after a condom burst in her stomach while she was flying back from Lima. She'd drunk a ginger beer, then fallen down, saying she was all on fire. She'd been rushed to hospital, he said, as soon as the plane landed, but it was too late. It had taken her six days to die.

She was next. Stepping forward, she felt the new bad feeling again, only this time it was stronger, clearer.

"*Goeie môre, meneer.* How are you, sir?" Her voice was steady, but she could feel sweat burning on her forehead and the backs of her knees. The heat from her gut enveloped her, then slowly sank away.

A policeman with a sniffer dog was idly circling the queue. She had not given herself away by any change of expression or sudden movement. She could count on that. After telling the official what he wanted to know, she would continue on her way at an even pace. Safe past the dog that was waiting to sniff her over, wanting to get the scent of her betrayal. Into the arrivals hall, alive with the warmth of families, their bundles and exclaiming relatives. She'd have done it.

"*Sawubona*, welcome to eGoli. And where have you come from this morning?"

Charnay gave him her biggest smile. That was an easy one. She began to answer, but found she couldn't remember the words. Instead, the pain was back again, the bird that was forcing its wings open in her stomach and pecking at her throat. And her heart was pounding loudly, making her feel dizzy and faint. She licked her lips, conscious of the officer with the dog coming up behind her on the left-hand side. Everything seemed to have gone still.

The official was looking at her expectantly, ballpoint pen poised. A queer sense of calm coursed through her as she lowered her head to her hands, resting her forehead against the booth's dusty glass. She was drifting away, feeling hands warm on her shoulders, the fragment of a bad dream – a crow pecking the seeds from a swollen yellow sunflower – already fading. The hands were gentle and firm and smelled of familiar things, soap and pipe tobacco. She felt ancient, older than the hills. In the noise and the clamour sinking behind her she could just make out a whistle blowing, someone shouting, a dog whining. But Oupa was pulling her towards him, stroking her forehead and holding her fast against his chest, and at last she was able to sleep.

She was rich with Friday-night wages, and there were swallows dipping and soaring in the mild October sun. The street where the Nigerian lived was lined with pawn shops and Greek restaurants, peep shows and pool rooms. Charnay had never been to Hillbrow before. Muscled men leaned on bar stools at the entrances of the strip clubs, talking to the beautiful girls in their high-heeled boots, smoking cigarettes and waiting. Out on the pavement, vegetable-hawkers guarded their stock – single cigarettes, butternuts, roasted chicken feet. She'd had to dodge out of the path of a Shangaan *mielie*-seller, heading home with a baby on her back and a brazierful of coals on her head. Black smoke had clouded her face, filling Charnay's nostrils and making her cough.

She'd still been coughing when she stepped into the restaurant, Bismillah's. Inside, at a window table, Pascal and Mr Femi were waiting. They'd been sipping tins of Black Label beer, into each of which, Pascal told her later, the Nigerian had dropped several hits of speed.

Mr Femi had seemed delighted to see her. He'd towered over her, tall as a preacher in his beautiful grey suit, his mirror sunglasses reflecting her uncertain smile. Ordered chicken and rice for them all with an expansive wave of the wrist adorned with the silver Tag Heuer watch. Then, in between mouthfuls, he'd told her the facts. A week's paid holiday at a luxury resort, cash for clothing and toiletries before departure, spending money while she was there, and R30,000 when she got home. Or rather, almost a year's worth of rent on a little flat, to make a nest for her and Pascal and the baby. Light and air had seemed to push up between his words, like tiny blessings.

Sipping her Coke, Charnay had considered the risks. What she could count on, she knew, was that the police would not be checking for someone like her – someone full of confidence, so pregnant and so white. Fact was the blacker you were, the more suspect in this rainbow nation. That's what had brought her and Pascal together. One time, the cops – four Zulu guys – had come to the bar searching for *makwerekwere*, cockroaches, foreigners without residence permits and skins a darker brown than your average South African *oke*. The street had been closed off, all the kitchen staff detained and asked for their papers. And if they couldn't count to ten in Afrikaans, they'd been thrown in the back of the van. Pascal had been lucky, brazening his way out by singing the words of the old song she'd taught him: *Ja, een ding kan jy seker weet, jy gaan jou brood verdien in jou gesig se sweet.* One thing you can be sure of, you have to earn your dough by the sweat of your brow.

Later, the deal sealed, Mr Femi had waved them goodbye with another expansive smile and they'd spun elated back onto the street to find a bus back to Berea. Up in his room, Pascal had made a shield from the wardrobe beside his bed, a signal to the other three men living there that this was his private time. He'd played her a song in French on his guitar. It was about her, he'd said, her beauty and courage and bravery, and when he got back to the DRC it would go straight to the top of the hit parade and make both their fortunes. Then he'd kissed her nipples and they'd done it from behind so as not to hurt the baby, and she'd fallen asleep with the smell of the squeezed sap from their bodies on her hands. His or hers, it didn't seem to matter.

Charnay awoke to the sound of a siren. Tubes dangled from the shiny white ceiling above her, swaying gently as they turned a corner. Her lips, underneath what she realised was an oxygen mask, felt dry and cracked. Her first thought was that she was back on the plane, but then it dawned on her. An ambulance. She was clear of the airport, *jirre*, she'd bloody done it. A man, someone wearing a blue paper mask and blue protective clothing, sat on the grey seat alongside her stretcher. He was reading, she noticed, a TAP in-flight magazine.

Pieter.

There was something very important she had to tell him. Her hands fluttered to pull away the mask, but by now he'd noticed that her eyes were open and he was moving towards her with soothing gestures.

"Michelle, my girl," he was saying, stroking a tangle of blond hair from her face. That smell again, on his hands. Tobacco and soap. "Michelle, you've gone into labour, but you're going to be absolutely fine. You're dilating very nicely and . . ."

Her voice, forced out of her with enormous effort, was hoarse. It sounded like somebody else's. "*Asseblief tog,* please. I don't want it any more, get it out of me. I don't want it to hurt . . . Baby, baby."

But the man was soothing her, telling her in a calm voice not to worry. "Breathe in deeply, now, Michelle, and relax," he was saying. "After all, you've got something very precious inside you, now haven't you? Something you really don't want to lose." And bending over her with loving care, he began fitting the mask back onto her face.

WITH HIS OWN TWO HANDS

Albert Garcia

My grandparents used to take the train from South Texas to Los Angeles' Union Station when they visited. They lived on a small farm outside El Paso. They had chickens, goats and a horse, and my grandpa said he built his house and the fence that surrounded it with his own two hands. "*Con mis propias manos hice esta casa y el cerco,*" he would say with his hands extended in front of him. I loved staying up late to listen to stories of how he learned to play the guitar as a young boy and how he sang to make money for his family instead of going to school. I used to stare at his hands and try to imagine the things they had done, but as I grew older, I started to look at him differently. I started to feel embarrassed about having grandparents who had a horse but no car. As a teenager in Orange County during the 1980s, I wanted to fit in and tried to act as un-Mexican as possible. I skateboarded and surfed and dated blondes named Mandy and Bridgette.

My grandpa had an old suitcase with shoelaces for a handle, and my grandma carried a wicker bag full of fruit and vegetables from their garden. My parents and I would pick them up at Union Station, downtown across from Olvera Street. They looked so much like the Mexicans I was trying hard not to be, my grandpa with his straw hat and overalls and the red handkerchief in his back pocket and their sandals made from car tyres. I hid the pictures of them and their farm when my friends came over. I don't remember when I started to feel like that, but I remember when I stopped.

Standing in Union Station, I can see the place where twenty years ago I met my grandpa for the last time. The rows of oversized, brown, leather chairs, tiled columns and the vaulted ceiling look exactly as I remember. Waves of people moving at different speeds rush from one end of the station to the other. The wood beams are freshly painted and the sun is pouring through the windows. I watch an old man walking with a cane in one hand and the other on the shoulder of a small boy. The boy is carrying a bag that looks too heavy for him.

The first time I saw my grandpa, I was four years old. It was on the farm, and he was splitting logs for firewood behind the house. As we drove up the dirt driveway, he raised an axe above his head and let it fall, exploding the piece of wood before him. He had a broad, muscular back and wore boots, and the straps of his overalls hung down by his sides.

He told me stories about how he bare-knuckle boxed with three, four marines a night for money when he was seventeen and how he had been a cowboy and travelled the whole of the southwest on horseback by the time he was twenty. He told me how he met my grandma while singing at a wedding in Juarez, across the river from El Paso, and how he had been drafted and fought the Japanese on the Filipino island of Leyte. My grandma would nod her head as he talked of the storm that lasted six months and nearly washed away their house, and she corrected him when he got his facts wrong. "*No, viejo,*" she would say as she gave me the right name or date. Sometimes he got angry when she challenged his memory, and she would wink at me and tell him he was right even when she knew he was wrong. To me he was bigger and better than any character in any story I'd read or any movie I'd seen.

When I was a teenager, I stopped listening to my grandpa's stories. By then his shirt no longer stretched across his back. His shoulders slouched a bit and his hair was almost entirely grey. We weren't from the same place or time. I was interested in playing Nintendo and listening to Run DMC. I could never be the man he was or do the things he had done. There were no logs to cut in Orange County, no frontier to ride out into. I wasn't a musician or an athlete. I was a city boy. My friends' grandparents were doctors and lawyers and spending their retirement in South Florida playing golf, not in South Texas growing cilantro and bell peppers.

This is my first visit to Union Station since the day my grandpa died. I've come to the station to pick up a colleague, a man interested in collaborating on the history of the El Paso-Juarez area. I'm a professor of Chicano Studies at a small college in North Los Angeles, and I've spent the last fifteen years earning degrees and teaching and lecturing about the importance of culture and how to best preserve it. It's easy to forget the shame I once felt to carry the name Enrique Guadalupe Sanchez. I remember when I wanted to be just Ricky S, an American teenager who had nothing in common with the Mexican on the corner selling oranges or a grandfather who had slept with a saddle for a pillow under an open sky.

My grandparents stayed for weeks when they used to visit. My grandma would make *menudo, pozole* and fresh tortillas, and she would sit at the kitchen table and prepare refried beans from scratch. When I was a boy, I would help her separate the beans one by one, and then we would soak them in a big pot. She would let me light the gas stove with a long match and taste the food as it simmered away.

As I grew older I started to feel embarrassed when the house smelled like a Mexican restaurant. I once came into the kitchen with some friends, and she asked me if I wanted to taste some fresh salsa. I said I didn't eat salsa any more, or refried beans or tortillas, and I remember how, as I walked away, her mouth curved down as she tried to hide her disappointment.

The last summer I went to the farm, I resented being there and spent the whole time watching movies and talking on the phone to my girlfriend back in California. My grandpa nodded when I said I didn't want to help him plant herbs in the garden like I used to, and his eyes narrowed when I didn't want to help him brush Reina, his horse. But when I told him I didn't want to play the guitar any more, his shoulders lowered and his face stopped straining to keep a smile.

For the rest of the visit, instead of telling me his stories, we argued, he in Spanish and I in English. He told me I was a Mexican-American, not an American-Mexican. I told him I was just an American and that we were living in the United States. I listened to my Walkman while he would ramble on about all the things he had done. "*Con mis propias manos hice esta casa e el cerco. Con mis propias manos,*" he would say as he held his hands out to me.

When I was seventeen, my grandma died. The following summer, my dad told me my grandpa was sick and he was moving to Los Angeles to live with us. I made my dad promise he wouldn't let my grandpa grow tomatoes in the back yard or wear his straw hat and overalls when he sat on the front porch. I had spent the whole of my adolescence creating the image of Ricky S. Only my family called me Enrique.

It was the summer before my senior year. I had just passed my driving test and I was supposed to take some friends to the beach. When I was packing the station wagon, my dad told me he had an emergency at work, and I had to pick up my grandpa. I was angry as I took my surfboard out of the car. I argued and yelled and threw my towel into the garage and slammed the door.

I took my time driving to the station, and when I arrived I parked and entered through the side doors. I knew my grandpa would be anxious as he waited for me and when I first saw him, I was shocked. He looked so much older. Hunched over, his clothes hanging loosely on his thin frame, he looked scared in the middle of the busy station. He scanned the faces that pushed through the doors as he stood between his suitcase and a wicker bag that was bursting at the sides. Wearing a *serape*, he held his straw hat in his two hands in front of him. He took out his handkerchief and wiped at his forehead as he searched the sea of people for a face he recognised.

He looked so many years removed from the man who had destroyed that piece of wood with one swift swing of his axe. I watched him as he walked towards the front doors with slow and short steps, looking back every few feet at his bags. At the entrance, he almost got knocked over as a young man barged through. He looked outside for a few seconds and then turned and walked back. His eyes were hollow and his mouth hung open. His cheeks were sucked in. When he reached his bags, he glanced around. Someone brushed by him, making him drop his hat. A thin hand extended from the sleeve of his shirt as he bent over and struggled to pick it up.

I started towards him. The station was crowded, and I had trouble walking through the streams of people. I got caught in a tour group and lost sight of him for a moment. I found his eyes as they scanned the faces around him. A briefcase slammed into my shins and I stumbled. When I recovered my balance I found myself in a school field trip, dozens of children and guardians with roller bags in tow. As carefully as I could, I made my way through the students, stepping over lunchboxes and avoiding knocking into small heads.

When I finally got near my grandfather, he was slowly sinking to the ground. He put his arm down to brace himself but it couldn't hold his weight, and I watched as he fell onto his case. A man in a suit stopped and bent down next to him. A crowd formed, and I was shoved away as they cleared a space for him. Someone called for a doctor. The man in the suit stood up and asked if anyone knew him. I felt my back strain as I wrestled through the crowd.

"My name is Enrique, Enrique Guadalupe Sanchez. He's my grandpa," I shouted into their midst.

People stood back and I helped the man in the suit roll my grandpa onto his back. Even though I was kneeling down next to him, he didn't see me. He was writhing slowly, reaching and grabbing as if trying to pull something away from his neck.

The paramedics arrived and surrounded him. They gave him oxygen, took his pulse, flashed a light in his eyes. People stopped and looked and then went on their way. One of the paramedics asked me questions about his health. I told him what little I knew. He wrote the answers on a clipboard and moved away speaking into a walkie-talkie.

After a few minutes, my grandpa stopped struggling. The strain on his face started to disappear and his eyes looked up to the ceiling. The paramedics stopped trying to revive him. I held on to his hand as the paramedics walked away one by one. The last two to leave covered his face with a white sheet, and placed him on a stretcher. A woman who was standing close to me started to cry. She didn't know him, but she cried.

I knew him, my grandpa. He was born in a wooden house with a dirt floor outside of Juarez, Mexico and he died on the terracotta tiles of Union Station in Los Angeles. He was a boxer, a cowboy and a musician. He was a husband, a father, a brother and a grandpa. He was a veteran of World War II and had a garden where he grew tomatoes, cilantro, and bell peppers. My grandpa's name was Enrique Guadalupe Sanchez, and he built his house and the fence around it with his own two hands.

AIR AND SEA AND SALT

Matthew Weait

Vivienne watches the sea breaking below her against the side of the ship and wonders what it would feel like to step over the railing, to launch herself into the air, arms spread, before being engulfed by the dark, roiling water. She does not imagine being conscious at the point of impact, or rather she imagines that she would lose consciousness at exactly that moment. In any event, it is not the experience of impact that intrigues her, or the shock of the cold, it is the seconds between, the fleeting, irreversible sensation of falling towards the water through the air, feeling its rush against her face and body, knowing that this would be the last sensation she ever felt.

Jim had been insistent about the holiday. The chance of a lifetime he had called it. For her part, Vivienne could think of nothing more dreadful. Two weeks imprisoned on the high seas with strangers for whom this was a grand ambition or, worse, a regular event; the only moments of liberation day excursions to towns whose economies depended on those excursions. But Jim – well, Jim loved the sea, and was practised in the art of managing rejection. To refuse him was to accept a period of silent and justified recrimination. And she was, she had come recently to realise, too old in the bones for this. She no longer had the energy to fend off the months of subtle hurts that would inevitably be inflicted, and which two weeks of gritted teeth would serve to avoid.

So here she was, somewhere in the South China Sea, on a ship too big to make sense of, watching the water, shifting her gaze from the sea to the sky, allowing herself thoughts that she had never before imagined herself thinking. It is approaching dusk. In the near distance the air is clear, becoming increasingly grey and milky towards the horizon until, at the limit of her vision, it appears as a line of slate occluding the distinction between sky and water. The sun, low but still strong, is burning the side of her neck and cheek. She dabs at them with her hanky and is about to move away from the rail to find somewhere shady to sit when she sees it. At first she thinks it's a bird, an albatross perhaps, but did they come this far north? She thinks not. It is certainly big, or seems to be, but it is impossible to judge distances. It could be something small quite near, or something larger much further away. She squints her eyes through her sunglasses. No, it isn't a bird. It is on the water – a motor boat. But a motor boat this far out? She looks around, wondering if there is anyone who might also have seen it, hoping to exchange a knowing or puzzled look, but she is alone on this part of the deck. Picking up her bag, she heads for the interior of the ship.

When she arrives back at the cabin Jim is lying on the bed, the book she suggested as a holiday read propped up like a scout tent on his mounding stomach. His comb-over has flopped onto the pillow beside his head and rests there like a hairy stain.

"I thought you would be at the bar," she says, placing her bag on a chair.

"I was waiting for you."

Vivienne slips off her sandals and sits on the side of the bed. She senses an arm being extended, a hand about to touch her back and being withdrawn.

"Do you suppose that motor boats would be out this far?"

"How do you mean?"

"I was out on deck. I thought I saw a motor boat."

"It could be anything. Not a motor boat, not this far out."

"That's what I thought. It was probably a trick of the light. How are you getting on with the book?"

"I'm just where the vase gets broken and Cecilia climbs into the pond to fish out the bits. Does anything much else happen?"

Vivienne allows herself a private, condescending smile and is immediately ashamed.

"This and that," she replies flatly. "It's worth persisting, if only for the unforeseen consequences."

"Well, they're the only kind worth having," says Jim brightly, pushing his hands down into the mattress and easing himself off his side of the bed. "Have a shower, get changed, and we'll go to the bar."

She turns to face him. His pubic hair shows beneath his Y-fronts at the top of each thigh, wiry and wild. The outline of his penis is visible, flaccid beneath the white cotton.

"No, you get dressed and go on ahead. I'll meet you there. I need to make myself up."

"If you like. I'll be in the usual spot."

Standing in front of the mirror in the steaming windowless bathroom, a towel wrapped around her, Vivienne wonders how it came to this: that she should be standing in front of a mirror in such a place, her reflection obscured by condensation; that her husband already has a "usual spot" on a ship they have been on for little over a week; that she knows where that "usual spot" is. She wipes the mirror with her hand. Instantly it steams up. She takes a flannel, holds it under the hot tap, squeezes, and wipes again, making an oval just large enough to see herself in. She runs an index finger under her left eye and observes the loose skin puckering before it. Her hair, released from its clear plastic shower-cap, is the colour of uncooked fish bone. She grimaces, baring her teeth. They are a good shape, small and even. "And at least you are all my own," she says out loud before tapping them with a fingernail as if for confirmation. She allows the towel to fall to the floor and pins her hair back with two black plastic slides. "You look like Baba Yaga," she says, and enjoys the reflected smile. After drying her face she smoothes on some foundation. She takes a lipstick, a new one from the ship's boutique, and carefully applies the creamy dark-bronze colour to her top lip before compressing it against the bottom one. She applies a smoky-brown eyeshadow, mascara and eyeliner. With tweezers she extracts a white hair from her chin, an errant one from an eyebrow. She pulls out the slides, draws a brush gently through her hair, once, twice, three times. She raises her chin and lowers it, turns her head slightly to one side, and then to the other. "Not bad for a hag," she says.

Back in the bedroom she is about to get dressed when there is a crackle on the Tannoy. She is so used to the endless announcements that she is ready to ignore it, but there is something odd about the timing. Usually they are left in peace in the evening, spared the otherwise endless information about volleyball tournaments, Japanese flower arranging, fat-busters. She lays the dress, still on its hanger, onto the bed. A different voice is coming through, a serious one she has heard only a couple of times since the beginning of the voyage.

"Ladies and gentlemen, this is the captain. Please listen very carefully to this announcement, which concerns your safety and security. I repeat, this announcement concerns your safety and security. Please stop what you are doing and listen very carefully. I am reading from a statement. The ship has been commandeered by –"

There is a brief pause. Vivienne cannot quite believe what she has heard. Did he say "commanded"? There seems to be some background noise, voices talking over each other.

"I repeat. The ship has been commandeered. You are to remain where you are and await further instruction. Anyone who resists will be shot. Any attempt to reach the bridge will result in the death of the captain and crew. That is the end of the statement. Ladies and gentlemen, and all crew listening, this is not a drill. I repeat, this is not a drill. Do exactly as you have been told and await further announcements."

Vivienne's first thought is not about Jim, it is whether she should put on the dress. If she is a hostage – for this is what she supposes she is – it seems a little much to wear a low-cut cocktail dress, especially if she is to remain alone in the cabin. But a pair of shorts and a T-shirt will look ludicrous, what with the amount of slap she has plastered on.

What she can't do is stand here dithering. Suppose the pirates – for that is the word that springs immediately to mind, a word that stirs something in her – are planning to get everyone out of their cabins, to round them up? She can't be found in her bra and knickers. She decides to put on the dress, if for no other reason than it is at hand. She slips it up over her calves, enjoying the momentary coolness of the silk. She finds a pair of smart shoes with a low heel – stilettos would of course be ridiculous – and sits down. Minutes pass. She runs the back of her hand under her chin. There is something missing. She goes over to her jewellery box and selects a twisted platinum chain, a gift from Jim on their thirtieth wedding anniversary. She clasps it behind her neck, allowing its weight to fall against her fingers, and adjusts it so that it forms a low narrow ellipse below her throat.

She slips off her shoes and inspects her fingernails. Her mind drifts slowly from the low, pale table with its bowl of tropical fruit to Jim. She can picture him precisely. He is sitting to the left of the horseshoe bar at a table for two, by the window. Before him on the table will be a bowl of pretzels and a whisky and soda, no ice. Worried by what is happening, worried about her, he will be intermittently wiping his brow with one of his many pale-yellow handkerchiefs. She should have told him to stay until she was ready, that it would be nice to go up together. That would have been the kind, the generous, thing to do; but it would not have been a true thing. She recalls the first evening on board, Jim taking her arm just before they entered the bar, what felt like a hundred pairs of scrutinising eyes turning towards them. It is not that she is embarrassed by Jim, or that she minds being his wife. She simply dislikes the idea of being assessed in relation to him, being judged by strangers as part of an ensemble of which she is the more decorative component. Since that first evening, she has managed to hold back, to establish a little distance.

The Tannoy fizzes. A different voice, confident but not English. No pleasantries.

"Attention. People in cabins to stand outside doors open. Do now."

Vivienne stands up and looks around her. She knows she must do as the voice says, and she knows she ought to feel more panicked.

What she feels instead, though, is a strange lassitude, a heaviness in her legs and arms. She puts her shoes back on and opens the door. In the short, narrow corridor others are lining up. Immediately to her left are a young couple. The man's colour is high, his eyes are darting. The woman's mascara has run and she is wiping her hands up and down the sides of her dress. Vivienne tries, unsuccessfully, to catch her eye. To her right, a little further down, is an elderly man she has nodded to in passing. They exchange tight smiles. Nobody speaks. She shifts her weight and concentrates on a spot on the opposite wall.

One of the reasons she had resented the idea of coming on the cruise was that she was finalising an article that was already overdue. A critical analysis of the work of Louis Lepassier, whose name comes to her unexpectedly as she focuses on the wall in front of her. He had been Secretary of the Académie de Toulon, between 1880 and 1893. "What," Lepassier had written in an 1892 lecture, "is the world but the sum of our experience of that world? I am told that I exist because I have lungs and heart and brain; because I respire; because the atmosphere contains a substance called oxygen; because oxygen is necessary for the proper functioning of cells and the pumping of the heart; because consciousness is nothing but the effect of synaptic connection. What impoverishment has such science brought among us! Does such analysis and equation bring us closer to an understanding of our capacity for hate, or for justice, or for compassion?" Vivienne remembers these words verbatim, but she has not, she now realises, really understood what Lepassier was trying to explain, or rather to excite; for what she feels at this moment is excitement: a buzzing of strange particles. She can see the opposite wall because she has eyes that communicate through retinal sensitivity and nerve cells, nourished by blood, by oxygen. But what is this sense of anticipation made of? What is its substance?

"You."

The voice is a loud, male one, at the far end of the corridor. She cranes forward so that she can turn to see, but thinks better of it and falls back. The voice is joined by another, and possibly another. Someone is crying. The couple to her left tense and straighten. The woman is whimpering, the man steeling himself, his fists clenching and unclenching.

"Just do exactly what they say. And don't make a scene," he says.

Hold her, thinks Vivienne. She needs you to hold her.

The couple are next. Two men and one woman stand before them, carrying guns and holdalls. As the couple are ushered into their cabin, Vivienne tries to think of the things in her own that they will want. There is quite a lot of cash, about two thousand dollars in notes and travellers' cheques, her jewellery. Enough to satisfy them. Enough for them not to question whether there is any more.

The pirates come back into the corridor and confront her.

"In," the woman says. She is slight, with dark curly hair. She is wearing sunglasses that are too big for her face. Vivienne goes into the room.

"Money," one of the men says.

Vivienne gestures to the chest of drawers opposite the bed. He opens the top drawer and takes out a large white envelope. He stuffs it in a holdall, his eyes searching the rest of the cabin.

"Jewels."

"There," she says. "In that box."

He takes the box and empties rings, bracelets, necklaces onto the bed. She watches him as he runs his hairy fingers through the silvery metal.

"Gold?"

"No gold," she says. "I don't wear gold. Sorry."

"Sorrreee," the woman laughs, revealing creamy, gappy teeth.

The other man, who has been standing by the door, comes further into the cabin. Bigger and darker-skinned, he has the swagger of leadership about him. He approaches Vivienne and lifts her chin with the back of his hand. She is taken aback by his raw, animal smell. A mixture of iron and fresh sweat. He slides a forefinger under the chain she is wearing, looping it once round a knuckle so that it tightens against her neck. She looks him in the eyes, but cannot hold the gaze.

"I would like to see my husband," she says. There is a stain on the ceiling that she has not noticed before. "I would like to be with him.

He is in the bar."

Does she mean this? Her skin is tingling, her mouth dry. She has never experienced anything this unpredictable. The man untwists his finger from the chain and allows it to fall back against her skin.

"Passports?"

The other man has taken these from the drawer and is holding them in his hand. He gives them to the woman, who flicks through one, then the other. Her nails are bitten to the quick. She is about to pass them over when she stops and reopens one of them – Vivienne cannot be sure which. The woman whispers something to the man whose hand has just been touching her. He looks down at the passport, back up at Vivienne and – for a brief moment – closes his eyes. His voice, when he finally speaks, is quiet; each word clear and deliberate.

"Come with me."

He takes hold of her forearm, firmly, but not aggressively. She can feel his strength, does not resist. *What is the world but the sum of our experience of that world?* The words of Lepassier run through her head. Is this what he meant?

"Where are we going? What do you want?"

The man does not answer. He guides her along the corridor, into the wide atrium from which three staircases ascend. It is deserted. All she can feel is the thrum of the ship's engines beneath her. She tries to get his attention, but he is ahead of her, pulling. His hands are rough, chafing against her skin.

"Please, you are hurting me. Please let go."

She is startled at the tone of her voice. It is that of a stranger. She has never pleaded before, only read about it in romantic fiction. Her voice has become that of a Victorian heroine – beautifully doomed. She tries to muster herself, as such a heroine would, but she has no energy. He is leeching it out of her. She trips against the edge of one of the steps halfway up the staircase and bangs her knee. She cries out involuntarily and, seeing him turn round, automatically covers her face with her free hand.

"Please don't hurt me. I don't know what you want. I don't want to die."

The man crouches down awkwardly. He lets go of her arm. She draws it towards her face but he catches it in a surprisingly tender grip.

"Sit. Take breath. Is OK."

She looks up. With his other hand he reaches towards her, causing her to flinch and him to hesitate for a moment. She remembers another hand reaching out, retracting, but that seems a long time ago, in a different world. This hand, though, is not drawn back; it moves slowly towards her head, and touches it. She closes her eyes and allows the hand to rest. It lies flat, dry and warm on her scalp. She lets out a quiet breath as the hand is drawn gently back through her hair.

"You must come. Come."

Vivienne blinks awake. She staggers to her feet. The man has taken hold of her arm again and is dragging her upwards. At the head of the stairs they turn left, past the boutique. Couples and groups are on their knees, huddled, cowering against the walls. Some look up as they pass, others stare at the carpet. They turn again, along another corridor. He is taking her to the bar, to Jim. They stop just before the entrance. The man pulls her round to face him. His eyes are wide, dark.

"Is bad. Not us."

She does not understand.

"What is bad? Tell me what you mean."

He does not answer, but holds her by the arm. As they enter the bar she senses people turning to watch. She dare not make contact with their eyes; she cannot imagine what they are thinking. This thin, awkward, silver-haired woman on this dangerous stranger's arm. She looks over to the other side of the room, beyond the counter, to where Jim should be sitting. The table is empty. She turns to the man.

"Where's Jim? What have you done with my husband?" she asks, her voice rising. She starts to batter at the man with her free hand. Her arm feels like a leaf fluttering against a branch. She starts to scream, to sob. The sounds that are coming from her throat are raw, primal. She has never made sounds like this before, has no idea where they come from. "Let me go! Let me go, you bastard! I want to see my husband!"

And suddenly, as if a silent lock has been turned, she is free and running past the counter, knocking against tables, chairs. And then there, on the floor, is Jim. He lies on his side, not moving. She falls to her knees and touches his head.

"Jim, it's Viv. It's me. Jim, are you OK? What happened? Did someone hurt you?" She looks around wildly. "Someone, what happened? What did they do to him? Tell me!"

Silence. A cough. Somewhere in the room, a woman is crying quietly. Vivienne bends her ear down to Jim's face, takes his wrist in her hand. He is still warm, but there is no breath, no pulse that she can feel. She rolls him onto his back, opens his mouth, inhales, and blows into his lungs. She kneels up, locates his sternum, and pushes down three or four times. It is what she has seen people do in movies. She does the same thing again; and again. She feels giddy, the muscles in her hands ache; but still she continues. Her thoughts eddy, her strength ebbs. Little by little her efforts diminish. She knows it is hopeless. She stops.

"Is heart attack, I think."

The man is kneeling down beside her. She ignores him, strokes Jim's forehead with the palm of her hand. It is still slightly damp. She is grateful that his eyes are closed. She could not have closed them; does not think that she could have closed them.

"Is very fast, quick. Is happen before."

She is aware of snot on her upper lip and wipes it away.

"Before what? Before you boarded the ship? Came into the bar? Threatened to kill?"

She does not expect an answer and does not get one. She stands up, scanning the room for something to cover Jim's face. No one looks directly at her, though she can tell that she is the focus of everyone's attention. On the bar, wrapped around the neck of a bottle in a metal chilling bucket, is a white waiter's cloth. She pulls it off, bends down and lays it gently over Jim's face, loosely, so that his features are not visible. Her hand hovers over his head. She wants to stroke his hair but cannot. And then they come, unwilled – hollow, guttural sounds, low and resonant, pulsing through her, wracking and spasmodic, uncontrollable. She has no idea how long these continue. They, she, are out of time. As her body heaves, releasing the years, her mind fills with disjointed images and recollections: watching Jim fill the birdfeeder from her study window; him listening attentively as she delivers a lecture on a subject in which he had no interest; her turning away as he attempted to make love; a painted seascape he loved and she tolerated; a yellow handkerchief; and then, nothing.

When she starts to waken she imagines she is at home. She reaches out for the glass of water she keeps on the bedside table and is momentarily disoriented as her hand meets no resistance. She opens her eyes. Pitch black except for a thin line of light on the far wall. A door. What door? Jim. She must go to Jim. And then she remembers him lying there, on the floor, a white cloth over his face. She stumbles up off the bed, tripping against something. Her shoes? She feels for the wall and gropes her way towards the door.

"Hello? Is anybody there?"

Movement outside, a shadow crossing the light. The door opens and she is blinded by the brightness. She shades her eyes. A figure is standing in the doorframe. She recognises the smell, duller now, less acrid.

"Where's Jim? What have you done with him?"

The man flicks the light switch. He comes towards her and she backs away, crumpling back onto the bed.

"Here."

He passes her a bottle of water, keeping his distance.

She takes it. Only when the bottle is half empty does she hand it back.

"Your husband safe."

"What do you mean, 'safe'?"

"Is in room."

For a moment she imagines he means that Jim is back in their cabin, his dead body lying on their bed, on sheets she has slept on. The look on her face must give this away because the man adds, quickly: "Different room. Safe."

She should know how to deal with this, and with this man. The choices and emotions present themselves to her in quick succession, none of them fixing. She feels tired, extraordinarily tired. A fruit machine spins in her head, the strawberries, lemons and plums whirring past each other. Grief? Not that. She remembers her outpouring, the moans, the snot. Grief, if it comes, is for later. Anger? Yes, she feels angry, but about what? Not about Jim's death. You cannot be angry with death. That is futile. Perhaps she is angry with this man, whose name she does not even know. Would Jim have died if he and the others had not boarded the ship? She has no idea. He had high blood pressure, suffered a mild stroke a couple of years ago, was bad at taking his pills, drank too much. She half remembers another passage from Lepassier, something about a wood and a girl. Like a fairy tale, but not.

"I want to see him."

"Later. After."

"After what?"

The man comes to sit next to her on the bed. She does not move.

"Is better in sea."

He is talking about burial! An emotion rises but is squashed back down before it can take root; a ripe peach beneath a heavy heel. She will not feel indignant. She will not be middle class. She shuts her eyes tight. What *is* that other passage, that fable, from Lepassier? Something about a girl building a dam. No. That's it. The point is she *doesn't* build a dam. She lets the water flow, and when she is asked why the water is flowing, she realises it would be nonsense to say "Because I didn't build a dam." So that's what Lepassier was getting at. Jim may have died anyway, but that is not the point. He is dead. Things have changed, and this man is implicated. She feels the need for justice, for a levelling, to make a difference. She turns to face him.

"A burial at sea seems to be the best thing. Yes. When?"

"Is better soon."

"Tomorrow morning, then. At dawn. I would be grateful if you and your – if you could get him ready. Outside."

The man nods.

"Until the morning, then. Goodnight."

She is already awake when he knocks on the door. Still in her black dress, which now clings to her body in strange, damp folds, she follows him. He makes no attempt to hold her arm or to guide her. From behind he resembles a bear: great, broad shoulders, shaggy, oily hair. He lumbers ahead of her, and she thinks of the previous evening when, before she knew that Jim was dead, she felt that surge of raw and instinctive erotic attraction. Now the feeling has gone, displaced by Jim's death, or what Jim's death has provoked. Now he is just a man, like all men; bulky, awkward, facile.

They exit through a door on the lowest of the open decks. The woman from the night before is standing just beyond a section of guard railing that doubles as a gate for passenger disembarkation. Jim's body, which they have wrapped in what looks like a tablecloth, is lying on its back, his feet parallel with the edge.

"I should like it to be just us," she says.

He looks at her quizzically.

"You and me. Tell the woman to go."

She points and makes shooing gestures with her hands. He barks a command and the woman disappears through a door into the ship.

The sun, even at this early hour, is furious. Vivienne can feel the sweat building in her underarms, between her legs. The light is grey white, blinding without her sunglasses.

"You want I help?" the man asks.

"Yes. Yes, I will need you. I just want a moment to think."

She lowers her eyes and the man withdraws a little, faces away from her as she kneels down next to the body and places her hands on it, one on the chest, one on the head.

"I am so sorry, Jim," she whispers. "I am sorry that I did not come to the bar with you, that I wasn't there for you at the end. I am sorry that I ignored you, that I was embarrassed by you. You did not deserve this."

She wipes her eyes with the back of a hand and leans down to kiss the cloth where it covers his face. There is a sudden gust of wind and then it is still again.

"I am ready now," she says, getting to her feet.

The man walks slowly over.

"If you go there," she says, pointing towards Jim's feet, "and pull"

– she makes a tugging gesture – "I will guide him. I will hold him."

The man nods. He steps across the line which separates the deck from the metal area and crouches down.

"Good," she says. "But first we pray. Understand? Pray?"

She holds her hands together, closes her eyes and bows her head.

The man lowers his own eyes, holding on to the railing for support. As he does this, she opens her eyes, slips off her shoes, takes one in her right hand and moves silently to the side of the body. She has not made up a prayer since she was a child and is not sure what will come out of her mouth. She tries to be as convincing as possible.

"Almighty God. I do not know if you will hear this. Jim Turpin, my husband, was a good man who thought well of everyone."

She moves a little closer to the railing and holds on to it tight with her left hand.

"Jim loved animals, especially birds. He loved the sun, and the earth, and the sea. I was not a good wife to him, although I tried to be. He was always patient. He always forgave."

She notices that the man is shifting his weight. She must be quick. She moves one step nearer to him. She's running out of things to say.

"We commend his body to your care. In the name of the Father, the Son and the Holy Ghost . . ."

These are words the man recognises. As he says "Amen", she brings down the heel of the shoe sharply on his knuckle. His hand flies up and for a moment he is toppling, like a child's toy, his arms waving comically, trying to regain his balance. There is a look of horror and incomprehension in his eyes. And then, just like that, his balance is gone, but not before he lunges forward, his hand reaching towards and catching at the chain round her neck.

They fall together, once or twice bumping into the side of the ship, arms spread, a clumsy tumbling couple. And this, Vivienne realises, is what it is actually like – the seconds between, the nauseating, horrific and irreversible sensation of falling towards the water through the air, elbows and shins and skull crushed and scraped against steel, small fragments of bone cutting through nerve and sinew, blood and lung and brain exploding; and what she feels, the last sensation she will ever feel, is not the freedom of being at one with nature, of being true to herself, but fear and disappointment and dread – the coldness of the water and the hardness of its black steely surface, which dislocates her neck, but not so that she instantaneously loses consciousness as she imagined, but so that she flails about unable to control her limbs or keep her head above water for any longer than it takes to recall the years she has dedicated to studying a dead, irrelevant pseudo-scientist, and her failure to acknowledge and reciprocate the love of the only man who ever loved her, albeit quietly and in his own ineffectual way. And as her throat and lungs fill with brine the last touch she has is not of cool sheets or warm skin but of the desperately grasping hand of a man with frightened eyes whose name she never knew or bothered to ask, whose death she has caused and who is the cause of her own, who tried to be good and kind in the only way he knew and to which she was wilfully and selfishly blind because she wanted to make a difference, to feel alive, because she wanted justice. And as the sea sucks her in and down she realises, too late to shout it out, that the girl by the stream in the wood is her; too late to shout at the world that the taste of justice is salt and does not quench.

GOOSE
Paul Martin

The canal is darker than the night above; floating cans and litter, constellations of half-dead stars. Trellick Tower looms large over everything in Ladbroke Grove, top lights like tyrannosaurus teeth. An anti-lighthouse pulling people towards its particular kind of rocks. Gregory stands on the bridge, inhaling the summer evening, looking for the geese he saw when he crossed here this morning.

He was late for work but the sun glittering on the canal had stopped him. Gregory saw two geese, one ahead of the other, their steady swimming motion tracing two Vs on the surface. He watched as the geese moved closer together, their Vs overlapping like butterfly wings, until they were finally side by side. A large fantail with nothing between them.

This image has stayed with him all day. Separation followed by togetherness. Alone on the bridge, Gregory is only just becoming aware of the space where his physical body ends and where his thoughts and desires stretch out, uncontained, spilling over.

The nature books he read when he was young said that geese can sound like dogs barking, particularly at a distance. Tonight they were not like dogs but they were honking hard. A loud nasal sound repeating a two-syllable tune like a trumpet calling.

The honking grows louder, followed by a bang. Gregory rushes off the bridge and runs underneath, hurdles the safety barriers and sprints along the canal's edge towards the noise. Another bang, another cry. Through the gloom a dark figure runs away. Two discernible features break up the shadow: long blond hair flowing in the wind and a chequered bandana sitting like a warped chessboard on top. Gregory does not give chase, drawn instead to the sounds coming from a bush by the water.

A bird is in distress. A Canada goose with its distinctive black head and long neck. The white chinstrap is crimson and its brown body is wet and bloody. It has been shot at close range and is now beating the ground with its wings in a slow, macabre rhythm. Soon it stops flailing. It lies there and hardly breathes, looking through Gregory with a black, glassy stare.

He fumbles in his pocket for his mobile and is not sure who to ring, the police or the RSPB. He wants to comfort the goose, hold it close to him, find the right noises that could communicate something, but he is too late. The goose convulses one last time and stops moving. Gregory picks up the still, warm body, opens his jacket and cradles the bird. He searches for a heartbeat but finds none and remains there for what might be three or thirty minutes, rocking backwards and forwards.

Two men walk by with a pit bull. They are both dressed in sportswear and oversize Avirex jackets with fancy dragon designs down the sleeves. The taller man wears black and the other red. The man in red breaks the silence.

"What have you got there, mate?"

Gregory opens his arms and his jacket falls open. They recoil from the package of blood and feathers.

"What have you done, fucked it to death, you fucking pervert?" shouts the man in black, as he lets the pit bull out on a longer leash. This would usually make Gregory back off. Usually, but not tonight. He lays the goose down gently at his feet.

"I didn't do this. Some bastard shot this goose. I heard a noise from the bridge and when I got here this is what I found. Do you want to help or what?"

The men retreat, drawing the dog closer to them. They look at him, at the front of his bloody jacket. They turn their backs and try to move away, but the pit bull smells blood and pulls against them. Gregory stares at the straining dog, prompting one of the men to yank hard on the leash, spinning the pit bull around. As the men leave, Gregory bends down, lifts the dead goose into his arms and walks back along the canal. The upturned shadows of the huge water towers loom in the distance. They are burnished orange by the neon Sainsbury's sign; the fingers of huge metal hands from some long-lost Atlantis. Gregory gazes at the water, transfixed by the lights from nearby buildings which highlight dirty white feathers floating on the surface like lost galaxies.

He moves off the canal and onto the bridge. There is a small black door on the other side that he's never noticed before. He crosses the road and walks over to it and finds that it's open. He pushes it further with his left foot. A sign declares "This way to the Dissenters' Chapel". The door leads to some steps which run down to a building that looks like a Greek theatre with its jutting columns. He descends into the gloom, passing the imposing edifice, and his eyes open onto a vast dark grassy expanse of statues and shadows. He realises he is in Kensal Green Cemetery. A place he remembers well.

The last time Gregory had been there was for Mac's funeral. Mac had been HIV positive for years before his body finally gave in at forty-four. The ceremony had been a colourful affair, West London likely lads mixing with the rude boys and dreads. The dub music of Toots and the Maytals strained the tinny speakers more used to high-end hymns. Mac's coffin finally disappeared behind the curtains to the sweet strings and skanking reggae bass line of Bob and Marcia singing Mac's favourite phrase: "Follow me; I'm the Pied Piper."

The wake had been an equally lively late-night session at the West London Working Men's Club. Torch singer David McAlmont had everybody in tears as he sang the old standard *Autumn Leaves*, while on the screen behind, images of Mac had flashed by. In one he was a young boy sat on a wet beach wearing striped swimming trunks, looking straight into the camera. Behind his head a line had been drawn in the sand. In another he was on the top of a red London telephone box outside the Vivienne Westwood shop Sex in the Kings Road, wearing a white sleeveless T-shirt and ripped bondage trousers. The sun from behind made his hair look on fire.

The dead weight of the goose is making Gregory's arms ache. He staggers on through a twilight world filled with mausoleums and stone monuments, angels and sphinxes. It starts to rain. He projects the faces of the cemetery's famous occupants on random gravestones as he passes. He sees Feargus O'Connor, the nineteenth-century Chartist leader, alongside Isambard Kingdom Brunel, buried next to the Great Western Railway he built; and Ossie Clark, the sixties' clothes designer. Mac must be smiling at the company he now keeps. The crucifix shadows and white stone angels with chipped wings chase the absence in his heart to the surface.

Mac always had a spliff to pass back and forth and a story to tell. He had acted with Ray Winstone once, and they had to reshoot the scene several times because they were laughing so hard. The scene was intended to be a poignant moment between the two men. Mac was supposed to say, "A good friend is hard to find, but I found one in you," after which they were meant to shake hands and hug. However, in the first take Mac had said, "A true friend is someone who thinks you are a good egg even though he knows that you are slightly cracked." Then he shook Ray's extended hand, breaking a hidden egg into it.

Mac was like that; he cracked people up and in the cracks people saw for a moment a glimpse of joy in him and then in themselves. He was fun to be around, even when he knew he was dying. Once, Gregory had asked him, "How come you never slow down?" Mac had flashed a half smile and quickly retorted, "Those not busy living be busy dying." He then turned to his bookshelf, pulled out an autobiography and handed it to Gregory. It was the story of Rubin "Hurricane" Carter, the boxer who had overcome drink and drug addictions to free himself from his desires.

In the main part of the cemetery Gregory can see freshly dug ground where a new wall is being built to run alongside Harrow Road. Two weeks ago a storm of biblical strength had knocked down part of the wall, and now green netting and metallic-grey poles let the street in. Car headlights throw halos onto the angels, highlighting their silence. Gregory thinks he finally understands that opening line from Rilke's *Duino Elegies*. "Who, if I cried out, would hear me among the angels' hierarchies?" He screams into the dead air.

He stops, bent over from exhaustion, and lays the bird onto a marble tomb, by the side of which there is some clumped soil. Falling to his hands and knees, he digs into the dirt. It's been years since he has seen anybody from the old days. Those days when he had an internal metronome that always found the rhythm in a tune. Those days when he danced between the beats, subdividing them with his feet. He rises as he hears a deep, resonant trumpet call: a single sound followed by staccato bursts. It's as if Toots and the Maytals were present and with his feet dancing he lifts the bird from the white marble now shining in the moonlight breaking overhead. He hears the horns of a whole chorus of geese, some of the birds taking the higher pitches, others the lower tones, harmonising like a New Orleans funeral band. He lays the goose down in the hole and sways, using his dancing feet to kick dirt over the body.

The following night Gregory can't sleep. He finds no peace in the silence of late evening. Every time he closes his eyes he sees a pair of spectral white wings beat the ground as they strain to fly. He hasn't dreamed of flying for a while, pinioned like the geese of moulten summer. Abandoning the idea of rest, he decides to head out for some fresh air. He looks in the cupboard for a jacket and sees his old cherry-red goose down at the back. Nowadays Gregory dressed down, his outward appearance reflecting his inner ghost. He had been an early adopter of the quilted goose-down jackets that were de rigueur with New York's hip hop style gurus and imported across the Atlantic in the eighties alongside the music. Mac was the first guy that Gregory had seen wearing one; his had been midnight blue.

Gregory passes the usual assortment of old men and youths hanging around outside Lick, the West Indian barber's shop. Gregory hasn't lived locally long enough to get a greeting, but now and then he gets a friendly nod. He stops for a minute to stare at the new development of canal-side flats. White fluorescent lights deep from within make the structure float in the air. He turns right at the crossroads. The shadow of the Gothic church opposite competes with the garish bright lights of the late-night chicken fast-food joint. The menus above the counter are tinged mustard yellow. Gregory ate there only when he was desperate and his stomach always regretted it. He decides on a nightcap, and heads up the road to the Lost bar.

Gregory pushes open the door and his eyes alight on the sculpture behind the bar. A figure with wings. There is no face and the body is turned away. Beneath it is the word "Fallen". Not many people are in tonight, just some noisy Italians. Gregory feels he's drowning, submerged in his thoughts; a far-off siren's song drones faintly in his ears. He is pulled towards the bar by a distant undertow. He's seen the barman somewhere before. He rubs his salt-stung eyes and orders a rum and Coke. As the man pours his drink, Gregory's memory surfaces like a diver from deep waters into light. Long blond hair and a black-and-white bandana. The barman also has a small goatee beard and is wearing a white vest. Around his neck is a silver chain on the end of which are looped several dirty cream goose feathers. He leans over to put down the glass. Gregory points to the feathers and says, "Are you a fan of plumage?"

The barman looks momentarily perplexed.

"Oh, you're referring to the feathers."

Gregory nods in confirmation but all he can think about are the final movements of the goose as it died. The way its eyes twitched like beating butterfly wings. The way it shuddered like an old wooden door slammed shut.

He finds himself stutter over his next words.

"D-d-do do you like like birds then?"

"To be honest, I can't say I am a big fan. Feathered reptiles is what I call them. Why do you ask?"

Gregory pauses before he answers, not sure what to say. He can feel the weight of the bird back in his arms again.

"No reason. I just noticed the feathers and thought they looked . . . kind of strange."

"Well, I guess that's why I like them."

Gregory just nods again in reply and picks up his drink and takes it to a nearby table. For the next hour he feels neither awake nor asleep. The objects in the bar have lost their sharp edges. Tables float like driftwood at sea. The barman appears like a giant caped Dr Strange from Gregory's childhood *Marvel* comics; his hands glow white, the glasses he fills are multicoloured jewels. Gregory drinks the same drink what seems like a thousand times until through the mist he hears the words "Last orders" reverberate like a timpani in his head. In need of some air, he pushes himself to his feet and leaves the bar. After inhaling deeply several times, he crosses the road and sits down on a bench by the bus stop opposite and waits.

As Gregory sits he hears a solitary honk from the direction of the canal. He wants to run and hug the goose inside his jacket, but he does not want to miss the barman. His nerves are taut like tent ropes. His heart feels like it's pushing through the fabric of his jacket as it races away at an apocalyptic drum-and-bass tempo. A further thirty minutes pass before the staff leave. He watches for the chequered bandana. The barman finally exits the building. He doesn't notice Gregory, and starts to walk towards the bridge. When he reaches it, he looks out into the canal.

Another honk. Gregory follows the barman through shadow like the tail of a black wedding gown gathered from the dark above. A rough caress like an old towel against his cheek has him fighting the desire to drift away. The barman is now on the other side of the bridge, his outline eaten by the night. Gregory knows he must be quick and throws himself over the side wall, dropping ten feet to land on a mud bank by the water.

The barman is on the opposite side of the canal, closing on the sound of the barking goose. He crouches down and reaches into his long dark coat and pulls out a hunting rifle. A reflection of burnt moonlight ripples in the water that separates the two men. Gregory stares at the metallic swirls and sees Mac's ragged mouth, a chipped yellow tooth next to a shining gold one. Mac broke his smile at a Toots and the Maytals gig at the Rainbow in Finsbury Park. He had climbed the huge stack of black bass speakers and was conducting the crowd, who were cheering him on. Then he stretched his arms out to his sides, held the pose, like the Redeemer over Rio, and threw himself into the throng.

There is no time to reach the other side of the canal. Gregory backs up as far as he can, throws a glance heavenwards to the moon, and the sad fuel of loss propels him to sprint. He launches himself between the night sky and the dark canal. He knows he will be both seen and heard and this is what matters. His body arcs and he prays for a bellyflop. He hangs in the late air as he waits for the splash of cold water.

LAST NIGHT OF THE

Ali Smith

Proms, I say.

Well, obviously, you say. OK then. I've got a great story about that. That's a really easy one.

We are sitting in our car round a corner then round another corner from our own house. Everything will be waiting for us at home just as we left it two weeks ago, unless we've been burgled, that is. The chairs will be there. The sofas will be there. There will be a pile of post on one of them. The answerphone will be making its regular little beeping noise. Its dial will be flashing, which is what happens when it has more than twenty messages waiting, as if twenty messages is the sane amount and any more than twenty is a kind of madness. The cat will be waiting at the front door, watching out of the glass panel, like she always is when we go away and come back. The bin in the kitchen will be full of the empty sachets from the cat food the sitter's been feeding the cat for fourteen mornings and evenings. The kitchen will smell faintly of rotten meat. The water in the kettle will be fourteen days old, from the breakfast we had before we went on our holiday. The laptops upstairs will, as soon as either of us switches one on to check fourteen days' worth of emails, cause that strange silence, unlike any other silence I've ever known, to come over us.

As we drove closer and closer to the house I had the urge to slow the engine. I let it dawdle to a near halt. There was a parking space outside a house that's simply nothing to do with us. I pulled in. I switched off the engine. I took the ignition key out and put it on the dashboard.

What? you said.

Then I picked up the key and put it back in, turned it one notch so that the radio came on again, something from the Proms.

What's wrong? you said.

Nothing's wrong, I said. I'm giving you a challenge before we go home.

What kind of challenge? you said.

I'm going to give you a subject and you've got to tell me a story about yourself that I don't know yet, I said.

How do you mean, subject? you said.

I don't know yet, I said. The end of things, maybe.

What, after twenty years you think we've maybe said it all? you said.

And every story's first line has to have the particular phrase I tell you to use in it, I said.

What? you said. What kind of phrase? You mean something like . . . like . . . It was the last night of the –

Proms, I said.

I waved my hand towards the radio.

Well, obviously. Aw. That's an easy one, you said.

You sit there, still seat-belted in, and you begin.

It's the last night of the Proms, you say. The last night. Again. That's a lovely thing, that there's always another last night somewhere in the future, that another last night will just come round again in the course of things. My mother would turn from the TV screen, and the screen would be buzzing with that too-high colour that early colour TVs had. The audience would be wearing their attention-getting hats and waving their flags. All those everyday people let in on the classics, singing the roof off the Albert Hall. Land of hope and glory. My mother would sigh at me on her knee. Or she would sigh at me, scab-kneed and older, in my bathrobe on the rug in front of the fire after my Saturday bath. Or she would sigh at me, fourteen and disdainful, sitting on the arm of the chair like I'm refusing to commit myself to the living room any more. And every year she'd say it.

Ah well, love, that's the summer over for another year.

We are both looking straight ahead, past the windscreen wipers and the scatter of dead insects over the windscreen, at someone else's bushes, at the bowing-down outgrown hollyhocks in someone we don't know's front garden.

Is that the end? I say.

She knew nothing about music, nothing at all, you say. At least, as far as I know, she didn't. But she once said to me, out of nowhere, that the thing she'd most have liked to do, even just one time in her life, was conduct an orchestra. We were in the kitchen, I was about twelve years old, she'd have been about the age that I am now. She looked at me over the ironing board, then looked down again at the tea towel she was ironing. *Ever since I was a girl,* she said, *smaller than you are now, ever since I was small enough to think that the trees shaking their leaves was the reason it was windy rather than the other way round, I've always thought it would be really something wonderful. I've always wanted to.*

But the nearest to anything classical we had in the house was a record she'd saved up coupons and sent away for, from John Player's cigarettes. She sent them away and three weeks later these three albums arrived, classy-looking and shiny, black like the packets of the cigarettes she smoked, with the same gold lettering on their front as they used on the packets. John Player Special Collection Jazz, John Player Special Collection Show Tunes, John Player Special Collection Classical. It's where I first heard Tchaikovsky, Waltz of the Flowers; Mozart, Elvira Madigan; a Chopin nocturne. It's where I first read the strange words. Rimsky-Korsakov. Rachmaninov. Paganini.

And every year the last night of the Proms came round, and it was as if she'd gone to her purse to see how much she had, but everything in it had simply been taken. She'd sigh, and she'd say it. *Well, love. That's the summer over.*

We nod at each other and sit in the silence after you stop speaking. Well, I say silence, but the radio is still on, low, the piece of music coming and going. I move slightly in the driver's seat and our luggage settles against itself behind me in the back. I have no idea what the piece of music playing is. The only piece of classical music I know is Sheep May Safely Graze, and I only know it because we were made to sing it at school. I imagine the eye of a sheep in winter, with snow lacing the wool above the forehead, a hunched sheep in snow, a random catch of snow just above the sheep's dark eye.

Someone switches a light on in an upstairs room across the road, and off again. The radio comes and goes, then comes again.

Last night of the summer, I say.

You think? you say. There's more summer to come, surely. Anyway, what summer? You can hardly call it a summer this year. It's like the whole year's been just one long season.

No, I mean, last night of the summer's your next phrase, I say.

Isn't it your turn to tell one? you say.

If you don't tell me a story that really happened, with last night of the summer in the first line, a true story I don't yet know about you, I'll drive us home, I say.

How will you know it's true? you say. How will you know I'm not just making it up?

I trust you, I say. Go on. Or . . .

I hold my hand above the ignition key.

It was the last night of the summer, you say really quick.

Ha ha, I say.

We're both laughing now.

It was the last night of the summer and it was back when I was a student. I had rented a room in a pretty horrible farm cottage on the coast road about ten miles out of the city, from two medical students, boys I hardly knew, friends of a friend. I had one summer to finish this thesis I was working on; it was about the use of the deathbed scene in Victorian literature.

Is that true? I say.

I thought you said you trusted me, you say.

I don't remember you ever telling me about a thesis like that before, I say.

There's a lot you don't know about me, you say. Anyway, I remember taking this room because I thought being with medics might be useful in the light of deathbed literature.

But what the medics *were* particularly good at doing was eating up, in the space of two days, all the food I bought to last me a fortnight. And only one of them was hard-working. The other slept in his room until four every afternoon then played his guitar until four every morning. He was tall. He stooped when he walked. He liked books, he told me with his mouth full, on my first day in the cottage, as I was unpacking my books and my records and he was eating the Cheddar I'd bought. He had it in his hand, its packet ripped open, a lump the size of his mouth bitten out of it. His favourite book was Lolita by a writer called something Russian. Did I know it? He peeled back the wax paper and took another bite.

The other medic, the hard-working one, had the biggest room in the cottage, the front room, the only room with any source of heat in it. He told me I should treat his friend gently. His friend's father had died in a sea accident a few years before. That was what made him erratic. That was why he sang Neil Young and Nick Drake songs all night in his high-pitched drugged-out voice, while I lay there on the other side of the wall unable to sleep, in the smallest room in the cottage, with the sea roaring away behind us just over the curve of the shore, onto whose sandy lunar landscape this same mourning doctor-to-be would, at one point, drive his car until he hit the wetter sand and its wheels sank too deep into it to move. And the tide was coming in. And the car sat there all night. The seawater rose up round its pedals. The next day the farmer who owned the cottages hauled it off the beach with a tractor and a tow chain and charged him fifty pounds.

So this was the shape of my days. The light would come up. The birds would start singing. The medic would stop singing. I'd finally fall asleep. I'd wake at seven, ragged with tiredness, get up, step over the steaming insides of a seagull or a rabbit or whatever the medics' black-and-white cat, which they never fed, had left uneaten in the hall, go out into the grey summer morning and get into my car. I'd drive two miles up the road to the petrol station, which sold packets of Danish bacon and multipacks of Golden Wonder cheese-and-onion crisps.

That's what I lived on for about two months. For the whole of July and August I stumbled about on the edge of things, took long stumbling walks on the shoreline, all banked sand, all plastic rubbish thrown off ships and washed up and embedded in the coast. I did no work at all. I started having dizzy spells, I think probably from the cheese-and-onion crisps.

Plus, the man who rented the cottage next door, and who seemed to have a key for ours too, had appeared at the side of my bed several times at two or three in the morning, though so far, luckily, I'd been awake, or at least I hoped I had. But, even worse to me at the time, someone had rifled through my album collection and taken several.

When this happened I put the cash for the next two weeks' worth of rent in an envelope. I went up to the big farmhouse and stood on the porch. I knocked on the huge front door.

Oh, it's yourself! Come away in! the lady who opened it said.

She said it so affectionately that I nearly burst into tears. She put her arm round my shoulders and bustled me into a big front room, the room was full of sun, everything was clean, every ornament on the sideboard promised a sort of decency. She sat me on a couch big enough for four people. She put a glass of white wine in my hand.

Thank you, I said.

Where's your car, dear? she said.

Up the road on the verge, with the other cars, I said.

Bring it closer to the house, she said. Don't leave it up there.

OK, I said.

Now, do you need a jersey or anything? she said. You're not cold, are you?

No, I'm fine, thanks, I said.

I sat back into the couch.

And how's your time with us been so far? she said.

Well, it's been a bit mixed, to be honest, I said, and now it's the last straw really, because my Bill Withers album's not there any more, both my Rickie Lee Jones albums are missing, and almost the whole of my Joni Mitchell collection's gone.

Oh dear, she said.

I know, I said.

Then two girls and a boy came in. They were about the same age as me. The motherly lady sprang to her feet.

Here they are at last! she said. Your friend got back first. She's been waiting for you.

They looked at me in bewilderment.

No, I'm from the cottages, I said. I'm the girl who's subletting from the boys at number two. I just wanted to give you direct notice of me moving out.

I held out my envelope.

Oh, the woman said.

She stopped being motherly immediately. She took the envelope from me. She took the glass of wine out of my hand and put it on the sideboard with the decent ornaments.

That's who you are, she said.

She led me through to the kitchen where there were chairs but I knew I wasn't meant to sit down. We stood in the kitchen and she told me things in no uncertain terms. She used the phrase in no uncertain terms more than once. She took the money out of the envelope, counted it twice on a sideboard. She told me to relay an angry message back to the others in no uncertain terms about their illegal subletting practice. She showed me out the back door.

The end, you say. Now it's your turn.

No, I say. Because that one doesn't count.

What do you mean, doesn't count? you say.

I don't see how that one's about the last night of the summer, I say.

It happened on the last night of the summer, you say. It's clear. I was very clear about that.

It could have been any season, I say.

No it couldn't, you say. It was summer. And what about the asking me did I need a jersey? That's proof. It was the end of summer. Not that you didn't always need a jersey on the Aberdeen coast, mind. Did you not like it? I can't believe you didn't like my story.

I liked it fine, I say.

You *liked it fine*, you say.

I loved it, I say. It was a very fine one. But it didn't meet the criteria.

Remember, you say, when we saw that Italian film about the prostitute who gets robbed by the man she thinks is in love with her?

I remember, I say. The man sweet-talks her into selling her house and tries to do away with her in a wood and runs off with everything she has

– yes, you say, but she comes out of the wood at the very end and round her there are lots of kids, and young people singing and playing their guitars, going along the road to some kind of festival

– and she walks along the road with nothing left, with them all singing round her, I say.

And remember, right when it ended, the word FINE came up really big on the screen, and remember that woman behind us said: *Well, that's the right word for it all right, what a fine film*?

I do, I say.

She was right, you say.

Very fine indeed, I say. I wonder what happened to him.

Who? you say.

That medic who sang songs in the dark, I say.

It wasn't dark, you say. It was too bloody light. Scottish summer.

The piece playing round us, whatever it is, reaches a fullness. Then it dims down to its end. In the echo of applause and voice-over I think about a story you told me way back when we first knew each other, about how, every morning, your mother would wet the ends of your hair and heat it with tongs into a pageboy style, and every morning you used to go along the road to school taking the condensation off the cars with your hands and pulling your hair straight again.

Come on then, I say.

What, home? you say.

You look at me in the dark. It's the moment on the radio before more music. The conductor raises a silent baton.

It has to be true, I say, and it has to be new to me.

When will it be your turn to do the telling? you say.

Next year, same time, I say.

You laugh. You settle back in your seat. You put your feet up on the dashboard.

What's the phrase, then? you say.

Um, I say. Last night of the –

Holidays? you say.

We both laugh.

Go on, I say.

IN SEKA'S COUNTRY
Olja Knezevic

I wake up before nine because my mobile phone rings. I mouth "Fuck it" fatly into the pillow. My upper lip feels too tight again because of the latest collagen injection, and last night I even noticed several small bruises above it. Fine. The doctor-dog will give me my money back, or I'll sue him Montenegro-style: take expensive things from his pathetic little clinic.

The phone screen flashes with the words "The Friend". Well, well. The Friend never calls mortals unless he's hurting.

"Hello Tiger." I like to be a peppy baby when he calls. "Why up so early? Pussy-craving for breakfast, aren't you?"

"That too, that too. Hello Peachlet," the Friend replies, attempting to sound breezy.

"Hmm, you're worried baby, I can tell," I say, holding the mobile phone to my ear while rushing to the toilet, where I try to urinate quietly, but it comes out insanely loudly, an enchanted river, waterfalls and birds, oh, and a prince, galloping on a horse across its shallow surface – that's a fart, in cadences.

The Friend answers: "Well, to be honest, Sonia's case is avalanching into a bit of a to-do. The Opposition want something big before the election and this is an unexpected gift for them . . . Sonia mentioned your name to the Shelter women and now I'm told you must be picked up by the police. You're better off checking into the police station voluntarily. They want you there today, at ten a.m. – now, in other words. Sonia will be there to confirm it was you who kept her in that flat and . . . you know . . . *rented* her."

"That ssscum," I hiss, still on the toilet, not wanting to flush while on the phone with the *president of the country.*

He calls her "Sonia" now. Not "that girl", "the Russian" or "the Russian girl", although, frankly, she's a Moldovan. Men are so easily manipulated by the victim role. All my girls are volunteers. Both the local and the imported ones. Why else would they travel across the border answering the agricultural ads that so poorly hide the fact they would become prostitutes? But, while I own them, if they prefer the victim role – I let them inhabit it.

"I know, I know," the Friend sighs, his thoughts already somewhere else, I can tell, but that's OK because I want to flush the toilet. And clear my throat, too; I sound more and more like a fifty-year-old with throat cancer.

"OK, I'll do this for you-know-who," I say, ungluing my thighs from the toilet seat. "For you and my son. I don't want the neighbours to see me get in the police car. It's good my boy is at my parents'."

"How is he?" the Friend asks, his voice trained to fall softly where bits of political kitsch are called for, like visiting the peasants with sick children during the campaigns.

"He's improving, thank God," I say. "Actually, thanks to your brother. Maybe the job in the car-washing department will make a man out of my little ape. But don't you worry, Tiger. I'll fix this. That Russian trash can't hurt me. Not in my country –" I bite my tongue. "*Our* country."

"Right. Well, keep a low profile, and don't be too late for the police officers. You know, they're like doctors – big egos. Kiss you, Peachlet."

"Mmmm, yeah, Tiger. See you later. Bye."

Back in my Fag Shui bedroom, I part my Hermès-pattern blackout curtains. The air in Podgorica is clean after last night's heavy rain, the colours outside so intense they make me sick. Why people adore spring is one of life's big mysteries for me. The iron deficiencies in the girls, those mood swings, the lunatic dreams, the migraines. The blue, green and yellow through my window will remain clear for another couple of hours. Then they'll become dimmed by clouds of diesel coughed out of jammed herds of ancient cars, milling up and down the main boulevard that runs, wide and tree-lined, through the whole town. Dimness works for me just fine. That's the time of day I'm ready to go out into this kingdom of bone-sucking dogs. They all look at me like: "There she goes again, the angry Madame Seka," but the sucker dogs would fuck me spermless if only they could afford it. So when I see them looking I say: "Found your bone yet, ssssssuckerss?"

What the fuck does the Friend's phrase "keep a low profile" mean? Maybe: "Wear long and shapeless pants"?

I go back to the bathroom where I strike the Arching Warrior pose under the immovable shower and wash only superficially because I'm not going to see the Friend anyway. To wash my pussy I have to thrust my hips forward and up as if gesturing to the shadow-enemy: "Suck it, loser!" I don't have time to do my hair, so I tilt my head away from the juddering water. Wash the pussy, keep hair dry. Hence the Arching Warrior. I want my Socialist-era shower back, the one that moved like a microphone. But, I paid a member of the working class in advance and this is what happens.

I wanted a purple bathroom with a golden bathtub of mutant dimensions in the middle of it and a throne-like, velvet-covered toilet seat. "Oh," the interior-decorator bitch said, "according to Fag Shui, that would bring more emotional tension into your life. Also, it's bad for your ego, the large objects." So now, everything is black, indistinguishable and tiny: the shower cabin, the toilet seat. It resembles Auschwitz more than anything else. (Who the fuck is this Fag Shui character anyway? Never heard of him, and next thing I know he's deciding what my place should look like.)

I put some make-up on in front of the mirror wall and decide to go for the black leather pants as something not very sexy, yet still definitely not shapeless. Semi-low profile. I match this with a see-through top – I just have to. Red bra underneath.

I go out. I get into my car. My big SUV baby. I adjust the rear-view mirror my way, so that I can see only my eyes in it. I have no stomach for the way others look behind the wheels of their silly cars, and besides, I start thinking this: Why's it *me* the police want? I'm just doing my job. I'm actually a new-age feminist: I think men are weaklings. Still, I've had all my unruly body hair permanently removed.

When I enter the chain-smoking-friendly premises of the police station, I bring sunshine in with me. The police officers' hard faces warn me to keep zitto unless absolutely necessary, and then to say just "Yes" or "No". Then, I have to stand with two extra-losers behind the ghost mirror and give Sonia a chance to confirm my ID and have me locked up. That might happen in Neverland, but not in my country.

So I mouth "You're dead" to the devil's window and give my Jack Nicholson stare and I feel her collapse out there. She's that scared of me. Better luck next time, slut-oh. For me, this operation has the duration of an uncomplicated abortion; for the Moldovan, it probably had the importance of childbirth.

But, the child is stillborn today. The police officers inform me that Sonia failed to ID me. They all look as if a heavy stone has been lifted from their chests.

"Don't worry," I console the police inspector, the one who likes putting rather sharp objects into my girls. "She is not a war hero, just a pile of human garbage from Moldova. Not even Russia. She needs a long time to be ready to face me, but she won't live to tell." I have to reassure him, gently though: men react strangely during a crisis; my strength ferments their hostility. I'm gathering reliable allies. I have the social-ritual cup of sweet Turkish coffee with the police inspector and his typist, while the Shelter-manager woman is screaming something behind the door of his office. "You are all rapists," she yells. "You're all murderers! It's not over!"

Afterwards, I treat myself with a slice of shopping therapy, just to scatter the hopelessness of the police patch off me; two lemon Cokes, three phone calls, and – what do you know – it's girls o'clock!

I hop into my SUV and turn the turbo folk queen's vendetta hit loudly on. I live her lyrics: *Welcome friends, freely visit our masqu-a-*

raded ball / It's no secret, just accept it – we're honest about it all / And the marital bed you see / Obviously made for three / Can't hurt you, can't hurt me . . .

So deep, that moment. Me-time. I start the engine.

I'm speeding up then down then up the main boulevard again, listening to my music and giving myself some coke before I go and act it up with the girls. I visit them every day, including weekends, including after-party massive-hangover days, every single day of the year at this time, around lunch, to make sure they are there and alive. I feed them – the hard workers can order Italian or steaks – and I deliver the needs stated the previous day. According to yesterday's whining, three of them need ultra pads for periods, and another three, tampons for the last days. One litre of boric acid. Toilet paper – they can never have too much toilet paper. Two lipsticks, screamer red. Sleeping pills, vaginalettes, camomile tea. Antiseptic cream, cotton-wool balls. And always this: stockings. Lord, if I could have all the money I spent on stockings back, I could retire to a Sandy Lane resort somewhere.

I park the car in front of the villa that has a neon sign saying "Hermitage" across its unfinished, unpainted façade. I own this marvel of architecture that not even Fag Shui could have made simpler. I keep the girls in a *garçonnière* above the nightclub I'm letting to some dirt-dog. Hermitage, the name, is my idea. Have to think of everything.

Not a sound is heard from inside. I take the items I bought for the girls out of the trunk. The spiral staircase takes me up, to the balcony of their dungeon. It takes awhile to unlock and lift all the bars and steel shutters, but when I do – boy it's loud in there! I leave the bags in the kitchen and walk through into their room.

All the girls are in some phase of menses. It happens when cats spend time together, and it's not good news for my trade. Tense, fragile, wired, quarrelsome. It feels like entering a beehive.

I erase the hype from my lips – no smiling during girls' time.

"Hey, *hey*, I'm in! I'm talking now. *Silence!* What's up with Enissa?" I ask.

"She has the blue-angel crisis again," one of the girls says.

Enissa is lying foetus-like on her mattress, staring at the opposite wall. Quietly wailing, stomach bloated.

The room smells of fungi in a turtle's shell. Bare mattresses disarranged on the floor; two wardrobes agape with nylon clothes pouring out; one naked bulb hanging from the ceiling, always turned on – no outside light coming in since the wooden shutters on the windows are closed and nailed, behind them, iron cage bars.

This room is aired only when I come and unlock the adjoining kitchen, where I open the balcony. This is how Sonia escaped. I came in, the morning after the party during which Marich-dog almost burned her cunt to ash. I came to help her survive it, and I saw her sitting in the corner while the others were still sleeping. She was smoking what must have been her ninety-ninth cigarette and the room looked like a battlefield after a rout. My lungs shrank into raisins so I walked back to the balcony door and opened it, to air the *garçonnière*.

At that moment, Sonia stretched like a puma, three leaps and a jump. She pushed me; I fell on the cooker. She was out, jumped over the rail and ran for her life. There was no chance of catching up with her. The other bitches woke up; I had to stay with them and scare the morning shit out of them.

I put the cage bars on the balcony the day after Sonia's flight. But I had already lost Sonia to the Shelter. The politically correct kind of shelter. Because these two rooms above the nightclub are also some fucking shelter, right? To hell with that. I have a job to do.

"Hey, Enissa, come back to reality!" I yell at the tiny blonde curled on the mattress.

"I'm pregnant," she says.

"No."

"Yes."

"No, you stupid bitch, you can never be pregnant. Get up and let me check you over. It's probably just your period. You motherfucking smell."

"I'm going to have a baby." Enissa's blue eyes light up.

"Hey, you stupid cow, read my lips. You. Are. A. No. Baby. Case. Now, get up."

"I can't. I have vertigo."

"*Vertig-oh*, huh? What is this? A philosophy class? Listen." I shove her hard, roll her over. "I'm in the right kind of mood to beat some loose bag up." I kick her half-heartedly somewhere in the kidney area.

Enissa's so petite, so gentle. Her face's cute: big blue eyes, tiny nose, sweet little mouth. She's the Friend's favourite poodle. I grow jealous at how much he likes to play with her. He tightens a leash around her neck and naked they stroll around the party. She's overused, Enissa. I hate giving her a break; I have dark urges to see her killed by fucking, but the businesswoman in me knows better. I can't afford to lose Enissa as well, after I lost Sonia, the dancer-made-of-rubber. They rarely come with some kind of talent, the girls.

I kneel on the floor, take her head in my hands and unstick her woolly hair from her face.

"OK, when she's past morning sickness give her something to eat and let her stay in, um, bed. She'll be unpregnant again tomorrow."

"Give her some sleeping pills. She screams at nights, so scary . . ." someone says.

"Get used to it already. She always screams the same angel bullshit. I'll shoot something into her. She'll sleep better."

"Can you inject something into me?" Daria, the dumb one, asks.

"You like to inject food down your throat, don't you, fat duck? Fatso? What do you eat? Come here."

Daria lazily approaches me. She is the only one bigger and taller than me. Never outshine the Master. Not even in body mass index.

"Have these." I take several laxatives out of my purse, and put them on Daria's sweaty palm.

"What are they?" she asks, her face doing the junkie jerk.

"What do you care? Take these, unwind. Happy?" I say, eyes narrowing.

"Happy?" Daria echoes.

"Yes, happy?" I'm losing patience. "What a waste you are."

"What?" Daria says, blankly.

"I ask the questions here. Don't be clever with me. It's not your job. I am very angry today. Angrier than usual. So: *happy*?"

"Yes."

"Good."

I get up with a little jump. I am very strong; gym clothes are my second skin. Even in high heels I can kick and run, hard and fast. I look at the girls, really look at them. One by one, very carefully. Who are these girls? Suddenly, this softness; I give a fuck about their biographies. Why? Age? My own boy growing up?

I will have to leave this job one day, and that day is just around the corner. I take a vial out of my purse and haul hard, like a horse, twice, discarding the previous weak thought. I'm not an addict, not that type. I simply always have the drugs on me, and like the bee-keeper has to try the honey, I try my goods, make sure they breed only good feelings.

Enissa's still moaning, a little dying kitten balled up on the floor, ribs prominent even through the three sweatshirts she has on. Always cold, like all women born and raised in poverty, their youth and beauty fading away early, leaving no trace.

"I want to see my blue angel, Sonia," Enissa says looking at me.

"Shut your filthy mouth. And for the record, Sonia is dead," I hiss back, taking the mobile phone out of my purse as a full-stop signal.

This news stirs the girls. They don't know what to think of Sonia's escape, but they probably think anywhere is better than chez moi. But if I say Sonia's dead . . .

Turning my back on this undercurrent of panic, I dial Marich. The man is the reason Sonia ran away from me in the first place, so I figure it's only fair to let him know that I play the supporting-wall role for many lover boys in my country, but mostly for him. And there's an extra charge in red-alert situations.

Marich, or the Boss, as everyone calls him, is about fifty years old. He used to be a *Gastarbeiter* in Germany where he worked in the food industry (he says). People say he killed pigs in a slaughterhouse near Frankfurt. These days, he dreams about frankfurters stuck up his nose, seeking revenge through apnoea death (his words).

In money terms, he is the real owner of Montenegro. He pays the police and state intelligence from his own pocket. He knows all the secrets. Marich keeps the president's, or the Friend's, own millions somewhere safe. The source of their huge wealth is simple and not even scary: cigarette smuggling. The Friend never gives me any money; we have a clean relationship. Marich pays me monthly, cash in advance, serious money, but he damages my girls. He tortured Sonia. Fucked her up the ass with Chivas bottles, kicked her in the mud during winter storms and burned her with cigarettes, stubbed them all over her. But that stupid bitch danced for him whenever he ordered her to dance, and what a dance it was. Hers was a dancer's body. A firm muscle of a butt that followed any rhythm. The beat of drums jumped off her flesh. She slithered like a cat, stiffened like a porcelain geisha, rolled herself softly into a cobra, her eyes devouring bewildered Marich as if he were her prey. Her wiry legs stretched easily all the way apart until her cunt rested on the table. Everyone was mesmerised. That talent came from her Gypsy father, she told me. She could do it on any surface, did it mostly on the tables for us. Her face became beautiful. Then Marich would take her out somewhere, and I'd find her hours later, a hairsplit from being dead.

Marich is a rather short man. His head and shoulders are towering, the rest of his body ridiculously small beneath them. He hides his greys with rusty highlights. He has a brutal jaw line. His eyes are two happy, scanning little devils. I don't like looking at him. He freezes my waterfall of words and that's why I want to have this conversation with him on the phone.

He always answers the phone; if the display flashed with the words "Death calling", he'd answer it.

"Hi, Marich, what's up?"

"Seka! Don't hide your number when you dial me, OK?"

"Why not? I want to surprise you, dolce-vita boy. I've had not-so-great a morning, *thank you*, and I want some comfort. Besides, don't you have some little device, Bond-like, that discloses who's calling, anyway?"

"I swear, people in this country – you included, madam – need real jobs to stop them idling and fantasising about James Bond and the superheroes."

"Well, give jobs to idlers."

"Nobody in this country wants a job-job," Marich says. "Everyone wants my job. They think it's easy. They don't know that it takes some natural M&A organisational skills, I kid you not –"

"What? To smuggle cigarettes? Don't make big mama cwy now."

The girls start fidgeting, then fighting over the goods I brought for them, their voices losing control in the hormones-filled room, becoming high-pitch hysterical; and with Enissa's constant moan, the place suddenly turns into a pigsty before an earthquake.

"And, are you in your whorehouse? Oh, please don't say you're calling me from there," says Marich angrily.

"SILENCE YOU SHITHEADS!" I yell at the girls. "I'll just kill them today, all of them, and who's gonna miss them? Oh, sowry, you and your buddies would miss them, probably. And, why not call you from here? Who's gonna spy on *you*?"

"Don't be so shallow, Seka."

"Did you say shallow?"

"Look, sexy, I'm not your ordinary little buddy who's gonna leak every time you call. And you phone me from your whorehouse and haven't as of yet told me why, so I'm guessing you need money. Is that it? Why don't you just say so? Don't pussyfoot around, you're not a teenage slut. *Quod licet Iovi, non licet bovi,*" says Marich, the Latin lover.

"Yeah, yeah, and *lick-et assum meum, dickheadus,*" I say, scratching his ear with my voice.

"Well, this is slightly amusing, otherwise I would completely cut you out of my life. I have two minutes. Why did you call?"

Marich is a late bloomer where his sex life and its deviations are concerned, and men like that I don't respect. But, having the Friend and Marich interested in you means mini-power, means money, means a future. I would do anything for my son, even quiet down the wounded dragon in me. And regress to a pussycat.

"Oh, amigo," I say, "you know, I just feel I'm all alone in this affair.

I mean, I was the only one interviewed in the police station – sense the scapegoat role, hate it, can't play it, can't keep my profile low enough to graze meekly, y'know. Sonia was still too weak to confirm the ID this time, but – well, it's not over. They are pampering her in that Shelter, but she has cigarette burns all over her vagina from you, man, so I reckon you and the Friend should protect me, you with your money and he with his actions."

I plan to provide some more reassurance, but Marich's end is suddenly mute as in hung-up-on-me mute. Conversation caput.

To hell with it. Enissa's still moaning behind me. Like a fire alarm in the Land of Elves, her moan. Uninterrupted, the lonely warning for the Thumbelinas of this world. This too shall pass. I need some fuel. Another year, another spring. I'll survive it, to hell with it. These girls are merely a bunch of wilting flowers and need watering to get through another day.

"OK, now," I yell above the sounds of the beehive. "How about this? No partying tonight. Today is my gift to you. I'll bring you a nice warm meal. This afternoon, we'll go and have some beauty treatments. It's springtime outside, you need to show some skin, and your skin looks old and tired. Well, mostly it's just dry. So, we'll have the all-inclusive spa revival, anti-stress cures are on. What do you say?"

"Drinks afterwards?" one of them asks.

"No," I say. "You don't ask for a fist when I give a finger. Or – you'll get the fist." I laugh at my own line. Have to do everything myself.

Then the thought strikes: they want me dead. Marich and the Friend – they don't want Sonia dead, they want her back in her own Moldova or Canada or the US – they don't care, just not Montenegro – but they want *me* dead because I'm an institution. And so are they: they are the state institution, and I'm the entrepreneur. They are still in communism and I've gone ahead, back to capitalism. It's kind of complicated for me to explain now, but I sense they want me dead because they know no other way to deal with the new-age capitalist entrepreneurial feminist – *moi*. It's the obvious clash of characters during times of transition.

Oh, fuck it, I always have to fight men. Even the ones listed as friends. I look at the girls – they are my employees, my soldiers, my army. I need to feed them well first and then start training them for combat. All I need to do is give the loaded Beretta from my purse to one of them – to crazy Enissa most probably; crazy as she is, she still has the biggest urge for self-defence – and send her to Marich for a night. That dog can't resist burning the cute ones. All I have to say to Enissa beforehand is: "Your blue angel told you never to let him hurt you." Nobody knows I have the Beretta, only the father of my son; he gave it to me a long time ago. The police only know about the Colt Combat .45. They issued a permit for me to carry that one.

That man, my son's father, used to be a famous footballer. He's not a person any more; now, he's a fluid, running like spilled brandy from one back street in this town to another. I see him sometimes and I put some money into his pocket. He probably loses it, the running-liquid ex-man. Anyway, he can't harm me. In fact, nobody can.

For years my father kicked the life out of me and I still have no idea why. He'd lock me up to sleep with the chickens in the barn; he'd shave my hair off the morning after. I looked around for my mother to ask her, "What is this, Mama? Why does he do this?" but she would disappear when this was happening. She'd have to milk the cow right at that moment, or go over to the neighbours' to have coffee and a cigarette.

So, one morning, smelling of chickens, my head half shaved, my father's bloodshot eyes directed at my face as if it was a gun that needed cleaning, I lost the fear, the confusion. I jumped away, grabbed a butcher's knife and pressed it to my father's throat, his skin rough like the wooden floor of our stable. "Hey, here, old man," I told him and I meant it. "Touch me one more time and I'll kill you." I cut him under the chin a little, just to prove it. The old man's blood was dark and slow.

Now, he and Mama are the mummified servants to my boy, the difficult grandson. I moved them to town, put them nearby, in a nice penthouse where, so my son informs me, they complain to each other about how the TV is too far away from the sofa, how there's no central bulb hanging from the ceiling, only the giant floor lamps they thought were vases, no lift in the building, no normal neighbours, only the passing-through foreigners.

See, I have to organise everything myself.

Now, first things first: feed the girls.

12 HOURS IN LE MANS

Josh Raymond

There's blood on my chips, but I'm used to it. Michelle told me shortly before I left Rouen that "*bien*" and "*cuit*" are two four-letter words her countrymen prefer to keep separate. I raise my glass to the empty chair opposite. Carafes somehow make anything drinkable. A song by Chris Rea is on the radio and, while practising French is pointless now, it's either talk or listen.

"*Il n'y a beaucoup de personnes ici.*"

The waitress is wiping down the bar. Blond hair, eyes that might be green, slightly crooked tooth at the front. She doesn't look like she wants to talk but it's OK. The mirror in the last *station-service* showed stubble, fatigue and, from somewhere, oil, and it's been *trois cents kilomètres* since then. I wouldn't talk to me either. After what seems a long time she shrugs. "*C'est hiver.*"

I take off my jumper and it joins my helmet and the box containing my saxophone in a black still life on the floor.

For dessert I have crème brûlée. I don't much like it but it's easy to order.

"*Tu viens d'où?*" asks the waitress. She has to step over the jumper on the floor and ends up standing close, and the smell of my sweet little pudding is complicated for a second by the smell of her: perfume and just a suggestion of sweat. She steps back, mistaking my silence for incomprehension, and returns to polishing glasses behind the bar.

My fifth cigarette of the day tastes as unpleasant as the previous four. "*Ils sont filtrés?*" I had asked the tobacconist. "*Oui oui, sans-filtres.*" Meanness alone stopped me throwing them away. I wave the packet at the waitress.

"*Tu veux?*"

She smiles and takes one as I blow smoke out towards the empty tables. You couldn't do this in London.

She asks me where I'm from again, in English this time. She sounds American, and I try to work out why as I answer: an English teacher at a school or . . . maybe . . . "*Tu es Canadienne?*"

She smiles again. "Yes," she says, "from Quebec."

Habit and principle make me reply in French. "*Pourquoi es-tu ici?*"

She doesn't answer, just shakes her head slowly and stubs out her cigarette in an ashtray on the bar. Her smile looks like she's forgotten it's there, and the thin grey wisps curl up towards the ceiling fan.

Michelle only smoked after meals, but that included breakfast. We would have it at the café underneath her flat sometimes, trying to eat croissants without making crumbs and laughing when we couldn't. She lived on a *route nationale* by one of those green *toutes directions* signs for truckers who don't want to pay tolls. It's hard to say when we started noticing the noise.

The coffee here is good and seems to be the only thing other than brandy to fill the time until my head hits the hard bolster pillow in room 429 of the inaptly named *Hôtel Première Classe.* I have a brandy. I also get out the map, tracing with my finger the road to Calais, where I will wait in cold drizzle to have my bike strapped down on the ferry by burly Greeks, like it's a mental patient. The M2 from Dover is hard to think about; London is impossible. I don't look up when the waitress comes over, but she puts a full glass down by my almost empty one.

"*Pour la cigarette. Gratuit.*" She looks over my shoulder at the map. "So what are *you* doing here?"

Her inflection makes me give up on French, and I explain that Le Mans was just where I had got to when I felt like a rest; that I wasn't here for any reason at all. She says nothing, standing close again, and it is suddenly hard to breathe. I think about something I have never dared to say.

"What time do you finish?" I have said it almost before I realise.

I used to finish at noon and eight p.m., with an old-fashioned three-hour French closure in the middle. I would shut up the shop, walk the narrow streets back to the flat and construct some lunch from leftovers in the fridge before falling asleep on Michelle's side of the bed. I never told her I did this. The afternoon was the same as the morning: putting on records and helping anybody who came in wanting to buy one. I knew little French, but a lot about records, and enjoyed many mutually baffling conversations with the punters. France is different from England: you make less money but somehow don't waste it in ways you can't remember. Michelle was a *fonctionnaire*: she did something for the government but I didn't know what. She would get home at six, and I would find the flat tidied in that feminine way I could never quite replicate, and some sort of dinner on the go.

"Dominique," says the waitress.

"Richard."

I want to shake hands but don't. She hasn't answered my question and her gaze is hard to hold. She looks down, and then up at me again, pushing a strand of hair from her face.

"I'm finished now," she says.

"Does that mean I don't have to pay?"

"No" – the smile is back – "you have to pay."

I've thought about *when* Michelle left me more than why. We lasted a year, starting in autumn with our best times in winter. Spring brought nothing new, and my only sense of summer was that the heat expanded us until we were in each other's way just being in the same room. We finished by a sort of leaden symmetry where we had started. Didn't I have to think about my life in London? I suppose I did. Autumn is the real New Year. The days' dark constriction concentrates the mind.

France isn't always warmer than England. I shrug on my leather jacket as Dominique locks the door of the restaurant behind us. The broad boulevard stretches away to either side and there are no trees or people, just tall dim street lights, one flickering over a parked car whose wing mirror hangs by wires. Le Mans, home of the legendary 24-hour endurance race, the *Vingt-Quatre Heures*, is deserted at *vingt-deux heures et demie.* I refrain from making the pun aloud. A dog barks far away and I imagine a scraggy brown mongrel snapping at the rubbish I can smell on the wind. Dominique pockets the key and turns from the door. Nowhere looks open for a drink. She indicates that we should walk. I say something about the emptiness and she shrugs. "*Le Vingt-Quatre.*" I saw the track on the way here. The road from Tours forms part of the circuit, criss-crossing the back straight and closed to traffic only on race weekend. The track itself is wide and smooth, trimmed with bright rumble strips and shadowed by great empty stands; a massive winding darkness on the edge of town. Le Mans exists to serve the track, she says. It fills and empties with the car parks and campsites, the stands and souvenir shops. For eleven months of the year there is nothing.

An engine far away grows louder until bright headlights swing fast into the road ahead of us. Race exhaust, dropped suspension, alloys and a skinny pale kid behind the wheel who shoots us an amphetamine leer as he dopplers past. "They're always here," says Dominique, "just waiting."

We stop at a central square. A woman sleeps sitting up on a bench by a supermarket trolley. Two people are arm in arm on the far side, shambling with drink, but they're too far away even to tell their sex. "*C'est comme après une peste.*" She seems to be talking more to herself than me, and it takes another second of looking at the empty square to realise she means plague. After a plague. For want of anything else to say I ask her what she would do, if she survived a plague. She says she would get petrol and live on a farm with a generator. I'm not surprised she thinks about petrol, living here.

"What would you eat?"

"Vegetables," she says, setting out diagonally across the square. "Was there a plague for chickens as well?" She is looking straight ahead but there is half a smile when I turn towards her. I want to see more of her face than I can.

"Let's say chickens were OK."

"Then chickens."

We keep walking. The shambling couple have gone. The shops around the edge of the square are shuttered and the lights in the windows above them dim and few.

"What about when the petrol runs out?" I ask.

"The world would get smaller then. Everything would have to be in place."

There is a bar by a church up a hill. The streets are narrower here, and the quiet less oppressive. I suggest that the track has sucked the life from the flat parts of town, but the hills are out of its reach. Dominique just thanks me for holding the door. A black man in a white shirt greets her by name from behind the bar, and they make small talk in French. "*Philippe, c'est mon ami Richard.*" She pronounces my name the French way, and I say, "*Ça va?*" and take Philippe's hand over the bar. His grip is firm and dry and lasts longer than I expect. We do not need to order the large brandies he pours. Able at last to look at her properly over our corner table, I notice Dominique's eyes are not green but brown and that the thinness of her face makes her look tired. I have not drunk with any woman but Michelle for over a year. Michelle turned heads in every bar we went to, and I wonder if one of those handsome Frenchmen might even now be pondering the way she puts ice in cheap white wine, plays Rachmaninov on the upright in her sitting room and has orgasms in silence.

The brandy here is better than in the restaurant, and Dominique asks me about where I have come from, and the black box I have placed under the table. I tell her about the jazz-improv night last year in East London: how the tall French girl accompanying me on the piano had ended up accompanying me home and how, when the time came for her to go back to France, it made wonderful, spontaneous sense for me to go too. I sense Dominique is not really listening, but I don't really mind. "So how about you?" I say.

Dominique looks down at the drink rings and scratches on the old wooden table. When she speaks her voice is small, and I realise she is close to tears.

"I had a boyfriend . . ." she says, and, as Philippe stops his cleaning at the bar behind me to listen, I know that I am about to hear something evil. She takes a breath. "Robert. He raced in the *Vingt-Quatre* two years ago. Motorcycles. Like . . ." Her voice catches and grows even quieter. "Like you." I drink and say nothing. "He lost it off the straight into Mulsanne. He tried to ride through but found grip too quickly. I don't know the English word for that sort of crash."

I do. If you lock the back wheel going into a corner and release the brake at the wrong time, the sudden increase in traction can make the bike flip with stunning violence towards the outside of the bend. A racer's crash. The very worst.

"A highside."

Dominique lifts one shoulder. It is the smallest, saddest gesture I have ever seen.

"He fell onto his back, and the bike landed on top of him. The front wheel went through his chest. I watched all his races, all of them, but that lap I went for coffee and I came back and he was dead." She lowers her head and does not move away when my hand finds her arm.

We sit there for a long time, like a sad sculpture. After a while I say, "Tell me about him," and, very slowly, she does. Born in Canada, Robert had risen from the ranks of dirtbike boy racers to be offered a factory contract with Suzuki France, as the second rider on their three-man team for the *Vingt-Quatre*. Dominique had moved here with him three years ago to be with the team. They came fifth in their first race and thought that another year of practice would get them on the podium.

"He trained so hard," she says. "The race was everything. To hear the three of them talk about it . . . I guess in the end it meant too much."

"What did you do all this time?" I say.

"I learned the bikes. I was hanging around the garages making the coffee, then got bored and asked the head mechanic if he needed a hand. That was it."

My surprise shows; the machines that race the *Vingt-Quatre* are not worked on by just anyone.

"Six months and they let me do tyre pressures," she admits. "A year later and I'm changing the oil." She drains her glass and stands. "Let's go. I want to show you something."

Philippe says, "*Bonne nuit,*" as we leave and catches my eye. He knows what she's told me.

The night seems warmer, or maybe it's the brandy. Dominique talks freely about how she conducted minor work on Robert's bike, timed his laps and helped him analyse his cornering using video she had taken from behind ad boards and tyre walls. My mind wanders back to the record shop in Rouen and how my saxophone sat dusty and unpractised under Michelle's bed.

What Dominique wants to show me is a view. Around the back of the church is a high mossy wall with a locked wrought-iron gate. I look through and see the town square and the houses beyond. It's unremarkable.

"That's the first view," says Dominique. "You need to see the second one to understand."

We walk up narrow streets between high-sided brown buildings. This is old Le Mans. An apartment block juts improbably from the top of the hill.

"I live here."

The lift has a metal grille that must be closed by hand, and doesn't sound like it's going to make it to the top floor. We walk across ageing yellow linoleum to her door, which she unlocks and opens.

"Coffee or brandy?"

Brandy has got us to here; no reason to desert it. She leads me into a clean white-tiled kitchen that smells faintly of bleach and pours two measures from a nearly full bottle. We clink.

There is a balcony outside the living-room window. We duck and step through. Dominique sits on a low wooden stool and invites me to look over the edge. The church is down to our right, and I see with a start that the iron gate is exactly, geometrically below and in front of us. The view from here is the same, but, being higher up, one can see over the final row of houses to where the twisting black hulk of the track wraps itself round the edge of the town.

"I am the only person who can see this," says Dominique. "I sit here pretty much every night."

We drink the brandy, then another. We smoke.

"Are you going to go back to Canada?"

"I don't know," she says. "I'm here now. The café, the *Vingt-Quatre* . . . It seems to come round quicker each year. The team has moved to Limoges but they always have work for me when they come over. They're good people."

I nod and drink and try to make out the shapes of the bends in the darkness.

We are on the sofa with the window shut when Dominique asks me to stay the night. "It's late," she says. "You can sleep on this." I have ridden five hundred kilometres and had a lot to drink. Sleep sounds good. She hugs me goodnight and fetches a blanket from a cupboard. I take off my shoes and lie down as she turns off the light and goes quietly away. I pull the blanket around myself and watch the ceiling, the brandy muddling thoughts of Michelle with the story of Dominique and Robert. She became a mechanic to help him and still looks out over the track that killed him. I had been a musician once. Not a good one, but not bad either, and I had met a girl who shared my ear and then what? Felt so adventurous in moving to France that I sat for a year in a record shop while she cooked my meals. I bunch the blanket in my fists and don't bother to flick away the tears.

The door opens and Dominique is there. "Sleep in my room, Richard," she says. "Nothing . . . just . . . it's warm." I understand. We lie together in underwear and T-shirts and find ourselves breathing in time.

Sun wakes me slowly in the morning. I use the bathroom and gingerly explore the limits of my hangover. Tolerable. I get back into bed with

Dominique and don't mean for the kiss I place on her neck to wake her up. She turns towards me, then to the bright rectangle of the window, and then back to me. "*Soleil,*" she says with a sleepy smile.

"*Oui, soleil.*"

"*On ne s'attend pas au soleil après une peste.*" You don't expect sunshine after a plague.

The road out of town is empty. Each motorcyclist killed near Le Mans is represented by a black cardboard cut-out at the site of the accident. In spite of this I ride fast, thinking about how Robert, second rider for the Suzuki France *Vingt-Quatre* team, would have done it.

Dominique wanted to see my bike before I left but I made an excuse. It's a trusty thing, and I didn't want expert eyes finding fault with it. She walked me as far as the church, and we said goodbye at the gate.

"You were the first man to sleep in my bed since him," she said. "I liked it."

"I liked it, too," I said, and we left it at that.

There's not much waiting for me in England now, but there is a new melody in my head. I take a sweeping left-hander with the throttle wide open, then shift up for the straight, unable to tell if I am singing out loud through the howl of wind and engine.

ALL OR NOTHING
Alison Huntington

Biggest tide of the year tonight.

At ten o'clock the Thames is low, lower than low, starting to show what its watery flesh has been hiding. Just a little peek, mind you, not very free with its secrets. Arrowheads and goblets and bottle-tops and bones. Bits of people, and bits of the things people have made. And bits of the things people have stole. Be quick and you might steal something for yourself. What's it to me? I wouldn't tell.

The river will rise over twenty foot by four in the morning. You'll be able to see it coming, lapping and slapping like a long-time drunk staggering sideways, but always, inch by inch, headed onwards. Anything you haven't picked out by then will swirl away, new with old, plastic with wood, dreams with rememberings.

On and on it'll come, creeping towards the pavement, licking at the stones. Like it's not satisfied with what's already in its belly. It's still hungry. It wants to empty the fridge. The Thames couldn't care less most of the year but this one night it makes a real effort, splashing up under the bridge arches, reaching, stretching its liquid fingers, stroking, straining, like it's after a hostage. It's calling. Come with me on a trip out to sea.

They once found a corpse weighted down with two hundred pounds in coins and a dictionary. I wonder what words escaped as the man went down. I fancy "pauper" might've made its way to Richmond. Or "trust fund" fetched up at Limehouse.

Tonight I'm in the same place I always am, in my cubbyhole on the South Bank, looking up at Waterloo Bridge. The cubby's right opposite the book market, in between two of the great coffins they use to store books. Words one side of me, water the other. I've got my best navy wool coat on. The buttons are pulling a bit.

I'm doing the usual, waiting for everyone to go home so I can have my nightly bit of peace with the river. Waterloo's not a very pretty bridge, but I like how those low arches bellyflop from south to north. I like that however much lighting they put in it's always dark underneath. But never too dark for Lizzie to see.

I open my faithful flask, have a few swallows to keep the damp out. I'm feeling a bit drowsy if truth were told. Normally I love a good story and there's always plenty on a big-tide night but tonight something's different. The damp is getting solid, sticking to walls and lamp posts and bridges. The air's turning to water. My eyes are swimmy with the wetness and my legs are rheumatic. It's raw for September and my lovely coat can't cope. I'm getting the shivers inside and out. I feel like making a nuisance till someone whisks me away in a nice warm police car.

And then they pull him out of the river in front of me, so I'm glad I stayed put.

I've just popped down onto the pebbles for a pee, when an RNLI boat comes speeding towards me and two figures get out, and another stands up in the water. This person is pulling someone else onto the shore. The someone else is very white, his mouth is all down on one side, and his eyes are closed in that screwed up kind of a way, like what he's been looking at is really bright.

Some of his clothes have come off, though not the ones you'd think. His trousers are half down but he still has his big coat on, all twisted and stuck to him so I can't see where his pants are. And one shoe. A big boot thing with shiny buckles. The other foot is bare, and pale blue with thin black veins spidering over it. I want to touch it. I've never seen his feet before.

All his clothes look black but that might be the night or it might be the Thames sucking on the material. I don't envy the rescue diving bloke who's had to go in and get him. He has a mask, but just think what you're swimming past. Not just beer cans and driftwood now, is it? There's tampons and condoms and shitty nappies and bits of drowned dog and the stuff that comes out of boats' toilets. Why would you want to drown yourself in that? Nicer to swallow bleach.

They put him down on top of the pebbles and the rubbish. Lucky the tide is so low, or not very clever of him, depending on how you look at it. And they bump the back of his head as they lie him down and it makes me think how close his skull is to the stones. And then it's just like something on the telly, lots of shouting, and a guy with a box runs up and starts pumping on his chest and to start with nothing happens, it's like he's been picked up and thrown by a giant and left there like a toy. Then I see water coming out of him. Dribbling and spilling and spurting then a gush and all of a sudden I'm thinking about those cartoons where goldfish pop out as well, dancing on a fountain.

The guy who's been doing the pumping shouts "YES!" and looks at me. I'm quite keen to stay in on this now as it's getting interesting, so I jump up and I shout "Thank Christ for that!" I get out a hanky like I'm crying and they seem to think that's the right thing to do, though why I should care I don't know. He's not my responsibility.

And then they're picking him up and carrying him, the three of them, it takes all three, what with his body of wet lead and his sopping coat and his boot and his bare blue foot. I look up and there's an ambulance parked on the walkway in front of the National Theatre. I've no idea how it got there. It's usually pedestrians only. I'm following as he's posted in the back, and a hand comes down and pulls me up inside. Because I've had a few I'm a bit emotional, and the wet on my face might well be tears. I suppose that's why they think we are together. I like the idea they think I'm his girlfriend.

I've never been in an ambulance before. And it's cold, so what the hell.

Inside two medics are getting on with it. They don't fuss over him, just pull back some of his clothes – which is tricky, like peeling skin – so they can hook him up to a machine. There's a mask over his face which reminds me of the diver who went to get him and I wonder where he's gone to get warm or dry and if he's allowed to have a bit of Scotch afterwards or if he's on duty which would be a bit rough I reckon, after swimming with all that muck. Someone told me Scotch is antiseptic so it might do him some good.

Funny, lying there like that, all grey from the water, it's hard to tell how old someone is, or rich, or funny, or proud. All I know is Marty has bones under his skin like the rest of us, breathes air like the rest of us which is why all that water turned out so disagreeable. The skin on his face has bumps of stubble, a few freckles. I can imagine the cheeky schoolboy he told me about. Nice eyebrows, neat, soft. Will he get whiskers when he's old? Who wants whiskers. Who wants to be old.

He was scared to death of it.

One of the ambulance blokes asks if I'm all right and I nod but I'm not really, I still need a pee. Everywhere I usually nip into is shut. I used to like the old Festival Hall best. The loo was down this narrow stairwell and there wasn't much room but when you came up after there was this little space with big mirrors for titivating, and I like pretending I'm checking myself out before I go on the stage and sing to hundreds of people. Gone though. With the renovations. Improving it to make it look like the 1950s again, which seems a bit odd to me.

I've only met him a few times when he asks me to come and see him play Brixton Academy.

I do as he's told me and go up to the door that says Guests and tell a suit as wide as he's high that Lizzie's here. And he gives my name a big tick and me a big smile and he stands back and I go inside.

Backstage smells of disinfectant and there are concrete steps everywhere and I don't know where to go. There's an arrow pointing upstairs with his band's name on it, but it's nine o'clock now and that's when he said they'd be onstage so I push the door ahead of me that says Auditorium. And I'm in Wonderland.

I'm walking up a slope towards a glittering pond of faces, a million starry eyes looking at me, and as I get used to the dark I can see them spilling from the tiers above me and the little gold-painted boxes hanging from the wall. I stick out my chest and pat my hair and they lift up their plastic cups and they look like dizzy glow-worms and they drink to me. And I nod and I smile and I'm wondering what to sing when there's a rush like a dam has burst and they're pouring towards me and the huge black robot with many faces next to me clicks and hums and explodes with noise and all I can hear is the roar that fills my eyes as I turn round and I see them, fifteen feet above me, spider men in black wearing silver guitars and in the middle stands Marty in a red satin dress and he's screaming the most beautiful scream I've ever heard, that crashes into the silver guitars and the robot speakers and kisses the watchers like a waterfall. The light is raining and he is a god.

Tell some lies, have some fun. Or like Marty, tell them the truth and hear them believe you. For an hour, while they're there. But then they go home, and leave him to the truth, all by himself. Which scares him shitless.

I want to go backstage to get a better look at his dress, see if it's silk after all. But I go home instead. Next time I see him he says it is, but I'm not sure I believe him.

They chuck the back doors open and two nurses are waiting with a trolley. They get him on like he's a baby, a long, skinny baby. One of the ambulance men taps me on the shoulder but I don't look back. I'm sprinting along the corridor behind this trolley so I don't miss what happens next. But after a couple of swing doors I get stopped by a great big schoolboy in a white coat with a label that says he's Doctor Spock or something and he says I can't go any further, they'll come and get me when there's news.

So I go and sit in the bloody hospital café and get a cup of plastic tea. I hate waiting. But someone always turns up.

"Who the hell are you?" First thing she says to me. Charmed I'm sure. Then she apologises. "Sorry. They told me you were with Marty and I don't know who you are."

"Can't know everything," I say to her with a smile and then I catch sight of myself in the glass door. I'm a fat spring roll with electrocuted hair and a too-tight coat with a bulging pocket. I look like I might ask her for money any minute. And I still might.

She says sorry again, then she holds out her hand and says, "I'm Sara. What do you know about Marty? They said there was no news yet. They said you came in with him. They told me to come and have a chat and a freaking cup of tea."

She looks like she's about to do major amounts of blubbing which'll make a horrible mess of all the gothy eyeliner she's got round her eyes. So I wipe the rim of my cup to be polite and pour her out the last of the tea. I'd be more upset, but it's pretty cold now and even though I've been to the loo once I'm getting towards needing it again.

"All right now, love? No need to get agitated. He's in safe hands." I sound about as reassuring as a bullfrog. "You've had a shock. This'll sort you out."

While she has a go at sipping I have another look at me in the glass. Some days I could pass for forty-nine, but this isn't one of them.

"You've got to squeeze the life out of the tea bags in here. It's like somebody's sucked them first. He'll be all right. Come on, lovely, have a good blow. Does he like a drink? Would've kept him a bit warmer in the water."

She sits up and wipes her nose.

"Yes, a bit."

Marty drinks like there's a prize for the winner. He's too thin to soak up pints so he practises with shorts. Jack Daniel's and Coke, mainly, but he loves his vodka, loves the burn. And that green absinthe makes him feel all decadent, really rock and roll. He keeps a bottle in the inside pocket of that great big coat and when he's feeling particularly passionate he takes it out and waves it around. The contents usually end up down his front and the bottle ends up in the river.

This Sara's too skinny. They must look like a set of pipe cleaners when they're out together. Face so white, looks like she only comes out at night. The tea's perked her up though. She's getting very chatty.

"He was supposed to be coming straight back. He's supposed to be packing for New York. He disappears. He keeps turning up in strange places, scary places, talking to tramps and mad people, giving them things out of that ancient grandad coat."

I've stopped listening.

I'm in the Embankment Gardens. I like it down here. It's close to the river and I always need to be close. But something's going on. Loads of people jammed in, seems like they're waiting for something to start, someone to say "go". I'd been planning on a sit-down, a fag, a little drink, get up enough strength for the bridge steps. There's nowhere to squeeze my backside so I have a go at getting through the crowd, but it's impossible. I keep getting stood on by old folks, young folks, people with kids in prams, mates on a big afternoon out. And suddenly there's this bloke walking backwards in front of me, clearing the way, waving his handkerchief, bowing like something out of Molière. "Look out," he says, "Milady's coming through." He's with some other boys, all of them dressed up in black, bits of make-up round their eyes. And he's smiling. Lovely face. Lovely smile. But mostly I remember his hair. Beautiful. Long, over his shoulders. And the sun's on it. Makes it look like dirty gold, like melting gold on a sunny day. Thick and soft. Makes me want to touch it.

I get to the gate, and his mates are all clapping. So I smile and I say "Thank you kind sir," and I swish through in my flowery red dress and he gives me a kind of a bow, and then he disappears back into the crowd.

I never imagined I'd set eyes on him again.

In the ambulance you couldn't see the light in his hair any more. It was like thick, dull dog tails just come out of a slimy pond.

Sara's making shapes with her finger in the spilled sugar. There's this pale blue light under her eyes where the fluorescent strips on the ceiling are shining through her magpie lashes. I wonder what they get up to in bed? Coal-black hair on blueing flesh. One big fucking bruise.

If she holds that cup any tighter her fingers will snap. I bet she clings to him. Hangs on like a delirious bareback rider. Rides him round the room squawking like an inky cockatoo.

"Do you love him?"

Oh my dear. That was meant to stay in my head.

She's looking down, like she's trying to read her own tea leaves.

"I can't stop myself. Is that love?"

Marty runs away, after gigs. The first time he fell over me by accident. Now he brings great cardboard cups of coffee and lets me steal the chocolate off his, while he talks. Once told me he could have any woman he wanted. Maybe that's why he wanted to jump.

Time to leave her to work out what love is. Out the café door there's a mile of green corridor, a white line painted all along at hand height to help the escaping blind. No wonder so many stop breathing in here, no air. Give me the cold, the wet. Give me the little soul lights on the river. Out the revolving doors, round and round, changed your mind or lost it? Round again. It's pouring black out here, the sky's collapsing in the car park, the stars have cried themselves shut. I don't know where I am but I can sniff the Thames. It'll be coming up fast, squeezing and squirting itself to the parapets, running away. No one on the streets but shadows, them as died in the hospital or before, before there was a house for controlled dying. Those whose days ended in the river. Coming out tonight. Their night for escaping, when the tide is right up, and creeping with their fingers, sliming a hold with their putrid hands. I'm not thinking about them. But I have to be there, just in case.

Five minutes from my cubby, just turning down my short cut, I fall over a girl. Her bum's on the pavement, but her legs and arms are on the road between two parked cars. Her head's lying on her briefcase on the kerb. She's been sick down herself, down her nice pretend-Chanel navy jacket. One of her silly high heels is off. There's a cut on her hand. It's made a mess of one of her cuffs.

Her eyes are opening. She won't recognise me, but I've seen her a million times. Another one who's missed the starting line. Another Marty, lost in the city, missing the point. Heading for the river.

"All right, love?" I say, but of course she's not. She shouldn't've joined in when the boys hit the vodkas. But she did, because she wants them all to love her. "Come on. Sit up. There we are."

"Sorry."

She looks like she's used to saying that.

"What for? You can't help it any more than the rest of us. Do you remember where you live?"

For a minute she doesn't.

"Putney."

"Come down on the tide, have you. I could send you back the same way, maybe. Float you."

"Which way's the night bus?"

She's crying at the thought of it, so why bother?

"You're not going to be very welcome on that, my love. You're smelling a bit ripe, if you don't mind me saying."

You can see where she's tried to cover her freckles with make-up.

"No, my love, no bus for you. This is a job for Tony-Boy."

"Don't leave me!"

They get like this. Sometimes I'm a bit pissed off they're not more scared of me.

"Well I can't carry you, can I? Stay put for a minute. He's just round the corner. Don't worry. He won't rape you."

She sits there, shivering, squinting like the street lamp's an instrument of torture.

Tony-Boy's minicab company is in the next street. Tony's sitting behind the grille with his stomach around him like a lifebelt.

"All right, Lizzie?" He looks pleased to see me but talking's getting to be a problem. Can't do it and breathe at the same time. He's got his shiny beige polo neck on as usual. He once saw Marlon Brando wearing one in a photo. The sign above the door says Marlon's Cabs but everyone ignores it. Everyone calls the place Tony-Boy's.

"Who've you got for me tonight?" he asks, wheezing like a squeeze box.

"Banker. About twenty-five. Round the corner between the BMW and the '78 Capri. Puked, but not too bad. She'll be good for the fare."

Tony-Boy presses a button.

"Freddy. Pick-up, base. Pronto."

I leave it to him. Tony-Boy knows what he's doing. We've worked together a while. Sometime in the next week he'll send someone down with a tip. I don't ask his methods but sometimes it's jewellery or a watch instead of cash. If it's pretty, I put it on for a bit. But it's usually too much hassle to sell. So I chuck it in the Thames for the skeletons to wear. And imagine them all the way down on the riverbed, dancing.

Biggest tide of the year tonight.

Probably because of the rain, no one is looking at Marty. Maybe someone gives him a sly sideways peek under their umbrella but no one bothers to stop and see if he's all right. Why would they? Got to look after number one. Staying dry's the priority, not investigating some lost boy intending to get wetter.

The damp is getting solid, sticking to walls and lamp posts and bridges. The air's turning to water. My eyes are swimmy with the wetness and my legs are rheumatic. I only look up to see if the lights on the bridge are working. And there he is. In his great big coat, elbows on the parapet, head on his hands.

I have a bit of a shock, looking up and seeing him there. That's where he stands and looks over, to find me. But he's supposed to be going to New York. I didn't expect to see him again.

I wave up and he stares for a minute. Then he waves back. I'm thinking he'll turn and come down as usual but he stays put so I have to go up the steps in the rain. I'm not very happy.

"Darlin'," I say to him when I get to the top, all out of breath. "What're you doing up here?"

He doesn't say anything, but gives me a hug, and for a minute we're a wet wool sandwich.

We stop together for a bit, resting against the stone, watching the boat lights fly by, on water we can't see. He's wearing a woolly hat pulled down to his eyelashes. They've got rain splashes on them. He hasn't had a shave for days. That lovely hair's all straggly on the shoulders of his stinky old coat. I can't tell what he's thinking but he's bitten the corner of his mouth and a tiny dribble of blood is mixing with the rain.

My shoes are filling up with water and I'm getting colder which he should have noticed, respect for the elderly and all that. I start shuffling about like I'm ready to go.

And then he has a rummage in this little canvas bag he's got slung over his shoulder and he brings out . . .

"You robbed a bank, have you?"

He shakes his head and tries to shove this wallet in my hand. It's bursting with twenties. There's got to be five thousand lovely pounds in there. Think of the trips round Harrods food hall.

I try to push it back in his hands but he won't have it. One of the twenties blows out and flicks and rolls into a puddle. In the dark it looks like any other bit of rubbish. A cab drives past and a wave of water washes over it.

And then I'm too cold. I leave him up there. He's pulling handfuls of notes from his pockets and he's throwing them in the river. And I head back to my cubby, to see what happens next.

It's no longer tonight, it's tomorrow. The water is carrying away the night and all those stories that have been upstream and tweaked before floating back down again a bit fresher.

A lot of bodies get pulled out of the Thames. You used to get a reward for rescuing people, but so many poor bastards pretended to have saved a mate who'd obligingly got himself wet that they changed it to a certificate instead. About as much use as a stack of sopping twenties.

I'm opening Marty's wallet. I'm scattering notes like marigolds on the Ganges. I really want to keep it, a kind of memento, so I hold it and stroke it for a bit, but then I throw it in.

You have to cry for all of them, or none.

NOTES ON CONTRIBUTORS

With the exceptions of Toby Litt, Sarah Salway, Ali Smith and Pete Williamson, all contributors are students on the MA Creative Writing programme at Birkbeck, University of London.

Thea Bennett is an actress and writer who grew up in South London before it became a desirable place to live. She has written novelisations of two children's TV serials: *The Gemini Factor* and *A Little Silver Trumpet.* Thea is currently writing a novel about the theatre.

Gul Y. Davis's novella *A Lone Walk* received the J. B. Priestley Award for Young Writers in 2001. His story "The Psychology of Dangerous Roads" was adapted for radio and broadcast on BBC Radio 4. His short fiction and poetry have won or been placed in a number of competitions. He is currently working on a novel.

Melissa de Villiers grew up in South Africa. She was a political prisoner there during 1984. She now lives in London, where she works as a freelance journalist and editor.

Jon Elsom was born in Southampton and lives in London. He is a creative director in a large advertising agency. "Commission" is his second published story. He has completed a dozen or so stories and is beginning his first novel.

Albert Garcia grew up in Los Angeles and, after attending the University of California, Berkeley, remained in Northern California working for the University libraries as well as the City of Berkeley Public Library. Albert is returning to California to continue writing and considers London a home away from home.

Anupama Kumari Gohel was brought up in Hampstead, London. From childhood she has had a passion for storytelling, which both drives and dictates the tempo of her life. She has travelled extensively and lived abroad. She is currently working on her first novel.

Pippa Griffin lives and works in London. She was longlisted for the 2006 Fish International Short Story Prize, and her story "Next Door" was published by Route in their latest anthology *Bonne Route*, in February 2008. She is working on a novel and a collection of short stories.

Anna Hope is a Mancunian actress living in Hackney. She has read her stories at Tales of the Decongested. "A Gap of Sky" is from a work in progress, a collection of stories set on the same day in London.

Alison Huntington grew up in South Wales, lives in London and writes about both. "All or Nothing" is adapted from a novel-in-progress.

J. D. Keith was born and raised in London and is a regular on the performance poetry circuit. He won Farrago's London Slam in 2006, and was a finalist in BBC Radio 4's Slam in 2007. He is working on a collection of short stories set in London and will be published in the *Tell Tales 4* anthology.

Olja Knezevic was born and raised in a country called Yugoslavia that doesn't exist any more. Now she has to say she's from Montenegro. She has been living in London for three years and is working on her first novel. She has two kids who sit on her shoulders while she writes.

Cynthia Medford Langley is currently working on a collection of integrated short stories. Her stories and essays have appeared in *Puerto del Sol, Beacon Street Review, Pangolin Papers, The Sun, Downtown Brooklyn Review, American Agriculturist* and *Biographical Memoirs of Fellows of the Royal Society.*

Toby Litt was born in 1968 and grew up in Ampthill, Bedfordshire. He is the author of *Adventures in Capitalism, Beatniks, Corpsing, deadkidsongs, Exhibitionism, Finding Myself, Ghost Story* and *Hospital.* His new novel, *I play the drums in a band called okay,* was published in March 2008. He is a Granta Best of Young British Novelist. His website is at www.tobylitt.com.

Philip Makatrewicz was born in London of Polish parents in 1981 and has also lived in Frankfurt and Manchester. He is currently working on a novel based on the short story "Boozehounds" that appears in this collection.

Paul Martin was born in London and has worked in the music industry for many years. He has been a DJ across the world as well as an A&R manager at various record companies including the cult label Talkin' Loud. He is currently working on his first novel.

Josh Raymond is a rowing coach. He has read short stories at writLOUD and Tales of the Decongested and sometimes writes book reviews for the *TLS.* He is working on a collection of integrated short stories, another of which, "The Giraffe House", will appear in *Tales of the Decongested* Volume 2 (December 2008).

Sarah Salway is the author of two novels, *Something Beginning With* and *Tell Me Everything* (Bloomsbury), and the short-story collection *Leading the Dance* (bluechrome). An Internet collaboration with Lynne Rees resulted in *Messages* (bluechrome). She currently teaches

Creative Writing at the University of Sussex.

Thomas Jerome Seabrook is a writer and editor based in Leigh-on-Sea, England. He is the author of *Bowie in Berlin: A New Career in a New Town* (Jawbone, 2008) and a contributor to a number of other books including *The Faber Companion to 20th Century Popular Music* (Faber, 2001).

Ali Smith is the author of three short-story collections and four novels. Her novel *Hotel World* (2001) was shortlisted for both the Orange and Booker Prizes for Fiction. *The Accidental* (2004) won the 2005 Whitbread Novel Award. Her most recent book is *Girl Meets Boy* (2007). She lives in Cambridge.

Matthew Weait's short story "As Red As" was a winner in the 2001 Fish International Short Story competition. He is a legal academic and his book *Intimacy and Responsibility* was published by Routledge in 2007. He is working on his first novel.

Pete Williamson is a London-based artist and animation designer, and is the author and illustrator of twelve children's picture books. His work draws on children's book art, early experimental films, late Rothkos and lost photographs in order to create eerie, dream-like images that charm and unsettle in equal measure. www.petewilliamson.co.uk

